LAW ON LEVELS

An addictive crime thriller full of twists

DAVID HODGES

Detective Kate Hamblin Series Book 11

Joffe Books, London
www.joffebooks.com

First published in Great Britain in 2023

Cover art by: Nick Castle

ISBN: 978-1-80405-821-3

This book is dedicated to my wife, Elizabeth, for all her love, patience and support over so many wonderful years and to my late mother and father, whose faith in me to one day achieve my ambition as a writer remained steadfast throughout their lifetime and whose tragic passing has left a hole in my life that will never be filled.

AUTHOR'S NOTE

Although the action of this novel takes place in the Avon &
Somerset Police area, the story itself and all the characters
in it are entirely fictitious. At the time of writing, there is *no*
police station in Highbridge. This has been drawn entirely
from the author's imagination to ensure no connection is
made between any existing police station or personnel in the
force. Some poetic licence has been adopted in relation to the
local police structure and specific operational police proce-
dures to meet the requirements of the plot. But the novel is
primarily a crime thriller and does not profess to be a detailed
police procedural, even though the policing background, as
depicted, is broadly in accord with the national picture. I
trust that these small departures from fact will not spoil the
reading enjoyment of serving or retired police officers for
whom I have the utmost respect.

David Hodges

BEFORE THE FACT

The girl had a perfect figure. Stretched out on the striped, blue lounger wearing nothing more than a thong and half a bottle of suntan oil, her shapely body seemed to shine in the blaze of the afternoon sun. It was as if it were a carved statue that had been polished by a skilled cabinet maker. Detective Sergeant Kate Lewis stared across at her with undisguised envy. Then glancing down critically at her own body in the miniscule bikini briefs, she gave a rueful grimace.

An attractive young woman in her own right, with sharp blue eyes and long slender legs, Kate certainly had the looks and figure to match her neighbour's. But with shoulder-length auburn hair and pale, freckled skin, she had to accept the fact that she would never achieve a decent tan no matter how long she lay in the sun. The most she had ever been able to achieve was what her other half had once described as a 'delicate glow'. Some tan that! Worse still, she couldn't even expose herself to its fierce rays longer than half an hour without suffering nasty sunburn. She was reduced to spending most of her free time on her lounger under the protection of a large umbrella.

She had always dreamed of visiting Mexico, and she wouldn't have been human not to have felt a little resentful over the fact that, having made it to this select holiday resort on Cancun's golden coast with its powdery beaches and dazzling turquoise ocean, she was missing out on the principal benefit everyone else seemed able to tap into. But the feeling was only fleeting, and she suffered a momentary stab of guilt for even allowing such a churlish thought to enter her head. Right now, she should consider herself lucky to have got away from the cold British winter at all. At least she was able to lie on a beach in the sun, unlike many of those back home. Furthermore, she had known the price she would have to pay for her pale, sensitive skin when she had chosen the land of *sun, sea and margaritas* for the relaxing break recommended by her shrink as a form of what he called recuperative therapy. She had certainly needed the break too after the series of traumas she had so recently suffered in her job as a police detective. They had nearly broken her mentally and had twice resulted in a period of voluntary psychiatric treatment at a specialist clinic in Berkshire. She had only been discharged from the clinic after her second period of attendance just before her vacation.

To be honest, when she had booked the holiday she hadn't intended lying on the beach all day sunning herself and knocking back the bar's over-priced drinks anyway. Sitting and doing nothing for two weeks was not her style. She was not made like that. She needed a goal. A challenge that would take her forward. Out of the dark place in which she had found herself. So she had signed up for a creative writing course at the Villa Ambrose as a means of injecting some stimulus into her recovery plan. She had long thought about trying her hand at writing a novel. This two-week introduction to the craft at this so-called writer's retreat had seemed to combine both a relaxing break away from home as well as an introduction to what could prove to be a brand-new, less stressful career. She had to admit, though, that since her arrival twelve days before, the Villa Ambrose's retreat had turned out to be more about retreating than creative writing.

There *were* lectures, seminars and group forums, of course. But these were voluntary and usually held in the conference room on mornings and evenings when it was cooler, with no one questioning non-attendances. There were also assignments to complete that were assessed by a dedicated tutor. Her first task, for instance, had been an introductory presentation about herself to the mixed syndicate group of would-be writers. Her ambitions, likes and dislikes The disclosure that she was actually a serving English police detective had certainly created a stir among the group, prompting a multitude of uncomfortably searching questions. The presentation had been followed by the submission of her first two short crime stories over the next few days, which had been put through the bruising mill of syndicate opinion before a critical but mainly complimentary assessment by her tutor. She was now in the middle of the second part of her final assignment. Writing the first ten thousand words of a crime novel she had initially presented to the syndicate in the form of a detailed synopsis. That was proving more difficult to write than she had expected. But despite the work she had been required to carry out, overall she had formed the impression that Villa Ambrose and its writing course was all a bit of a con. An excuse for lounging about on the beach and eating and drinking to excess. Somehow she didn't think it would be of any help in turning her into a professional crime novelist. Furthermore, from her perspective, the majority of the other thirty or so 'students' on her syndicate were not exactly the most gregarious kind. She wondered whether her disclosure that she was a serving police officer had made them a little wary of her. She had encountered this sort of reaction before from people back home when mixing outside the job, so she wasn't particularly surprised. She wasn't particularly bothered either. Though happy to engage with everyone at the seminars and to exchange pleasantries with them in the normal course of association, she hadn't come here to socialise. She had come to repair the damage that had been caused to her emotional psyche and to relax and enjoy a peaceful, uncomplicated break.

Furthermore, her fellow students were a real mixed bunch, and she felt little, if any, affinity with any of the ones she had spoken to so far. To be fair, both sexes were represented. Young and not so young. They also hailed from a variety of different countries, including France, Spain and Greece, though with a predominance of Brits and Americans among them. So diversity was well represented. But that didn't make things any easier and for the most part, in her present state of mind, she couldn't help seeing the syndicate as a largely characterless, amorphous mass. Just an incessant droning, wittering sound that went on around her like insects in a meadow, or a stream constantly tumbling over rocks, as she struggled with her disordered thoughts and her new realities.

There were one or two notable exceptions, of course. People who stood out for one reason or another. People who struck her as different, interesting or amusing.

The two well-upholstered Maxwell sisters from Surrey, for instance. Doris and Mary. Both chatterboxes of the sort that Kate suspected would belong to a local writing group's 'knitting circle' back home. Middle-aged ladies who bored everyone to death at the seminars reading out pages of text from their two cosy crime novels and bickering constantly over everything. Then there was Gabriel, probably not his real name, with his dreadlocks and forage cap, who spent much of his time spouting about deep philosophical truths and trying to look like a creative intellectual instead of actually producing anything of substance. Conversely, twenty-five-year-old, left-wing firebrand and declared activist for the LGBT movement, Jenny Latham, certainly produced the goods, but her literary offerings were intensely political and filled with a raw passion that certainly raised eyebrows among the more conservative members of the group. This was especially true of hard-bitten American journalist Gary Tomlinson. He seemed to take a great delight in goading her. But there again, he did the same with everyone else and his dark, saturnine looks and acid tongue soon guaranteed his isolation from the rest of the group, including Kate, whom he also frequently taunted. Entrepreneur Tom Leakey was

4

the total opposite. Effeminate and overtly demonstrative with a ready smile that matched his sharp wit, he was also well skilled in creative writing. But he had a habit of button-holing people and pouring out his own personal woes with the speed of a ticker-tape machine, and should, Kate thought, have worn a sign saying, 'avoid at all costs'. He was told as much by badly scarred former squaddie Jedd Roberts. Discharged from the army after suffering serious IED injuries in Afghanistan and looking to write a crime fiction series set in a military environment, Roberts brutally cut him down the first day of the course in front of everyone, which reduced him to tears and caused general embarrassment. Other members of the group included retired history teacher, Joseph Solomon, with his poorly fitted toupee and lisping, condescending tones that got everyone's backs up, and the student who liked to be called Ash. An intense, middle-aged loner with a pasty face, a discomforting stare and a propensity for grilling other students, particularly Kate, on every minute detail of their presentations.

It was hardly surprising that Kate found none of the group appealing. They were just not her type or on her wavelength. Nevertheless, she had tried to fit in as best she could during the relatively short time she had been at the Villa and at least her own work so far seemed to have impressed the course tutors. Plus the fact that there was the sun, the sea and those margaritas to enjoy, plenty of which seemed to be on offer. So what was there to worry about?

She allowed herself a crooked smile, thinking of Hayden, her other half who was stuck back home in Somerset, unable to get time off. He would have really loved the Villa Ambrose, though without the creative writing bit, which would have definitely not been his thing. Committed to a laissez-faire philosophy in which indolence played a major part and work was an irksome, though unavoidable, reality, her clever ex-public schoolboy husband and detective partner would have eagerly embraced the opportunity of a fortnight's eating, drinking and lazing on a beach. But most definitely *not* the sight of his wife lying topless on a sun lounger among the hotel's other half-naked guests. That would have been right out of order for him. Horrifying his prudish, old-fashioned sensibilities and winding him up into an indignant fit. She was almost tempted to send him a selfie on her mobile just to get him going.

She was still turning that idea over in her mind when her phone bleeped. It was a text message and she stiffened when she opened it up and read it.

> *Hi Kate. Are your detective skills as good as your boobs? Maybe we should find out some time, eh?*

She frowned and scanned the beach from behind her sunglasses. Trying to spot who could have sent the message. There were half-naked bodies sprawled everywhere, some shielding under brightly coloured parasols, others braving the full heat of the sun. She could see no one with a mobile in their hand or anyone studying her. She turned and stared back at the wide terrace fronting the hotel behind her. Again, people everywhere at the little plastic tables, but no one apparently showing any undue interest in her. Yet someone had been watching her without a doubt.

She checked the text message again, but it was unsigned, and the ID was shown as just a telephone number, which she didn't recognise. She guessed the caller was using an untraceable burner phone. But why the hell would someone send her a message like that? It had to be one of her writing group. Whoever was behind it would have needed to know who she was and what she did for a living. Everyone on the syndicate had been required to share their mobile phone number, allegedly to aid group cohesion, and it would have been easy enough for the texter to have contacted her anonymously. But why? Was the sender some kind of pervert, like the stalker she had been hunting on one of her last police investigations back home? Or was this just someone with a misplaced sense of humour?

Infuriatingly, there was no way of knowing. But what-ever the truth was, she had no intention of ringing the caller back to give him a piece of her mind. That would have simply pandered to his warped mentality. Instead, she made a note of the number on a little notepad she always had with her in her beach bag, before deleting the message altogether. Then, her relaxing afternoon in the sun ruined and suddenly feel-ing conspicuous and embarrassed in just her skimpy bikini bottoms, she slipped her T-shirt over her head, scooped up her beach bag and headed back to the hotel.

The foyer was cool and almost empty. She nodded to the woman on reception before taking the lift to her room on the first floor. She had a couple of hours to kill before evening dinner, so there was just time for a shower and a change into something cool and elegant before pre-dinner drinks.

The air conditioning was off in her bedroom. But the thin, gauzy curtains over the doors to the balcony were stirring gently in a draught. As usual, the doors had been left ajar to let in some cool air, no doubt by whoever had serviced the room. She took a long shower, luxuriating in the hot, soothing jets. Then she donned the hotel robe and returned to the bedroom to pour herself a G and T from the fridge, which she took out on to the balcony while she checked the list of members' mobile numbers the course director had circulated to everyone. Needless to say, her mystery caller's number was not there. As she'd thought, he was probably using a burner phone.

From the balcony she had an uninterrupted view of the beach a hundred yards or so from the hotel. The sea was on its way back in now and showing signs of agitation. The foam-crested breakers were more prominent than before, and it was apparent that most of the other sunseekers were already in the process of following her example by calling it a day.

She went back into the bedroom to the small built-in wardrobe and selected a little off-the-shoulder black dress and high heels, then gave herself the once-over in the full-length mirror. It was as she was treating herself to an indulgent twirl that she noticed for the first time that the single drawer of the desk with which each room at the hotel was equipped was not closed properly. It only contained the hard copy plot plan of the novel she was working on for her next assignment. But knowing she had put the ten-page document away neatly between stiff cardboard file covers after running it off on the hotel's communal printer, she was curious as to why there now appeared to be a piece of paper sticking up through the gap.

Frowning, she went over to the desk and pulled the drawer fully open, discovering at once that the errant piece of paper was part of a document projecting from the folder. Further investigation revealed that someone had taken the manuscript out of the folder and leafed through the contents before putting it back. It was now creased, well thumbed, and had a couple of the pages out of sequence. Knowing that the young woman who serviced Kate's room spoke no English, Kate decided it was most unlikely that she would have been the culprit. Which meant that someone else must have been in there. With the balcony doors regularly left ajar and a fire escape close to one end of the whitewashed balustrade, it was not difficult to work out how they had gained access either. She remembered thinking when she had first arrived at the hotel that their laissez-faire attitude towards security was like an open invitation to a would-be thief. Well, it seemed someone like that had taken advantage of it, but not to steal anything. As far as she could see, nothing else had been touched. Clearly, they had been solely interested in her manuscript, but what on earth for?

It wasn't long before she found out. She had only just re-closed the drawer when her mobile gave a soft 'bleep' from the bed. A text message. Thinking it could be Hayden checking on how she was getting on, she scooped the phone up with a grin and checked the message. Only to have her momentary good humour evaporate.

It was a message from 'Mr Anonymous' again and on the same mobile number.

Hi Kate, I liked the outline of your crime story. A woman pushed off the balcony of a luxury hotel by a psychopathic killer? Interesting scenario, I felt. By the way, when I questioned your abilities earlier, I was referring only to your police investigative skills. I didn't realise you had the gift of clairvoyance as well.

She reread the message and frowned. Clairvoyance? What the hell was he on about? She hadn't said anything about being clairvoyant in her introductory presentation to the syndicate, merely that she was a professional detective. She shook her head irritably. The man (she assumed it was a man after reference to 'her boobs' in the previous text) was becoming a pain. She would have to speak to Martin Keogh, the course director, if the harassment continued and maybe tell him about the intruder in her room. But there again, perhaps it was best just to let things lie. She had come to Cancun to relax and that's exactly what she was going to do. In the meantime, Mr Anonymous was best forgotten. Deleting the text, as she had before, she grabbed her handbag and headed out the door to dinner.

* * *

Kate did not receive any more irritating text messages that night. In fact she was able to sleep peacefully until around 2 a.m., but her peace was then shattered. She was torn from her dreams by terrified screaming. She shot up in bed just in time to see something flash past the gauzy curtains drawn across the balcony doors, followed by a loud crash as it must have landed on one of the plastic tables. There was a brief pregnant hush before a babble of raised, excited voices erupted from all around her. Doors slammed and she heard the sound of running feet.

Grabbing her robe from the end of the bed, she stepped out, barefoot, on to the balcony. There were globular lamps on short metal stems lining the top of the low wall bounding the outer edge of the terrace running the length of the hotel below. In the bright light they created, she saw that there was a contorted shape lying on the flagstones beside an overturned table and chair a few feet from the steps leading down to the hotel's gardens and beach. Even from where she stood she could see the dark stain spreading out across the slabs from under the body of what seemed to be a woman with long black hair dressed in a flimsy nightdress.

Kate didn't need to see anymore. Appreciating the urgency of the situation, she returned to her room, unlocked the outer door and raced for the stairs to the hotel foyer. The reception desk was in darkness, having closed at midnight as usual. But the door to the terrace was never locked. In seconds she was feeling its gritty surface beneath the soles of her bare feet.

The woman was not moving and even as Kate bent over her to check her pulse, she knew she was dead.

'Looks like she fell from up there,' a large balding man dressed in just a pair of shorts shouted from behind her. Automatically, Kate glanced upwards and traced the line of balconies rising towards the face of the moon. Now a small crowd had formed a short distance away and she quickly took charge of the situation.

'Get on the emergency phone in the hotel foyer and call for the police and an ambulance,' she instructed her fellow guest.

'Not much point getting an ambulance if she's dead,' he muttered.

'Just do it, will you,' she snapped irritably. 'And like now!'

As he obediently trotted off in the direction of the hotel lobby, Kate carefully ran her gaze over the corpse. She could see that the woman had suffered horrendous injuries. Her skull was split right open, leaking blood and other fluids. One arm appeared to be shattered and both her legs were twisted at impossible angles. From the look and feel of her, she suspected she had also broken most of the bones in her body, including her spine.

Then the next moment the uniformed hotel security officer arrived and excitedly ordered everyone back to their

10

rooms. Seeing no point in remaining there, Kate left her name and room number with him as a possible witness and made her way back to her own room. But for her, sleep was now impossible and following the sound of approaching sirens, she returned to her balcony instead and watched the uniformed police and ambulance personnel arrive to deal with the situation.

Seeing the corpse of the woman being taken away as the police officers wandered about the scene, talking and gesticulating towards the upper floors of the hotel, she was conscious of an uneasy twisting feeling deep inside her. She had witnessed the effects of violent death many times in her police service and although shocked by what had happened here, she was not unduly fazed by the physical aspects of the tragic event. But something about it all was bothering her. When she returned to her room an hour or so later, after the emergency services had gone, she sat for a long time on the edge of her bed with another gin and tonic from the room fridge for company, mulling over what had happened.

On the face of it, the woman had either fallen or jumped from a balcony on one of the upper floors. But Kate was not convinced. If she had accidentally fallen, her screams would have accompanied her downward plunge in the terror of the moment. On the other hand, if she were a 'jumper' and had intended to kill herself, she would hardly have stood on the balcony screaming her head off before throwing herself over the edge. Yet there had been a definite time lapse of several seconds between the screaming that had woken Kate and the brief glimpse she'd had of the body flashing past the balcony doors and crashing into the table on the terrace. This suggested that the woman had been in the grip of unimaginable terror well *before* she had actually parted company with the balcony, which raised a very big question mark over the whole affair.

On top of this, the fact that the tragic incident seemed to mirror exactly the plot of Kate's novel was disturbing enough in itself. But what made it even worse and sent an icy chill down her spine was that the reference Mr Anonymous had made to the novel in his last text message had been accompanied by the thinly veiled hint of what was to come.

His words whirled round and round in her head, jarring her senses. *I didn't realise you had the gift of clairvoyance as well.* Had that been a deliberate hint as to what was going to happen or an unfortunate Freudian slip on his part? Either way, in the overall context of the message, what else could it have meant other than that the fictitious scenario in her novel was about to become a reality?

Kate's mind was in overdrive. Had the mystery texter himself randomly selected some innocent guest staying on her own at the hotel just to make a horrific point? She visualised him creeping into the woman's bedroom. Seizing her from her bed and dragging her struggling and screaming on to the balcony. Throwing her off . . . The very idea seemed preposterous. Why would anyone do a thing like that? Furthermore, why would they declare their intention of doing it in advance? Surely she was letting her imagination run away with her. She swallowed hard. Maybe she was, but if that was the case, the fatal fall, so like the one she had created in her novel, had to be one hell of a coincidence.

There was something else to think about too. It was plain that someone on the writing course had developed an unhealthy interest in her. But of those fellow students who stuck out in her mind, none seemed to fit the bill, despite much in-depth pondering on her part. Looking at things logically, the culprit could have been any one of the thirty odd students on the syndicate anyway, whether she had noticed them or not, so trying to work out who it could be without more to go on was a pointless exercise. Primarily, the reason for the interest in her seemed to be because of her job as a police officer. This invariably tended to obsess most aficionados of crime fiction. But she couldn't help thinking that somehow she could be to blame for it all by disclosing her profession at that first introductory forum. If, as she suspected, the woman who had plunged to her death from the hotel balcony *had* been murdered, then was that her fault too for stimulating the warped mind of some crazed psychotic?

One thing seemed clear. It was her duty to pass her information on to the police. After all, it was what she would have expected any self-respecting citizen to do in similar circumstances back home in England.

Very public-spirited of you, the voice in her head mocked, but what are you going to tell them? That some anonymous screwball has been sending you messages and you suspect he may have planned and carried out this woman's murder? So, where's your evidence? Well, I don't have any real evidence, officer. Just a hunch. But you see I am writing this crime book about a woman being thrown off a hotel balcony and in his last text message hours before the incident here, the man said I had to be clairvoyant. This suggested I was already aware of what was going to happen before it actually did. That would look really good, wouldn't it? Either the police would think you were a nutter or that maybe you had something to do with the woman's death.

She shivered. The cautionary voice was right. She had absolutely no evidence of anything and if anyone was likely to be considered a suspect, it would be her. This was Mexico, not England, and the criminal justice system here did not have the best of reputations in the way it treated suspects. The prospect of being shut up in a Mexican jail on some strand of manufactured evidence while the police went through the laborious process of an investigation was not something she felt like risking. So, a woman was dead and the thought of doing nothing about it weighed heavily on her conscience. But her suspicions could be completely groundless and anyway, what alternative did she have under the circumstances except to keep silent? The answer had to be none and to make sure she could not be accused of involvement in the incident, she went straight to her mobile's recycle box and deleted both text messages completely.

Her interview by a local uniformed police officer, in common with a number of other witnesses, was not until a good twenty-four hours later and it was apparent from the start that the authorities had already decided the death was accidental and there would be no further investigation. Apparently, the dead woman, who had been identified from her passport as a Brazilian national named Ana Barros, was a regular at the hotel. She evidently had a reputation as a high-class *meretriz* or prostitute, who offered her services to other guests, which though not condoned, was tolerated by the management, probably because they got a rake-off. She also had a history of drug addiction and LSD tablets had been found in her room. So as far as they were concerned therefore, it was an open-and-shut case.

'Maybe she thought she could fly, senora,' the elderly policeman chuckled after he had taken Kate's brief statement, but she didn't bother to reply.

A few hours later Kate had checked out of the hotel and was easing herself into her seat on her flight back to the UK, strangely relieved to be leaving the land of *sun, sea and margaritas* behind. The bleep of her mobile shortly afterwards came as a big surprise.

There was just one text message waiting for her and it wasn't one she had wanted to receive.

> *Hi Kate. Nice to be heading home, isn't it? Incidentally, what did you think of that woman's death at the hotel? Accident, suicide or something else? The incident could have been straight out of your book, couldn't it? After all, you had already foreseen it happening, hadn't you? Didn't push her did you?*

Kate instinctively twisted round in her seat to try and get a look at her fellow passengers. But she was by a window and it was only possible to see those immediately next to her or in the row opposite her across the gangway. It wasn't clear from the wording of the text whether her texter was actually on board the aircraft with her, or whether he had sent the message from somewhere else, like the airport itself. But she couldn't help feeling a sense of foreboding at the possibility that he had followed her on board. Angrily deleting the message as she had done the others, she turned off her mobile in compliance with the instructions now being issued over the aircraft's PA system. For the moment she pushed all thoughts about Mr Anonymous and his texts from her mind as she was left with no option but to press herself back in her seat to try and compose herself for what she always regarded as the worst bit about flying, the dreaded take-off.

The next instant the aircraft had pulled away from the stand to creep stealthily towards the runway. Minutes later it was vibrating heavily under the cacophonous thrust of the powerful jet engines before racing down the runway at breakneck speed and lifting off into a cloudless blue sky. With a sigh of relief — they were now safely up — she opened her tightly closed eyes and unclenched her hands. Forcing a weak smile, she threw a guilty glance at the elderly man in the seat beside her, hoping he had not noticed her moment of cowardice. She was rewarded with a snore, suggesting he was already fast asleep. Adjusting her seat slightly and settling her head back against the padded headrest, she closed her eyes, determined to seek refuge from her returning worries in the all-embracing blackness of a deep sleep.

But sleep evaded her. Instead, her thoughts kept returning to the Villa Ambrose and all that had happened there. Conjuring up a succession of vivid flashbacks of the woman plunging to her death from the upper balcony. A scene Kate feared would become indelibly etched on her memory. On top of this she found herself constantly going over the part-remembered content of the anonymous text messages she had received in a vain effort to make some sort of sense out of them. Trying to assuage the guilt she was still feeling over her failure to pursue her suspicions with the local police and failing miserably.

Some relaxing break this has proved to be, she thought ruefully. Definitely not what her shrink had ordered. She was probably more stressed now than when she had first arrived in Cancun. She felt she might even need another break if she were unable to come to terms with everything. Her only consolation was that the traumatic job issues necessitating her holiday in the first place had now been pushed to the back of her mind, replaced by the more horrendous, new event she had witnessed.

What was the truth behind the woman's death? Was it an accident, suicide or murder? As a cynical detective, had she herself jumped to unfounded conclusions over the tragic circumstances? Could the whole thing have been coincidental to the plot of her novel? Was she reading too much into it all, including her suspicions about the anonymous texter? Was there a link between him and the incident, or was he just some perverted voyeur seeking to capitalise on it? The questions swirled around inside her head like a succession of never-ending breakers hitting the shoreline. But she got nowhere. There was nothing there to grasp. Not even the tiniest element that could lead to some answers.

In the end she gave up, donned the earphones that were provided and selected some soothing music to listen to. Moments later she was asleep.

She was awakened some time afterwards by meals being delivered. But the flight attendant need not have bothered. Kate wasn't in the least bit hungry and after nibbling a roll, she ordered a glass of wine and concentrated on that instead before falling asleep again.

When she awoke for the second time, they were on the final descent to Gatwick. Shortly afterwards they had landed and as soon as the seatbelt signs were extinguished, she pulled on her short coat and in common with the rest of the passengers, climbed to her feet to retrieve her luggage from one of the overhead lockers. But as was usual in such situations, the crush around her resulted in a virtual melee. Everyone seemed desperate to be first to the exit, almost as if they thought the aircraft was about to catch fire. But hauling their cases out of the lockers without regard for anyone else, they simply cut across each other in the process. Kate ended up being sandwiched between two large men, with her own bag jammed against something inside the locker. She was relieved when someone behind, a man she thought from the look of the arm that reached up over her shoulder into the locker, freed the bag for her, enabling her to pull it out. But when she turned to thank him, there was no one there, just a stream of passengers heading out of the aircraft along the narrow gangway. He had disappeared.

Shrugging off the mystery, she followed everyone to the baggage hall and then through a deserted customs post, wheeling her suitcase, with her cabin bag over her shoulder on its long strap. She was soon in the airport bus and heading for the long-stay car park to pick up her Mazda MX-5 for the long drive home to Somerset. Tired but relieved to be back on *terra firma* again. But her relief was short-lived. She found the paper napkin bearing the logo of the airline in the pocket of her coat when she reached for her ignition keys in the car park and the short message scrawled on it in red block capitals could in no way be interpreted as a 'welcome home'. It simply read:

SEE YOU SOON, KATE.

Remembering the man, who had freed her case for her from the overhead locker, she felt an icy chill travel down her spine. Mr Anonymous! It had to be him. He must have slipped the napkin into her pocket after she had pulled on her coat in the aisle. She turned quickly to study the car park. Several people were getting into their cars and driving away; there was no sign of anyone watching her. Yet she could feel eyes fixed on her from somewhere along the lines of parked vehicles. As she had feared following that last text message, the bastard had actually been on the plane with her, and whether he was actually returning home or had booked the flight spontaneously, one thing was clear. He fully intended keeping in touch . . .

CHAPTER 1

He had never been to Somerset before, let alone that wide expanse of flat marsh and moor identified on his map as the Somerset Levels. He made a disagreeable face as he struck off across the dismal, waterlogged countryside through the mist. Acutely conscious of the narrow reed-and-willow fringed 'rhynes', as the internet had called the narrow drainage ditches lining the road on both sides. Wary of the potholes, sudden dips and adverse cambers in the tarmac, which could easily snatch the steering wheel out of a driver's hand and pull him over the edge.

He had made good time from the airport at Gatwick. Sticking to the route the sat nav had dictated. Joining the M5 motorway from the M4 just three hours after reclaiming his baggage, passing through customs and picking up the car he had hired on a month's contract from the car rental company at the airport.

That left him a good two hours clear to enjoy a leisurely lunch at a café in the Cribbs Causeway shopping outlet near Bristol and then do a bit of essential shopping before meeting up with the man from the letting agency who was renting a cottage out to him near a small village called Catcott. He'd got the details from the internet before catching his flight out of Cancun, and a quick phone call, backed up by his Visa card, had secured the property right there and then. All he had to do now was find the letting agent's office and be shown out to the property so he could settle in.

It was a real quirk of fate that had led him to Cancun. He could have picked a writing course from any number of so-called writing retreats advertised on the net. But for some reason he had been drawn to the Villa Ambrose on the Mexican coast. Maybe it was meant to be. What was it the Arabs called something like that? *Kismet*, that was it. Fate. In any event, it had resulted in him discovering Kate Lewis. A would-be writer like himself, but more crucially a real-life, professional police detective who had actually investigated the sort of serious crimes that made the greatest novels in the genre.

Personally, he didn't like the woman at all. Any more than he liked any woman. In fact, like the true misogynist he was, he despised the entire sex. Always had done. But this one really got to him. He particularly resented her career success and the fact that she was still not satisfied with what she had already achieved in life but wanted even more. Plainly, as well as being some sort of ace detective, she saw herself as a future crime novelist too. Pure selfish greed, he felt, when others like himself had yet to achieve anything in that respect.

What really galled him was the fact that she had only just started creative writing, while he had been trying to break into the craft for years. He had the rejection letters to prove it. From those who had bothered to reply to him anyway. Yet she seemed to have it all made for her. On the course, what work assignments she had put in had consistently received high marks for structure and authenticity, while his had been just as consistently marked down. His plots lacked realism, they'd told him, and his characters were too wooden. Just like the publishers and agents who had rejected him in the past had said. He well remembered one agent who had written back to him after he had asked her for some advice. She had told him to stick to sorting books in the library where he worked as he

19

had as much chance of writing a successful novel as becoming a rocket scientist. Another bloody woman, he'd mused, his anger boiling over. The unfairness of it all had really wound him up, feeding on his inherent misogynistic paranoia and acute sense of envy whenever he thought about it.

Nevertheless, putting all that aside, he had to admit that it was Kate Lewis herself who had unwittingly given him the brilliant idea that now dominated his every thought. Okay, so it was only an embryo of an idea at present and it needed a lot of work on it to firm things up. But it at least offered a potential breakthrough that could enable him to put his years of frustrating literary rejection behind him and at last establish his legacy as the best-selling crime novelist he'd always dreamed of becoming. He knew he had a high IQ. He had been told as much way back in his school days after being put through the Mensa assessment process. But he felt sure this irritating cop would make a worthy protagonist in the ambitious game he had devised. She was smart, determined and, from what she had suggested in her introduction to the writing group, very experienced and competent in her role as a police detective. Well, it wouldn't be long before he would be in a position to see just how good she really was. Just a week or so of research for his 'project', including necessary familiarisation with the area he would be operating in and he would be ready to start. As for the principal criticism he had received on the course about his writing lacking realism, if realism was what the bastards wanted, then he would soon give it to them in bucketloads!

* * *

The one-bed thatched cottage in the little village of Burtle was cold and unwelcoming when Kate turned her key in the front door. The log fire had been lit at one time, but now all that remained was a pile of ash and she'd already noted the absence of her husband's red Mk II Jaguar usually parked in the driveway at the side of the cottage, indicating he was out

20

somewhere. No doubt still at work. There was ample evidence of the fact that he had been home at some time, but it was difficult to tell from the empty bottles of wine and dirty glasses littering the coffee table and the pile of dirty dishes piled up in the sink how long ago that had been. Hayden was the untidiest, laziest person she had ever encountered, and she was not surprised to find the place in such a state. Her 'big affable bum', as she liked to call him in her despairing moods, didn't know the meaning of order and he had been like that ever since they had met as detective constables at Highbridge nick. How her eccentric, workshy husband had managed to survive for so long in such a frenetic CID environment she hadn't the faintest idea, especially as it was most unusual for married couples to be allowed to work together in the same department. But Hayden was the quintessential survivor and if there was a god of survivors, he was doing an excellent job watching over him.

She shivered, acutely conscious of the damp atmosphere rising from the adjoining marshes after the heat of Cancun. It seemed to be creeping into her very bones. Dragging her suitcases upstairs to unpack, she dumped them on the bed, then slipped out of the clothes she'd been stuck with since leaving Cancun and abandoned herself to the hot, soothing jets of the shower.

It was as she wandered back to the bedroom, vigorously towelling herself down on the way, that she heard her mobile bleep. Thinking it might be a text from Hayden checking to see if she was home, she retrieved the phone from the pocket of the coat she had shrugged off on to the bed and opened it up.

The message was short, but certainly not sweet, and once again it wasn't from Hayden.

Hi Kate. Enjoy your shower? You have a great body for a lady cop. Speak to you again soon.

It was apparent that the message had been sent anonymously no doubt on a burner phone again, just like the

21

others she had received. So her tormentor must have followed her all the way from the airport to her home address and was somewhere outside watching the cottage. Possibly using binoculars. What the hell did he want with her? Once again she wasted the message, stabbing the delete key with a force that threatened to punch a hole in the phone itself.

Her insides were churning as she hastily pulled the big bath towel around herself, and instantly regretting the fact that she had not drawn the curtains across the bedroom window, she shrank into a corner out of sight.

For a few seconds she remained there, heart pounding. Then curiosity got the better of her and she edged along the wall to the window and peered around the folds of the curtains. The small back garden was deserted and beyond the boundary fence an expansive marshy field scattered with patches of brown teasels and thorny scrub stretched away through a faint mist to a fuzzy line of willow trees bordering a rhyne. There was nowhere for anyone to hide and no sign of anyone loitering in the vicinity either. The watcher must have already made off.

Pulling the curtains across, she finished drying herself and quickly dressed in jeans, a long-sleeved blouse and a thick woollen sweater. Even then she still felt cold and putting her concerns about her 'voyeur' to one side for the moment, she went downstairs and out into the garden to collect an armful of logs from the log store. She had cleaned out the fire and made it up again when she heard the sound of a powerful engine beating off the wall at the side of the cottage and breathed a sigh of relief. Hayden's Jag. He was home. She applied a match to the firelighters and met him at the door. But if he was expecting a loving embrace in her present state of mind, he was disappointed.

'What the hell is all this?' she snapped, waving an arm towards the bottle-laden coffee table. 'Been living like a slob as usual, have you?'

The smile on the big man's face vanished as he stepped over the threshold, and he ran a podgy hand through his thatch of uncombed blond hair.

'Well, nice to see you too, old girl,' he retorted, closing the door behind him. 'You've obviously missed me!'

She ran a critical eye over him. The badly creased green trousers, crumpled pink shirt hanging out over his belt on one side and the scuffed suede shoes. All typically Hayden. She didn't need the detective skills of Sherlock Holmes to know that he had had lunch either. The yellow stain on the breast pocket of the shirt told its own story. The only thing that wasn't clear was which lunch day.

'This place is a tip,' she continued brutally. 'You might have cleared up before I got home.'

He winced. 'Sorry, old girl, I was going to, but I didn't expect you back so soon today. I *have* been working, you know.'

'Well, that makes a change for you!'

His resentment flared immediately. 'That's not fair,' he retorted. 'It's all right for you, sunning yourself on a beach in Cancun. The rest of us have been stuck here on twelve-hour shifts with days off cancelled because of operational commitments and staff shortages.'

Kate saw tears in his eyes and suddenly she felt as small as she could possibly feel. She was totally out of order and was taking out her stress over all that had happened to her on him. Lunging at him impulsively, she threw her arms around his neck, sobbing.

'Oh, Hayd, I'm so sorry,' she choked. 'I've missed you so much and I didn't mean to be such a cow.'

He gave her a powerful hug, then very gently pulled himself free and held her at arm's length, his face wearing a worried frown.

'Gordon Bennett, old girl, what is it?' he exclaimed. 'I thought you went away to relax. But you look about all in.'

She took a deep breath. 'Something happened, Hayd,' she replied, 'and I'm not sure what to do about it.'

'What kind of something?'

Leading him to the settee, she sat him down beside her and told him everything.

* * *

The man stood for several minutes in the doorway once the letting agent had driven off after showing him to his new home. The three-bed cottage he had seen advertised as a long-term let on the net was detached, fully furnished and obviously very old. It had thick stone walls stained with damp, a red tiled roof and in the reality of the cold grey afternoon light it looked nothing like the photograph on the website. It was enclosed by flat, waterlogged fields bordered on three sides by willow-lined rhynes and concealed from the road by a patch of scrubby woodland. It was miles from anywhere, though with easy access to the main road, and it had obviously once been a smallholding of sort. A large stone barn and several sheds with patched corrugated iron roofs stood in abject dejection around the overgrown yard at the front, adding to the property's unprepossessing appearance. According to the agent, the previous owner had died intestate, and his family, who were now living overseas, had sold the place at a knockdown price to his agency to clear their late father's death duties and other outstanding debts. The agency's middle-aged, pipe-smoking proprietor was clearly anxious to secure a long-term contract for a property whose maintenance had been burning a hole in his wallet for a long time and he wasn't too fussed about the bone fides of the client who was offering him a way out. The cottage may not have been everyone's idea of a cosy nook, but for Mr Anonymous, it was perfect. Just what he had been looking for. Consequently, a deal had been struck without a single quibble.

* * *

For a few moments after Kate had finished recounting her experiences at the Villa Ambrose and all that had happened since, Hayden sat staring at her in stunned silence. Then he gave a disbelieving shake of his head.

'I repeat, I thought you were supposed to be away on a relaxing break?' he said.

She treated him to a small, weak smile. 'So did I, Hayd,' she replied. 'Seems fate had other ideas.'

'But why would this character latch on to you especially? I mean, it appears from what you've said that there were a lot of other writers in your group.'

'I can only think that his interest was aroused after my introductory presentation to the group when I revealed the fact that I was a police officer.'

There was a suspicious glint in his blue eyes now. 'You sure that's all? Did you sunbathe on the beach while you were there?'

She shrugged. 'On occasions, yes.'

'Wearing what? I suspect that you have caught the sun in a lot more places than your face.'

She tensed, thinking of the first text Mr Anonymous had sent after her topless exposure, which she had been so careful to omit from her story. 'An overcoat, Hayden!' she threw back at him, keen to laugh off the issue. 'The one with the Astrakhan collar! What the hell do you think I was wearing? My bikini, of course. In common with most of the women there, I actually flashed my belly button!'

'Which could explain why he became so interested in you,' he said pompously. 'Lying there half-naked in full view of everyone? Gordon Bennett, you must have really turned him on, and you know how I hate you flaunting yourself like that.'

She was angry now. 'I was not flaunting myself, Hayden. I was just trying to get a bit of sun. Bloody hell, man, we're not living in the Victorian era anymore. They've stopped using bathing machines now. Strangely enough, women wear bikinis, and they actually lie on beaches sunbathing. It's about time you joined the twenty-first century.'

He held up both hands defensively and abruptly changed the subject.

'Okay, okay, keep your hair on. But going back to the death at the hotel, I really can't understand why your man would decide to toss some poor woman off a balcony simply to ape the scenario in your novel. What would be the point? Sounds a bit far-fetched to me. Maybe the woman *did* accidentally fall or commit suicide and you've put two and two together to make five?'

'Don't you think I've considered that? But however you look at it, the fact remains that by suggesting my storyline indicated I could see into the future, he was actually telling me what was going to happen just hours before it actually did. And what about the further message he sent me on the plane as I was leaving? It was so blatantly pointed.'

'So why did you delete it?'

'I really don't know. It was an instinctive reaction, as it was with the earlier text. I wanted him out of my head and as I was leaving Cancun anyway, what was the sense in keeping it?'

He released a heavy sigh. 'You should have told the authorities about your suspicions in the first place, you know that, don't you? You had your chance when the police interviewed you.'

'I tried, Hayden, I honestly did. But they had already made up their minds that the woman had committed suicide and without those texts, I had absolutely nothing to back up my suspicions. Even worse, because the scenario in my novel was identical to the one at the hotel, I might well have ended up as a murder suspect myself.'

He ran one hand through his untidy thatch and made a face. 'I do see your point there, I really do. But you seem to have got yourself into a pretty fix this time and no mistake. Whether your man is a murderer or not, he nevertheless seems to be obsessed with you. He has not only followed you all the way back to the UK but has found out where you are living and was actually outside somewhere watching you just this afternoon. Hence that last text. We have no idea what is motivating his obsession, or what he wants out of it, and that is very worrying.'

'Tell me something I don't know already.'

'And you say you have no idea who could have slipped that message into your pocket on the plane?'

She shook her head. 'There was a crush of people getting stuff out of the overhead lockers and after someone had helped me out with my bag, I turned round to thank them, but by then everyone had moved off.'

'So your courteous helper could have been our man?'

'Possibly. I can't think of any other time anyone was close enough and I had my coat on the floor at my feet the whole flight, so it was never out of my sight.'

'Except when you were asleep or went to the loo.'

'Yes, but I was at the end of a row of seats next to a window, so he would have had to squeeze past a couple of other passengers in the seats next to me to get to my coat and I can't see him doing something as brazen as that.'

'Maybe he was sitting in the seat right next to you?'

'Maybe he was, but as I had no idea what this character looked like, I had no reason to scrutinise my fellow travellers and all I can remember about the man next to me is that he was about seventy, had grey hair and was sitting between me and an elderly lady who seemed to be his wife. Hardly a likely suspect. No, I think the napkin was slipped into my pocket while we were all retrieving our cabin luggage from the overhead lockers.'

He nodded. 'Which means he must have been standing very close to you when he performed his sleight of hand, and he is obviously keeping close tabs on you. I think the sooner we pass this on to the guv'nor, the sooner we can get some sort of protection for you just in case this nutter's obsession with you turns violent.'

'No way,' she cut in quickly. 'This stays between you and me.'

'What? But — but it can't. For goodness sake, Kate, you could be at risk here.'

'As I have been on many an occasion in this job before. I mean it, we say nothing to anyone about it. The department already sees me as flaky after my near breakdown. I can't afford to give them more ammunition. '

'So what the devil *do* we do?'

'We sit tight and wait to see if anything else happens. I have another week's leave to go yet, so I don't want to jump too soon. Maybe Mr Anonymous is just some harmless voyeur who will eventually lose interest in me altogether.'

'Yeah, and maybe he's anything but. And that's what really worries me.'

CHAPTER 2

Just a week later, the subject of Kate and Hayden's conversation parked up outside a small village church late in the
afternoon and spent a few minutes studying the times of
the services on the noticeboard just inside the gate. He was
particularly interested in a side notice giving all the regular
events taking place at the church each week, and he read them
aloud. 'Band practice. Women's Fellowship. Bible Studies.
Youth Fellowship. Bell-ringing practice.' He stopped short at
the fifth entry and ran a finger along it with a sharp intake of
breath. Bell-ringing practice the following evening. Couldn't
have been better. He didn't bother to look any further but
casting a quick glance around to ensure no one was watching,
he walked briskly up the path through the graveyard and into
the porch. The latch on the heavy wooden door issued a loud
'crack' as he raised it and pushed the door open. He stood for
a moment in the doorway as if reluctant to enter, studying
the gold-coloured dust particles floating in the fragile shards
of newly arisen sunlight filtering into the nave through the
stained-glass windows, before stepping over the threshold.

He spent fifteen minutes wandering around the church,
noting in particular the ancient door giving access to the bell
tower, which proved to be locked. Then he slipped cautiously

29

into a small side chapel separated from the nave by an ornate carved screen. The chapel contained about a dozen chairs placed in front of a clothed altar table, which was set with a simple brass cross flanked by a pair of matching candlesticks. Picking up one candlestick, he fondled it thoughtfully for several minutes as if to test its weight, and when he finally left the church to return to his car, the sacred artefact was no longer in evidence on the table but carefully concealed under his anorak. Then he brazenly sat in his car for several more minutes, drinking from a can of Coca Cola and allowing his gaze to rove around the exterior of the church and its surrounds, taking in everything that he could for future reference. He seemed in no real hurry to leave, which was surprising under the circumstances. Though he would never have admitted it, he had always feared churches and he hated all that they stood for. They reminded him too much of his own frailties. For some reason, maybe due to a deep-seated primal instinct that he didn't fully understand, they also unsettled him and caused him to reflect, albeit briefly, on the possibility that there might just be a higher authority somewhere above, watching his every move.

Not that he actually regretted anything he had done in the past, or anything he was contemplating doing in the future. His twisted brain didn't work like that. It told him that you did what you did simply because you could, and legalities and moral values were irrelevant. Life was about getting what you wanted, nothing more.

He had learned that from his mother, and he thought about her as he sat there slowly sipping from his can. He could still see her in his mind's eye. The drunken bitch with the gimlet eyes and acid tongue. No one could have been more selfish or disreputable than her. She had always done exactly what she'd wanted to do ever since he could remember, and she had never considered anyone else in the process. Not even the old man. The hypocritical lay preacher at the local church who had eventually walked out on her after his secret gambling addiction and womanising had cost them their home, forcing them into a rundown council house on a sink estate. The cow had never worked throughout her whole miserable existence and when his father had left, she had relied on benefits and what she could 'earn' from the carnal services she rendered to a succession of so-called uncles. The only time she had ever exerted herself was to knock her only son about, or to reach for the bottle of cider she had bullied him into stealing from the local supermarket.

For his part, he had simply taken it all, too frightened of Iris and her violent temper to protest. He had always been a wimp where she was concerned, he knew that. Academically very clever, but otherwise a bit of a joke. His father had said as much when he was in his teens. 'Born without a backbone, that one,' he'd sneered. 'He's no son of mine.' In fact, he wasn't sure he was his father's son anyway. His mother had always had a reputation where men were concerned.

Iris had played on his weakness for all she was worth. Putting him down at every opportunity. Demeaning everything he did. Particularly in relation to his ambition to be a successful writer. Destroying any confidence he might have had in himself, while at the same time brazenly living off his salary after he secured a job as a library assistant. In fact, incredible as it seemed to him now, she'd continued to have the same inexplicable hold over him well into his forties, long after he should have moved out and embarked on a career that matched his intelligence and qualifications.

Instead, he had stayed on at home, putting up with everything she'd felt like dishing out. Too much in thrall to her to look for somewhere else to live. Too lacking in self-esteem to apply for the university place he wanted so much to enable him to study creative writing. Unable even to strike up a relationship with a member of the opposite sex because of a growing awareness of his own sexual impotence, which he had secretly researched and put down to a genetic mutation at birth.

But then on his forty-second birthday, he had suddenly undergone a dramatic change. After all the years of pent-up misery, the proverbial worm had finally turned. Ironically, the catalyst for this was the manuscript of his newly completed novel, which the old woman had accidentally discovered on his computer when he was at work and in a fit of jealous spite had completely deleted. She really shouldn't have sneered at him when admitting what she had done because something snapped inside him. Hauling her out on to the landing in a cold fury, he had deliberately pitched her headfirst down the stairs, breaking her scraggy neck.

There were no repercussions. The police were satisfied she had tripped on her carpet slippers, and after the inquest and funeral he was able to rent a small flat in town. Then after a few more years, with some more of the money he'd saved, he booked a place on the writer's retreat course at the Villa Ambrose and handed in his notice at the library, determined to at last realise his dream.

Even now he felt no guilt or even satisfaction over killing the old lady. It was just something that had needed to be done. Something he'd been wanting to do for such a long time. But it had taught him an important truth. Killing someone was no big deal. Even if it was your own mother. In fact, he had concluded that people were actually nothing more than pawns on the giant chessboard of life, to be played as the grandmaster thought fit. Almost immediately he'd felt a sense of liberation, as if he had broken out of some ethereal chrysalis or had been born again.

Later, killing the young woman at the Villa Ambrose after using a measure of persuasive chat-up charm he hadn't realised he possessed to inveigle himself into her room, had ultimately posed more of a challenge. It had been his first premeditated hit as part of the newly hatched plot he had devised to rattle Kate Lewis's cage. Though it had largely gone according to plan, the final act had not been as easy as he had anticipated. His plucky victim had struggled and screamed like a banshee when he'd carried her from her bed out on to the balcony. So much so that he had almost panicked and abandoned the attempt. But in the end she had gone over the edge without too much difficulty, enabling him to get clear of the scene in plenty of time. He hadn't realised just how much strength he actually possessed and that was a comforting discovery for the future.

Giving Kate's room the once-over after hatching his plot at the start had already enabled him to check the airline tickets she had left in a drawer. They had told him when and on what flight she was returning to the UK. Then it had simply been a case of booking the same flight back home and keeping tabs on her thereafter. He knew his texts and that last message he had slipped into her pocket at Gatwick would spook her. But that was the whole point of it all, wasn't it? Wind her up and keep piling on the pressure until she cracked completely.

So far everything was going according to plan, and he felt very pleased with himself as he plotted his next move. He was so looking forward to everything that was to come, and the prospect of being able to humiliate that detective bitch in the process, as he had been humiliated by his own mother all through his life, would be the icing on the cake. A satisfying accompaniment to the legacy he would have created for himself.

Then as he sat there, revelling in the lurid pictures his vivid imagination conjured up for him, another figure in a distinctive cassock walked past his car from the manse next door, heading for the church. The cleric paused a moment to peer across at him and he met his curious gaze with a smile. 'See you later, vicar,' he said softly, and gave him a cheerful wave as he restarted the engine and drove off.

* * *

Kate didn't expect the 'royal welcome' she got when she walked into the CID department at Highbridge police station for her first tour of duty after her ill-fated leave. Even Hayden looked taken aback when the half-dozen detectives seated at their desks in the big general office let loose a rousing cheer. She ought to have known there would be more to it.

33

'Welcome back, skipper,' the civilian office manager, Ajeet Singh, said quietly from his desk, though unlike the others, he looked subdued and even a little embarrassed.

Kate responded with a brief, all-encompassing smile. But she looked bemused as she dropped her briefcase beside her desk and pulled out her chair.

It was Hayden who spotted the photograph and his explosive exclamation drew her attention to the noticeboard on the far wall. Curious, she went over to see what he was looking at and immediately regretted it.

A colourful picture postcard was pinned to the cork display and beside it a much larger version blown up into A4 size. It bore the slogan in big red letters, *Greetings From Cancun*, and depicted a beach scene, with most of the focus being on an auburn-haired sunworshipper lying on her back on a sunlounger under an umbrella wearing nothing but a pair of miniscule white briefs. A woman clearly recognisable as Detective Sergeant Kate Lewis!

Kate felt sick and turned away in embarrassment as Hayden, his face white with fury, ripped both pictures down and spun round to glare across the room at his colleagues, all of whom were now innocently hunched over their computers, studying the screens.

'Who — who did this?' he choked, spittle forming at the corners of his mouth. 'What rotten waste of a skin put this up here?'

No one replied, but Kate could see the shoulders of several of her colleagues shaking in obvious hysterics.

'Okay, you lot,' she snapped, taking the bull by the horns, even though inwardly she was quaking. 'So your DS has a pair of tits. Well, what a surprise. I hope seeing them has satisfied your dirty little schoolboy minds. Now the piss-take is over, maybe you'll be able to get on with doing the job you're paid to do.'

She hardly dared look back at Hayden as she returned to her desk and dropped into her chair and when Ajeet Singh, as polite and reserved as ever, came over to her, she treated him to a smouldering stare.

'It was delivered by hand in an envelope this morning to the front counter, Sergeant,' he said, his gaze downcast. 'I am truly sorry for what has happened. I wanted to put it in the bin when it came up here with the post, but—'

'Someone told you not to,' she finished for him.

He nodded and flinched when Hayden barked at his elbow, 'So who was it?'

'Leave it, Hayd,' she said. 'It was just a piss-take. I'm more interested in who delivered it.'

Singh shuffled his feet. 'I don't know who delivered it,' he replied. 'The station duty officer said it was just left on the counter with the rest of the post. It was a busy morning, and anyone could have put it there.'

'Put what where?'

The speaker, a slight, dapper man, with jet black hair and a keen gaze, and wearing a neat blue suit, had entered the room quietly and apparently unobserved by anyone. Acting Detective Inspector Charlie Woo, the head of the department and a former member of the Hong Kong Police, was not someone to make entrances, but he exhibited an air of quiet authority, nevertheless.

Before Kate could stop him, Hayden held the partially torn A4 picture up in front of him. 'Some lowlife in this department enhanced a postcard sent here this morning and stuck it up on the wall,' he exclaimed. 'It's a darned disgrace.'

Woo's eyes narrowed and he threw a quick glance at the other detectives sitting at their desks. 'Holiday snap, Kate?' he said drily.

She made a rueful grimace. 'Not from me, guv,' she said. 'Someone must have sent it from the hotel where I was staying.'

He nodded and handed it back to Hayden. 'Perhaps we ought to have a little chat, Kate,' he said and led the way across the room to his glass-panelled office in the corner.

'Good break?' he queried, sitting down behind his desk and waving her to a chair opposite.

'Until this happened,' she replied.

'So, why would anyone take a pic of you and send it here? What would be the point?'

She froze inside. The last thing she needed was for all the details of what had transpired in Cancun to come out.

'I, er, met a lot of people there,' she said. 'They would have known from the writing course I was on what I did for a living. Maybe someone did this as a joke.'

He obviously wasn't convinced, but he chose not to pursue his question. 'And some dingbat here chose to take things a lot further as a tasteless joke?' he suggested.

She nodded.

'So, what do you want to do about it? Clearly it's a breach of police regs and on top of that, a possible offence of sexual harassment.'

She shook her head vigorously. 'No, leave it. They've all had their fun. It's best to forget it.'

He appeared to carefully consider that. Then he shrugged and sat back in his swivel chair. 'Your decision, Kate. Anyway, it's nice to see you back. Cancun good, was it?'

She hesitated. 'In some ways, yes.'

'Except that you seem to have attracted an unwelcome admirer.'

'What do you mean?'

'Well, someone obviously took that pic of you lying on the beach and went to all the trouble of sending it here. Could be trouble on the horizon.'

She swallowed hard, conscious of his gaze fixed on her. Charlie Woo was nobody's fool, and it was obvious that he suspected there was a lot more to the incident than she was admitting.

She treated him to the semblance of a smile. 'I can handle it,' she said dismissively and stood up. 'Anyway, better get on.'

He grinned. 'I don't think Hayden will want to let this go. He looked pretty angry to me, and I reckon you're in for some grief later.'

'I can handle him too.'

He chuckled. 'Oh, I'm sure you can. But make sure there's no blood left on the carpet.'

Hayden was not in the general office when she walked back in and there was an uneasy silence among the detectives still sitting at their desks with their heads down, pretending to be engrossed in whatever they should have been doing. She said nothing but marched straight across the room and out of the door at the end.

She found her husband where she expected to find him, sitting at one of the corner tables in the canteen, a mug of coffee in front of him and a lardy cake halfway to his mouth. She drew up a chair and sat down facing him.

'We'd better get this out the way,' she said.

His face was still flushed, and he glared at her as if she had mouthed an obscenity. 'Get what out of the way?' he grated. 'Oh, your naked exhibition, you mean?'

She glanced around her self-consciously but found that only a couple of the other tables were occupied, and they were well out of earshot.

'I wasn't naked,' she snapped back. 'I was topless.'

'Same thing.'

'No, it isn't, and I wasn't "exhibiting myself" either as you put it. I was trying to get some sun.'

'You told me lies.'

'I did no such thing.'

'You said you were wearing a bikini. You didn't say you were showing your, er, your thingummies.'

Kate released an unintentional snort. 'My thingummies?' she echoed disparagingly. 'Oh come on, Hayd. Get real, will you? They're called breasts. I just can't believe that a man of your age, and a serving police officer to boot, can be so unworldly. It's like you're living in a parallel universe, untouched by the twenty-first century. You — you're so pompous and narrow-minded, it's not true.'

'You're my *wife*,' he hissed through his teeth. 'Don't you get that?'

She stood up with a heavy sigh. 'Yes, Hayd,' she agreed, 'I am your wife, but not your bloody property!'

Then she left him sitting there, gaping after her.

* * *

Charlie Woo met Kate as she returned to the CID office. He was waving a piece of paper in one hand and Kate's eyes narrowed. A single piece of paper was always a problem in the police service. She had learned that a long time ago. A bundle of documents was usually okay, but that one sheet often spelled a 'just' job and she was right this time.

'Reverend Joshua Strange,' he said, handing her the missive. 'Been on the phone to me.'

She glanced at the address he'd handed her and raised an eyebrow. 'And?' she said warily.

He made a face. 'Some lead was stripped from the roof of his church a week ago. Second time the place has been done this month apparently. About a fortnight ago someone broke the padlock on the donations box and nicked the money. He's just rung me to complain that someone has now stolen an altar candlestick and that he saw a sus car outside the place yesterday afternoon.'

'Job for the local plod, I would have thought?'

He made a face. 'Ordinarily I would agree with you, but the thing is, he's a bit of a persistent complainant. Always on the phone to uniform about cars obstructing the church gates or speeding through the village and kids mucking about in the graveyard, and he isn't too happy about the service he's received from us in the past. I thought it would be politic to send a DS this time to keep him happy.'

She nodded. 'Thanks. I'll say a prayer for you while I'm there!'

He coughed and scratched his nose. 'Er, Hayden okay about things now, is he?'

She snorted. 'Is he ever? He's still convinced he's married to a scarlet woman.'

38

'Well, I have to say, that pic was very attractive.'

'Only if you're a perv, Charlie!'

* * *

The village church was situated opposite a small post office and within spitting distance of the Goose and Feather Inn. The noticeboard just inside the wrought-iron gates said it dated back to the fourteenth century. The slate roof bore evidence of recent damage, clearly visible from the road, which was partially covered by a green tarpaulin, and hideous gargoyles adorned the walls below the bell tower's crenelated parapet.

Kate had telephoned the Rev Joshua Strange in advance of her visit and he was waiting for her in the porch.

A rotund little man, almost bald, with a military-style moustache and horn-rimmed spectacles, he reminded Kate of the comic character Captain Mainwaring in the old TV series, *Dad's Army*. That he was possessed of the same irritably, fussy manner soon became evident.

'You're late, Detective Sergeant,' he snapped pompously. 'I'm a firm believer in punctuality.'

She smiled wryly. 'Sorry, sir. Been a busy afternoon, has it?'

He appeared taken aback. 'Well, no, actually, but that's not the point. Things to do, though. Can't hang about all day.'

Kate was tempted to add for him: 'There is a war on, you know,' but thought better of it, saying instead, 'Then we'd better get on, hadn't we, Reverend? I understand an altar candlestick has been stolen from the church?'

'Yes, from the Lady Chapel.'

'Lady Chapel?'

'Yes, I'll show you.'

Kate followed him into the church, and he waved a hand towards the main altar on the other side of the chancel rails before turning off the nave into a small side chapel with perhaps a dozen chairs set before a modest altar bearing a cross and a single candlestick. 'There should be two candlesticks here. One has disappeared.'

'And I gather you saw a suspicious car here yesterday afternoon.'

He nodded brusquely. 'Very much so. Some sort of what I think they call a utility vehicle, a UV. Black with a white roof.'

'Did you get the index number?'

'Er, no. Fellow drove off at speed when I was about to approach him.'

'So the driver was a man? Can you describe him?'

'Not really. Just an average sort of chap dressed in an anorak and a baseball cap. Didn't see much of him.'

'What made you suspicious of him?'

'Just a feeling really. Saw him from the manse next door coming out of the porch here and getting into the vehicle. Then he sat there for several minutes, apparently staring around him. Casing the joint for later I believe the police call it—'

'Not really, sir. That's just on television.'

'Oh I see. Well, anyway, he was certainly very interested in the building and its surroundings. That's why I went out to see what he was up to. I expect you know we've recently had money stolen from the church and lead stripped off our roof?'

'So I believe. I'm afraid that sort of thing is becoming a national problem. Have you checked to see if anything else is missing from inside the church this time?'

'Yes and everything appears to be in order. But I thought I'd let you people know about this latest incident. Just in case, you understand.'

'Quite right, Reverend, and I'll ask our uniform patrols to give the church passing attention from now on.'

He hesitated, then added, 'My daughter was in the police, you know.'

Kate picked up the sense of pride in his tone. But there was something else with it she couldn't put her finger on, almost like regret or disappointment.

'Oh, where was that?'

'In the Met.'

'Good force. You say "was". Did she pack it in then?'

'Not quite.' He took a deep breath. 'Unfortunately Claire was attacked one night by some drunken ne'er-do-wells and was badly injured.' He coughed. 'Sadly, she, er, died shortly afterwards. She was just thirty.'

Kate felt her stomach wrench. For a moment she just stared at him, not sure what to say, suddenly seeing him in a completely different light.

'I'm very sorry to hear that,' she said quietly. 'How are you managing?'

He gave a thin smile. 'Not very well, I'm afraid, even though it was three years ago now. It hit my wife and me hard. God is a great comfort, though, and we trust in him to help us through it.'

To Kate's surprise he reached forward and squeezed her arm. 'The Lord be with you, my child,' he said, 'and please, take care of yourself. Life is so short.'

Then with his eyes filling up, he turned and disappeared through the half-open doorway into the nave of the church.

Kate felt quite emotional as she returned to the CID car and drove off. She had never been a churchgoer and if she was honest, she found churches quite scary places. But the faith and fortitude that the obviously still distraught minister had displayed despite his terrible loss gave her food for thought. Maybe there was something in this religion thing after all. An all-embracing goodness that rose above the filth and depravity of human nature? But if there was, it would need to go some way if it was to replace the weary cynicism that her years of policing the gutters of society had instilled in her. And she was soon to find out just how deep and unfathomable those gutters could be.

CHAPTER 3

The man Kate called Mr Anonymous was tired, very tired. Hardly surprising really. He'd been busy for the past week with all the research and preparations he'd needed to carry out before the commencement of his 'game'. Now, after the visit to the church, finally everything was ready. Tonight would be his debut and he was desperate to get on with it. In fact his whole body was tingling with anticipation as he bolted the takeaway he had purchased from the chippy in the village of Street. Then he quickly dressed himself in the khaki coat, jeans and baseball cap with *New York* emblazoned on the front he'd bought from the retail outlet at Cribbs Causeway en route to Somerset the week before.

'All set then?' he said to himself. He slipped the brass candlestick he had stolen from the church into a long pocket inside his coat, grabbed his camera and headed for the door. 'Bell-ringing practice tonight, old son, so we mustn't be late, must we?'

There were several cars parked alongside the wall of the church and a ghostly glow emanated from a crack in the door and from the half-dozen stained-glass windows. Lights also smouldered in the mist from the lancet windows of the square tower and even as he drew up he heard the peal of bells. So they were all in there. Brilliant. Now all he had to do was to wait for them to leave and trust in the minister to lock up and close the church afterwards. Even if he didn't and it was someone else, it wouldn't really matter. After all, one person was as good as another in these circumstances, weren't they?

Parking his car in a patch of gloom on the opposite side of the road so that he could keep an eye on all comings and goings without attracting attention, he settled down low in his seat and chewed a chocolate bar as he waited, determined to be ready when the bellringers left.

That happened just over an hour later and he was nearly caught napping. Literally so. He must have dropped off soon after finishing his chocolate bar and he was awakened by the sound of cars starting up and voices calling their goodnights. Two cars were already pulling away and another three were in the process of doing the same thing. As he watched, the road outside the church emptied of vehicles completely, leaving just a couple of muffled-up figures heading off into the village on foot.

He waited a few minutes to make sure there were no stragglers. Then slipping his camera over his shoulder on its long strap he quit the car and headed briskly across the road just as the lights went out in the church tower's lancet windows. Damn it! He would have to move fast. Whoever had turned them off was obviously about to leave.

The Reverend Joshua Strange was in fact in the process of locking the door to the tower when he strode into the nave, and he turned at the sound of the shoes ringing on the stone-flagged floor.

'Sorry,' the minister called. 'I'm just closing up.'

'Gee, that's a pity,' his visitor said, putting on a fake American accent. 'I was hoping to get a quick look around the tower.'

Strange pocketed the keys and shook his head. 'I'm afraid it's too late for visits. You wouldn't see much in the dark anyway. You'll have to make an appointment and come back during the day.'

The other grimaced. 'Fact is, that ain't possible. My flight back to the States leaves first thing in the morning from Heathrow, so this is my last chance.'

Strange sighed. 'I'm awfully sorry, but it is rather late, and I have an early start myself in the morning.'

'Yeah, and I don't wanna take up your time, but I'm only on a short business trip here and I wanted to be able to tell the folks back home that I'd seen inside the church my grandpappy visited when he was over here in the Second World War.'

Strange hesitated. 'Your grandfather?'

'Yessir, Hiram G Rhodes. He was a fighter pilot. Volunteered for the RAF when war broke out and was stationed somewhere, er, near Taunton. He was killed in action over Normandy in 1942.'

It was a plausible story, even though it had just been made up in the car, and fortunately Strange seemed to swallow it.

'Well,' he faltered, 'if you're not too long, I can give you a quick tour. Say ten minutes?'

'Gee, that'd be great. I'll take a couple of pics too if you don't mind.'

'No problem, but tread carefully on the stairs. They are very narrow and are badly worn, as you'd expect for a six-hundred-year-old building.'

'Hey, no problem,' he said, fingering the brass candlestick in his pocket, 'I'll go careful. Quick look from the top of the tower would be good

too . . .'

* * *

Kate didn't sleep well that night. As before when she had had a row with Hayden, she left him to the big double bed upstairs and made use of the settee in the living room for herself. She could hear his snores as she lay there staring at the dwindling fire. He was still mad at her for her topless episode in Cancun and the way their CID colleagues had produced the 'evidence' for all to see. He couldn't seem to get it that she was the one who should have been upset about the photograph, not him. He failed to understand how she could simply dismiss the issue as just a good-natured wind-up by the team. He had gone to bed still muttering angrily to himself and she had given up trying to placate him.

It wasn't the first time in their tempestuous relationship that they had fallen out over something. She felt sure it wouldn't be the last. Though it was plain they were both devoted to each other, they were chalk and cheese as far as their personalities were concerned. She was a thoroughly modern, independent woman. Up until her near breakdown the previous year, she had also been a headstrong, dynamic go-getter, prone to going against the rules to achieve a result. He on the other hand was a cautious, methodical thinker and totally laissez-faire about everything. His only real hang-up was the use of bad language, which he abhorred, and matters of female propriety. Then his narrow, old-fashioned outlook rushed to the fore. As if he was living in some sort of time warp. He was particularly self-conscious in matters of sex. In the last few months of their marriage he had developed almost an aversion to the physical side of their relationship, shying away from it as if scared of the very prospect. It always amazed her how someone who had been exposed to so many years of raw policing could be so out of sync with the real world. He seemed to be totally miscast as a copper. The proverbial square peg in a round hole.

Yet despite his funny ways and her much more liberal attitude on such things, deep down she had to admit that on this occasion she herself was more than a little disturbed about the situation she was in. But it was for a different reason, and it wasn't because of the photo of herself half-naked. Because she was a police officer, that didn't make her any different or more scandalous than any other topless woman. She was not ashamed of her body. What concerned her was why the man stalking her would go to such extreme lengths as to take a picture of her and send it to Highbridge police station. She guessed he had taken the photograph the same day he had commented on her 'boobs' in his text. But then to have had the picture produced in what seemed to be a professional looking greetings postcard, complete with its fancy caption, must have taken some effort and expertise. But with what object? If he was just some voyeuristic pervert, why adopt such extraordinary measures just to humiliate her in front of her work colleagues? As far as she could remember, she had not choked off or upset anyone while at the Villa Ambrose, so what the hell was his motive? Even more worrying were the text messages he had sent her tying her novel in with the suspicious death of the young woman at the hotel and the fact that he had then tailed her thousands of miles across the ocean all the way to Somerset. It all suggested he was someone suffering from some form of obsessive psychosis and she had to admit that was quite scary.

Maybe she *should* have followed Hayden's advice and reported the whole thing to Charlie Woo. But as she had tried so hard to explain to her husband, after the near breakdown she had suffered, which had already cost her temporary promotion to acting DI and a lot of professional credibility besides, she desperately needed to build herself up again in everyone's eyes. She couldn't afford to load herself with even more baggage by creating the impression she was relapsing. She had to do this thing on her own and she saw no other alternative. Even if that did mean a virtually estranged husband until he decided to come around again.

In the meantime she could do nothing but wait for her stalker's next move whatever that turned out to be. She was still dwelling on that when she finally dropped off to sleep and the next thing she knew was that the phone was ringing. For a moment she didn't have a clue where she was. She jerked up into a sitting position, straight out of a nightmare of flashing camera bulbs and sneering laughter as she wandered naked through a maze of decomposing corpses stacked higher than her head on both sides.

She shuddered, shaking her head violently to clear away the last of the fading images, and stumbled up from the settee like someone who had had too much to drink. She probably had too, she thought, glancing severely at the two empty bottles of red wine on the coffee table. The phone continued to ring, but she knew there was no chance of Hayden answering it. Once he was asleep, the Battle of Britain wouldn't have woken him.

Crossing unsteadily to the halfmoon table to one side of the stairs, she picked up the phone and grunted a response.

'Kate? It's Dick Cave, night turn skipper.'

She refocused her eyes and got a grip on herself. 'What's up?'

'Were you asleep?'

'What do you think? It *is*—' she glanced at her watch — 'four in the morning.'

'Yeah, well sorry about that, but we've got a funny job on, and I gather you had some dealings with the guy involved so might be able to throw some light on things.'

Kate frowned and ran a hand wearily through her tangled hair. 'It would help, Dick, if you were to tell me the name of "the guy" and what the hell this is all about? Especially at four in the bloody morning.'

'The Reverend Joshua Strange. I hear you responded to a complaint from him yesterday re a suspicious incident at his church.'

'A sus car, yes. But couldn't this have waited four hours until I was back on duty?'

'Not really. It might be relevant.'

'Relevant? Relevant to what?'

'To his death.'

'His death?' The cobwebs instantly cleared from Kate's mind. 'You're saying he's dead?'

There was a sardonic note to the other's tone when he replied. 'Yeah, you know, sort of no longer breathing. Which is not really surprising as it seems he jumped off the church

47

tower earlier tonight. Made a bit of a mess in the churchyard too. I'm at the scene now.'

'I'll be straight over.'

'That's nice to hear. Wrap up well, though, won't you? It's cold out here and you don't want that cute little chest of yours getting cold.'

The snipe ended in a gurgle of mocking laughter and before she could say anything else he cut off. So Dick Cave knew about the postcard too. Probably the whole nick, maybe the whole police area, knew about it as well. Wonderful!

* * *

Dick Cave was talking to a uniformed police constable when Kate pulled up in her MX-5 in the car park of the ancient church, and she nodded as she approached him along a narrow gravel path running down the side of the building.

Ironically Strange had landed on top of a large stone tomb in the graveyard at the rear of the church. His corpse lay at the foot of the tower, grotesquely illuminated by the moon, but thankfully out of sight of the line of cottages opposite the main entrance. He was lying face down, dressed in an anorak and dark trousers. His arms were flung wide as if he had been trying to embrace the canopy of the cracked, weathered tomb on which he had landed, and his visible injuries were horrific. What had once been his head looked as though it had exploded on impact like a ripe pumpkin, propelling blood, brain tissue and bone across the canopy as well as over the grass around the tomb and up the wall of the church. The one part of his face that was visible was just a gory mess of partially congealed blood, torn flesh and pieces of projecting white bone from which a single eye bulged in a demoniac glare like that of some maniac doll in a horror film. As for the rest of him, it was to be assumed from the general state of his bloody contorted body that most of his bones had been shattered on impact and both his legs appeared to be broken in several places and skewed at impossible angles.

Kate was immediately taken back to Cancun and the woman who had pitched from the balcony on to the terrace below her room. Automatically her gaze travelled up the wall from the corpse to the crenelated ramparts of the tower.

'Obviously jumped from there,' Cave said at her elbow, his tone suitably mollified now. 'Must have been desperate to do something like this. Police surgeon's en route by the way.'

Kate nodded, acknowledging that the procedural formality of death certification had been followed. 'Nasty way to go.'

Cave shrugged. 'Quick, though, wouldn't you say?' Then he added curiously, 'One funny thing.'

'What?'

He pointed at the grass curling round the bottom of the tomb. Kate peered at the spot. There was something lying just below the outstretched hand of the corpse. She bent closer, then stepped back quickly.

'What the hell's that?'

He shrugged. 'Looks like a dead crow to me. Maybe he was trying to grab it up top and lost his balance?'

'And why would he do that? Talk about fanciful notions. The thing's probably been lying here for a while.'

'Just a thought. Anything he said to you when you saw him yesterday that would suggest his death could be linked to the complaint he was making? You know, someone with an axe to grind against him who may have come back some time after you'd gone.'

'You sound as if you're trying to interview me, Dick,' she censured drily. 'But no, nothing like that. I just think he was paranoid about prowlers after his church was done previously. I said we would pay passing attention and that was that.'

'Did he appear depressed at all?'

'Well, he did tell me his daughter was killed by some thugs three years ago while she was a serving copper in the Met and he and his wife were still having difficulty coping with it. But though the tragedy was obviously still haunting him personally, he said God was helping them through the

49

situation, and I didn't sense anything in his manner to suggest he could be contemplating something like this.'

'Could be a reason for him to take his own life, though, couldn't it? You know, long-term trauma, PTSD or whatever,'

'It's possible, but why now after three years? And why the very day he had gone to all the trouble of reporting seeing a suspicious car outside? That doesn't sound like the mindset of someone who is bent on suicide. Why would he bother?'

'True, but who knows how the minds of depressives work?'

Kate eyed him narrowly. But there was nothing in his expression to suggest he was having another dig at her after her recent breakdown issue. She told herself she was being over-sensitive and let it go.

'How was he found?' she asked.

'His wife telephoned us. Apparently he attended some bell-ringing practice thing at the church in the evening, and she went to bed early because she wasn't feeling well and fell asleep. When she woke up around three in the morning and saw he wasn't there, she rang us in a bit of a panic.' He nodded towards the other uniformed officer. 'George Titmuss over there found him like this.'

'Has the wife been told?'

'Helen Strange? Yeah, I left her with one of our women officers. She's remarkably calm, but people often are in these situations, until later when things really hit them.'

'I shall have to have a chat with Mrs Strange. But I can't see her accepting that her husband killed himself. After all, that would be a sin in the eyes of the church and also suggest he had taken the quick way out and abandoned her.'

'Could be he accidentally fell, of course.'

'That's something we'll have to look into. Have you been up to the top of the tower?'

'Not yet. Not been here long.'

'Then I suggest we take a look now.'

There were around seventy odd steps to the top of the tower and Kate only made a brief stop on the way to check out the bell room. But there was nothing to see in there except the coloured cords, which had no doubt been tied up for safety reasons and were now hanging in loops from the shadows of the vaulted ceiling like sinister snake-like coils.

Kate was privately pleased to see that Cave was more out of breath than she was when they finally emerged at the very top, and she left him bent over and wheezing to cross the roof to the crenelated parapet directly above the point where Strange must have gone over.

The young police officer left guarding the scene waved when he saw her head appear and she shuddered. It was a long way down and from her viewpoint, the uniformed figure looked more like a model soldier from some kiddies' toy set than a real person.

She turned as Cave joined her. 'Well, one thing's clear,' she commented. 'You couldn't accidentally fall off this tower. The parapet must be at least four feet high. You'd need to have intended to do it.'

She peered at the section in front of her, then clicked her fingers. 'Have you got a torch? Quite a bit of shadow here.'

He handed her one and she ran the beam slowly over the parapet, then straightened with a grunt, handing it back to him. 'No distinctive scuffmarks to indicate that someone has climbed on to the wall. But there again, the stonework is already scored and weathered with time, and they probably wouldn't show up anyway.'

'So what's the verdict, Sherlock?'

'There isn't a verdict. How could there be? It's possible a determined jumper could have forced himself through one of the gaps—'

'They're called crenels.'

'Aren't you the clever one? In any event, the gap between them and the—'

'Merlons.'

'Thank you, Einstein.'

'Einstein was a scientist.'

'Whatever. You're beginning to sound like bloody Hayden. The thing is, the gap between these *merlons* of yours

must be around eighteen inches. Wide enough for a determined jumper to squeeze through.'

'Suicide then? Or maybe something else, do you think?'

'Don't even go there.'

* * *

The police doctor arrived ten minutes later, and his assessment was predictable. 'Multiple injuries consistent with a fall
from a significant height,' he said.

'Anything else you can tell us?' Cave asked.

The medical man gave a grim smile. 'Other than that he's
dead,' he said, 'not a lot, but it would have been instantaneous.'

'Any thoughts on time of death?' Kate added.

He considered the question. 'Not easy in this case,' he
replied. 'But from my examination just now, I would say
he's been deceased for about six to seven hours, give or take.'

'So around nine then?'

'If you say so.'

Kate made a wry grimace. 'Thanks, Doc, you've been
a real help.'

'I always try to be.'

The manse was right next door to the church and the
front door was ajar. Mrs Strange was sitting quietly on a
wooden chair at the kitchen table and the young police-
woman rose from her own chair beside her when Kate and
Cave walked in after a peremptory knock.

The elderly lady had been crying and her drawn white
face contrasted with the puffy redness around her brown
eyes. Small and thin with her grey hair hanging loosely to
her shoulders, she was still dressed in her long nightdress with
a long-sleeved blue cardigan on top. She looked so frail and
lost and Kate's heart went out to her.

'Detective Sergeant Kate Lewis, Mrs Strange,' she said
quietly, 'and this is—'

She nodded. 'Yes, Sergeant Cave. We have already met.'

'Can I say how sorry we are that such a terrible thing has happened,' Kate went on, occupying the woman officer's chair. 'But unfortunately we have to ask you a few questions.'

Mrs Strange gave a weak smile and to Kate's surprise, reached out and squeezed her hand. 'I understand, dear, and you have a rotten job to do.'

For a moment Kate was completely taken aback and before she could say anything else, the old woman went on speaking.

'He's with the Lord now, bless him,' she said, 'and I pray he will be forgiven for what he has done.'

'How do you mean?'

'Taken his life like this,' came the prompt, if whispered, reply. 'It's a sin, you see. Only the Good Lord has the right to take a life. But poor Joshua never did get over what happened to Claire. It plagued him all the time. I feared that one day he would submit to the devil's wiles and the anniversary of her passing was just two days ago.'

'Did he ever say anything about doing something like this?'

'He didn't need to. I knew he couldn't rest, and I was always afraid for him.'

'So you think things may have actually got too much for him in the end?' Kate went on gently, still shocked by the woman's surprising control and fortitude.

Another sad smile and a few more tears ran down the pale, lined face. 'Men do not have the moral strength and resilience of women, Sergeant,' she said. 'They are physically strong, but weak in other ways. Poor Joshua was a dedicated Christian and a devoted husband, but it seems he could not endure the loss of his beautiful daughter any longer.'

Kate nodded and threw a quick glance, first at Cave and then at the woman constable, compressing her lips with an air of finality.

'Is there anyone you would like us to call to sit with you when we leave here? Another relative? A neighbour perhaps? Or your doctor?'

She shook her head. 'I shall be fine, Sergeant, honestly. I have the Lord to help me.'

'I've already telephoned the church warden and she is on her way, skip,' the woman officer said, 'and I'll be staying here with Mrs Strange until she arrives.'

Kate nodded her thanks and reluctantly stood up. 'Well, if you need anything, Mrs Strange, please do not hesitate to contact me. I'll leave my card here on your coffee table just in case.'

'Suicide for definite then, you reckon?' Cave said to Kate once they were back outside and out of earshot.

Kate stared at the doors of the church, which were now closed, and nodded slowly. 'Seems like it, Dick. Anyway, I'm going home for some breakfast, so I'll leave you to finish up here.'

'Don't CID always?' he sniped.

CHAPTER 4

Debbie Moreton turned up for work with a massive hangover from a party the night before and she had barely dumped her oversized canvas handbag on her desk in the newsroom of the regional tabloid when the phone rang.

'What?' she responded with characteristic politeness through a mouthful of gum, pressing the phone against her ear with one hand as she tried to comb out her spiky, pink-dyed hair with the other.

'You the crime reporter?' a voice said.

'You got it.'

'I have something for you.'

'Such as?'

'A murder.'

Moreton froze. 'Is this a wind-up?'

'The Reverend Joshua Strange wouldn't think so. Especially as he's the one I killed.'

The comb dropped out of Moreton's hand as if it had suddenly given off an electric shock, and she fumbled for her notebook and pen in her handbag.

'*You* killed him?'

'That's what I said. Tossed him off the bell tower of his quaint little church last night.'

'That sounds like a load of crap to me, mister.'

'Does it? Then maybe you should check it out. I'll give you the address.'

With her hand shaking, Moreton scribbled down the details he passed to her.

'But — but why would you kill a minister?'

'I just felt like it and I found it quite liberating actually. Anyway, I suggest you get over there and take a look at the top of the tower before someone else finds what's up there.'

'What *is* up there?'

'"Seek, and ye shall find." Luke eleven, verse nine, King James Bible.'

'So why are you telling me this?'

'I wanted to show you just how incompetent the local police are. Especially Detective Sergeant Kate Lewis. She still thinks this was a suicide, the stupid cow, but she didn't do much of a scene search, did she?'

'Who am I speaking to?'

'Don't be silly.'

The caller cut off.

* * *

Hayden was not yet up when Kate got back to their cottage in Burtle village, and she could hear his snores from the bedroom as she opened the front door. She made herself some toast and marmalade and strong black coffee and settled on to one of the stools at the breakfast bar in the kitchen to reflect on the morning's events.

Something was bothering her about the death of the Reverend Strange, but she couldn't home in on what it was. It was just an uneasy feeling deep inside her that wouldn't go away. Nothing more than that. Okay, so all the facts pointed to a straightforward, if messy, suicide. No suspicious circumstances had been evident and even Strange's wife had been convinced that her husband had killed himself after suffering long-term depression over the loss of his daughter.

56

Furthermore, it had been plain during the conversation Kate herself had had with the minister the afternoon before, that the tragic event was still plaguing him. He had even named the issue to her completely out of the blue, as if he were seeking some kind of support. Yet despite all this something did not seem to gel. Perhaps she was just overtired and that coupled with the recent stresses she had experienced was creating problems in her mind that weren't really there. She hoped that that was all it was.

She was still thinking about things when Hayden stomped down the stairs in his dressing gown, bleary eyed and wearing a truculent frown. So sleep hadn't mellowed him in the slightest, she mused, and he was obviously not in any mood to acknowledge her presence. He didn't even ask her why she was up and dressed so early and it was apparent that he wasn't even aware of the early morning call-out. She watched him with cynical amusement as he manoeuvred around her in the small kitchen and poured himself a coffee from the cafetière before slamming two slices of bread into the toaster with such force that one sprang out again and landed on the floor.

Shaking her head at the childish display, she made no comment, but eased herself away from the breakfast bar and dumped her used crockery and knife into the sink. Then returning to the living room and grabbing her anorak from the peg by the front door, she went out to her car and left him to it.

She had reached Highbridge and was pulling into the yard at the back of the police station when her mobile shrilled.

'Yep,' she snapped, thinking that maybe Hayden had had a change of heart and was on a peace mission. No such luck. The voice on the other end was cold and smooth. Nothing like Hayden's.

'Hi, Kate,' the caller drawled. 'Back on the job then?'

She frowned. 'Sorry, who is this?'

There was a series of tuts. 'Oh dear, have you forgotten your phantom texter from Cancun already?'

She stiffened and glanced quickly at the unfamiliar number on her phone.

'Yes, you're quite right,' the voice added with a chuckle, effectively reading her mind, 'I *am* using a burner, as I did with the text messages. These old phones are very cheap, though quite limited in scope. Furthermore, their data can be wiped or burned, as they say, immediately after use and they are untraceable. I got mine just by handing over a bundle of cash, including paying for "X" number of minutes in advance. I gave a false name and address, declined a receipt and walked away with a nice little Nokia. I take my hat off to twenty-first century technology—'

Kate gripped the phone so tightly that it made a loud 'crack'. 'Enjoy drooling over my photo, did you, you dirty little pervert?' she cut in through gritted teeth.

There was a heavy sigh. 'Not really. I just wanted to get your attention after I failed to do so by chucking that stupid woman off the hotel balcony. As for the "dirty little pervert" bit, now that is a gross insult. I'm not interested in your cute little body, Detective Sergeant. Sexy as it may be with all its freckles.'

'In which case, what is it you want?'

'What do *I* want? Oh dear, you do have things arse about face, don't you? I don't want anything, my dear. You are the one who wants things. Or rather will want them. For a start, you'll want to know who tossed poor old Reverend Strange off the bell tower of his own church and also why they did it.'

Kate swallowed quickly. 'I hate to disappoint you, but the minister committed suicide,' she retorted, though her tone was slightly shaky and lacked conviction. 'So, if you're trying to make something out of that, you can forget it.'

'You sure, are you? Then how would I know his name and what happened to him? Especially as the news hasn't been released yet. I just wondered how thoroughly you checked the scene? Not very well at all, I would suggest. Otherwise you would have found the evidence.'

Kate felt the acid bile surge in her throat. 'Evidence? What evidence?'

'Now that would be telling, wouldn't it? Well outside the rules of the game.'

'Game? What game?'

'Why, the game you and I will be playing from now on. You know, to test those vital powers of perception and deduction that you told all of us budding literary sleuths back in Cancun go to the make-up of a good detective.'

Kate could hear the rising emotion in his voice now.

'Remember? You were so full of yourself standing up there with all your so-called superior knowledge. Pretending to be one of us, but underneath it all, holding the lot of us in contempt. I couldn't help thinking at the time, what makes her think she's so special? What gives her the right to see herself as the world's greatest detective and the world's future best-selling author all rolled into one?' He snorted. 'No right at all. In my opinion, you're nothing more than an arrogant, conceited little bitch who deserves all that's coming to you—'

Kate cut in on his mini rant. 'So that's what all this is about, is it?' she mocked, trying to wind him up still more in the hope that he might inadvertently say something that would lead to his identification. 'Jealousy. Pure and simple. Because you've been an inadequate and a failure all your life, and you resent anyone who appears to be proficient in what they do.'

She heard him catch his breath and his tone was suddenly laced with naked malice.

'Is that what you think? Well, little Miss Perfect, you'd better pay attention. The game I mentioned just now has already begun. I have thrown the first dice and you'll need to get yourself in gear if you are going to have any chance of catching me up. You see, over the next few days I will be providing you with a number of nice fresh corpses. The Reverend Strange was the first. We won't count that silly mare in Cancun. As I said just now, she was killed just to attract your attention. The other stiffs will follow in due course, the second in a few days, then the third and the fourth and so on as the mood takes me. All you have to do to stop the carnage is what I believe you coppers would call "feeling my collar". Quite simple really.'

'You're off your trolley.'

'Now that's also insulting. Just think of it as a battle of wits. Yours against mine and may the best brain win. Probably mine actually as I have a very high Mensa score and you are nothing more than a self-opinionated copper of very average intelligence. It'll be a bit like playing that well-known board game, Cluedo. Oh by the way, did you find my rather gruesome calling card at the scene?'

'Calling card? What are you talking about?'

'The crow, my dear. I left it in the good old minister's hand. Must have fallen out.'

Kate's mind flashed back to the dead bird Cave had pointed to at the foot of the tomb. 'You really *are* crackers.'

'Not really. Just well read. You see, the crow has long been regarded as the harbinger of death and the ancient Romans associated it with murder too. I thought it was a rather appropriate thing to use. But enough of this chat. You'll want to get back to the scene of the good minister's death PDQ. Before the reporter from the local paper gets there, I mean. Could be a tad embarrassing for you otherwise.'

* * *

Kate almost hit a parked patrol car as she reversed her MX-5 into a corner of the yard before turning round and racing back out with a swirl of tyres, heading for the Levels. Fifteen minutes later she was swinging across the road into the church car park. She was relieved to see that Dick Cave's marked patrol car still occupied its original parking space. At least he was still there. But there were two other unfamiliar cars parked close by and she felt her stomach muscles tighten. Her worst fears were realised when Cave strode out through the doors of the church as she pulled up just feet away.

'Kate,' he exclaimed as she clambered out of her car, 'am I glad to see you. We've got a problem.'

She nodded, her expression tight-lipped. 'I can guess,' she replied.

'Press,' he blurted, 'a woman reporter and a guy with a camera. They sneaked into the church as I was sorting out the removal of the body with the undertaker. I'd already sent Titmuss back to the nick with the wopsie, er, PC Baker that is, so I was the only one here. They're up in the tower now taking pictures. I shot out here to call you up. Signal's naff inside.'

Kate pushed past him into the church. 'Okay, okay. What are they taking pictures of?'

'Dunno,' he replied, close on her heels. 'But I had no power to stop them going up there. It's not a crime scene.'

You could be wrong about that, Dick, she mused grimly and ducked through the open door leading up into the tower.

She came face to face with the spiky-haired reporter at the top of the stairs. She recognised her immediately. Debbie bloody Moreton. A regular pain in the arse!

She controlled herself with an effort. 'Hello, Debbie,' she said in as even a tone as she could manage. She pressed forwards on the narrow stairs, forcing the journalist to move back through the low doorway out on to the roof of the tower and then in turn the plump, bald-headed man with the expensive looking camera who was directly behind her. 'Up and out before breakfast then? That's not like you.'

In the sunlight streaming through a gap in the clouds she saw the reporter smirk.

'I go where the news takes me, Kate,' she replied. 'Like to a potential murder scene where the police have yet again cocked up.'

'It was a suicide, not a murder.'

'Not what my source told me this morning.'

'What source?'

'Some mystery guy who claimed he actually killed the good reverend by pushing him off the tower.'

'A hoaxer you mean.'

'Oh, I don't think he was a hoaxer, and guess what, we've got some great pics of a weapon too, which he obviously used to smack him over the head with first.'

The cameraman nodded and half-turning, pointed across the tower to something lying against the parapet. 'Nice bit of blood on it too, Sergeant, though of course, being responsible citizens, we haven't touched anything.'

'Wouldn't want to compromise a *crime scene*,' Moreton added with emphasis on the last two words.

Kate pushed past her and bent over the object. It appeared to be a brass candlestick, maybe from the church altar, and the dark gunge covering part of the base looked unmistakably like blood. Her mind flashed back to Strange's complaint about the theft of just such an artefact from the Lady Chapel and she felt sick.

'That wasn't up here when we checked the tower earlier,' she said before she could stop herself.

Moreton scribbled quickly in her notepad. 'Famous last words, Kate,' she mocked. 'Don't suppose you would like to follow them up with an interview?'

'Piss off!' Kate snapped back, only to clamp her mouth shut when she saw Moreton writing again in her notebook.

'Obviously we won't actually print that remark,' the reporter said, 'seeing as our readers might be offended by the use of such a crude expletive. But I think I can convey the drift in my piece.'

'I think you'd better leave,' Cave butted in. 'Or you could find yourself under arrest for obstructing—'

'A crime scene?' the cameraman finished for him with a loud guffaw.

Then both he and Moreton turned and pushing past Cave, disappeared down the stairs.

Cave pulled a packet of cigarettes out of his pocket. 'I have a horrible feeling we're in the shit on this one, Kate,' he commented.

She gave a short unamused laugh. 'That could be the biggest understatement you have ever made, Dick,' she replied. 'Now I'd better get Scenes of Crime down here. What is it they say? Better late than never?'

* * *

Charlie Woo was not happy. He stared at Kate for several minutes while he chewed over what she had told him. A dying fly buzzed and wriggled on its back on the windowsill and in the DI's otherwise silent office, the sound seemed magnified to the level of a road drill.

'Bit of a cock-up then,' Woo summarised with a heavy sigh, and he sat back in his swivel chair, playing with his pen. 'Looks like Strange's candlestick thief and the perp who stiffed him are one and the same person.'

Kate nodded but said nothing.

'I've already had a reporter from the regional daily, some-one called Debbie something or other, on the phone asking me about the incident,' he went on. 'Apparently your mystery caller rang her to fill her in on the details of his crime, though he doesn't seem to have shared the bit about the dead crow with her. I refused to comment obviously, and it took me a while to convince her to go and play on the motorway instead.'

Kate winced. 'On the face of it, I know it looks bad. But that candlestick was definitely not on the roof of the tower when Dick Cave and I first checked the scene. It was not fully light then, I admit, but it was light enough for us to have seen something like that if it had been lying by the parapet. As for the dead crow, why should I have regarded that as anything significant? It was just a dead bird.'

'So you're saying this character must have returned to the scene after you had gone and while Dick Cave was oth-erwise engaged, to plant the candlestick there?'

'I don't reckon he ever left entirely. I think he was hiding somewhere nearby and was monitoring everything we were doing so he could choose the right moment to do the job.'

'But what I can't understand is why he would do this in the first place. It suggests he's got it in for you or for the police generally and wants to rubbish reputations. That's why he got in touch with the local rag so quickly. Plainly the Reverend Strange was not murdered for any personal reason. He was just the means to a specific end. The scumbag was after us, or rather you in particular.'

She hesitated a fraction, feeling another acid surge in her stomach. Then gnawing at her lip for a moment, she tried to decide whether to unload everything on her boss or continue to keep her mouth shut about all the other baggage she was already carrying. But he then took the decision right out of her hands.

'Okay, Kate, let's cut to the chase,' he said quietly. 'What else have you got to tell me? I'm not a fool and I know there's a lot more behind this business than you've told me so far. Is it linked to Cancun and the postcard that was dropped in at the nick, by any chance?'

She took a deep breath and nodded. 'I've got quite a lot to tell you actually,' she admitted. 'But you're not going to like it.'

'Try me.'

So she did.

* * *

The fly was dead and the silence in the room seemed even more pronounced than the creature's death throes. In the general office on the other side of the glass partition that separated it from the DI's inner sanctum a telephone rang, and someone asked who wanted coffee.

'Why didn't you tell me all this when that pic of you went up on the wall?' Woo asked finally.

'Embarrassment primarily, I suppose. Maybe also an element of trepidation about how it would be perceived after my recent mental health issues.'

He nodded as if he sympathised with her feelings, but he didn't comment on the explanation. 'And you feel sure the woman in Cancun was deliberately thrown off that balcony by the man who is now stalking you?'

'After everything that's happened so far, I think that's a pretty fair conclusion to draw from all that he's said.'

'His motive being what? To destroy you simply because he doesn't like women police officers, or because he has a thing about women crime novelists?'

'Both probably. For some reason, he appears to have taken an intense dislike to me after I gave my introductory presentation to the syndicate in Cancun. The way I put it over, something I said, I really don't know.' She thought of what Cave had said to her about depressives and added, 'Who can fathom how a crazy's mind works?'

'And you reckon that the same character was on your plane back from Cancun and that he stuffed that napkin in your coat pocket?'

'Who else knew me or would have known I was on board?'

He glanced down at the napkin she had placed on his desk. 'I can't see us getting any forensic evidence, like prints, off this sort of material. But I'll pass it to SOCO anyway,' he said. 'Could be it carries some other DNA traces, but they could have been left by anyone. Especially if this arse-hole picked the napkin up from another seat. Furthermore, unless he's already on our PNC database, there wouldn't be anything there for us to use to identify him anyway.'

She nodded. 'And if we did manage to tie the napkin to the right man, he could always claim he didn't write the message himself but had left the napkin he was using on his seat before quitting the aircraft.'

'Precisely. But back to his texts, we'd better have your mobile phone. I'll get the technical crew to see if they can do anything with it re the messages he sent you.'

She looked dubious. 'Unfortunately I deleted them all, and I believe he was using a burner phone anyway, so even if they manage to turn the messages up, the phone is likely to be untraceable.'

He shrugged. 'We'll give it a whirl anyway. I'll get hold of another temporary phone for you in the meantime and you can retain the same number just in case he calls again.'

He threw her a keen glance. 'As a matter of interest, didn't spot anyone from your writing school at the airport or on the plane as you were leaving, did you?'

She shook her head. 'Sorry, but it might be useful to get hold of a copy of the passenger manifest from the airline, plus a list of those attending the writing course from the Villa Ambrose, to see if any were on my flight.'

'Which would prove what?'

'Not a lot really, I must admit. But we have nothing else to go on.'

He sighed heavily. 'Well, it's worth trying anyway. But the long and the short of it all is that we could have a potential psychotic killer out there somewhere, who is just getting started—' he shrugged — 'and heaven knows what his ultimate goal might be.'

'As I told you, he said in that last phone call that he wants to prove he is cleverer than me. He sees it all as some sort of intellectual game.'

'Great, and it seems you have failed the first round.'

'Thanks for reminding me. But what now? Do we put something out to the public through the media, warning them to be vigilant, or do we say nothing on the grounds that it could cause a panic?'

'That decision is way above my pay grade. But I think we shall certainly have to pass what information we have on to the police in Mexico in case they want to re-investigate the death of the woman at the hotel. Unlikely though that might be in view of what you've said about them, there's an outside chance it could throw up the names of any likely suspects after they've actually reinterviewed staff. I will have to speak to Mr Ricketts about the public announcements issue, though—'

Kate winced again, fully aware of the antipathy the area's detective chief inspector had towards her personally. 'Our "golden boy" will really love to hear of my latest faux pas.'

'I doubt it very much. Especially as we will very likely be fighting a rear-guard action against the local paper when their next edition comes out screaming CID incompetence. At least you got SOCO down to the scene PDQ and the suspected murder weapon will soon be with Forensics.' He frowned. 'Pity we couldn't have got the forensic pathologist to the scene while the body was in situ, but that can't be helped now, and we can still ensure that the omission of an expert witness in that regard can be partially corrected when the post-mortem is conducted. I will get hold of the coroner's officer to set things up straight after we have finished here.'

'I can do that.'

He shook his head firmly. 'No way. You are too personally involved in this thing to have anything to do with the investigation and when I speak to the DCI and tell him the circumstances, he will almost certainly decide that you're going to have to sit this one out. There's likely to be an internal inquiry over the handling of the original incident anyway.'

Kate clenched her fists tightly in her lap. 'I must be part of the crime investigation. I can't be left out of things. I am what this case is all about. He'll be expecting me to be an integral part of it and I don't know how he'll react if he learns I've been sidelined.'

He snorted. 'The day we take into consideration the feelings of a suspected murderer will be time to pack the job in altogether.' He treated her to a faint smile. 'As I understand it, this won't be the first time you've had to be taken off an inquiry because you yourself have become the issue. So you should be used to being sidelined by now, and this time it will give you the opportunity of sorting out your latest spat with poor old Hayden.'

Kate's mouth tightened into a thin, hard line as she remembered the cases he was referring to, the last of which involving the ruthless killer, Frank Tannahill, had sent her on the downward path towards a nervous breakdown. She knew Woo was right. Officially, she couldn't be allowed to investigate a case in which she was personally involved, but somehow she didn't think Mr Anonymous would see it that way . . .

CHAPTER 5

Kate found it a long day after all that had happened. For the first time in her service she clock-watched after returning to her desk from a solitary lunch in a corner of the police canteen as she began to unenthusiastically tackle a pile of paperwork that had been dumped in her 'in' tray by the office manager.

Ajeet Singh returned from his own lunch as she was scanning a burglary file one of her team had submitted for a decision by the DI. He approached her desk, profusely apologetic.

'Sorry, Kate,' he said, 'but you're the only DS on the department at the moment and it has all sort of built up while you were on leave. We've been sending some of our work over to one of the skippers at Bridgwater, but now you're back—'

She waved his apologies away. 'No problem, Singh,' she replied, the bitterness evident in her tone. 'It's all part of the job and it doesn't look like I'll be doing much else from now on.'

He shuffled his feet and glanced quickly around the now empty office. 'Look, skip, I don't know whether there's anything in it, but the postcard that was pinned up on the noticeboard. You know, the one with—'

She half-closed her eyes. 'You don't need to go into chapter and verse,' she said. 'I haven't got that short a memory.'

He compressed his lips in a rueful grimace. 'Yes, of course, but there's something I've been wanting to tell you about it.'

'Like, who blew up the image and put it there, maybe?'

He shook his head firmly. 'No, I can't tell you that. It would be like informing on a colleague.'

'Then what?'

'Well, I came in yesterday morning a bit earlier than usual and I think on reflection that I may actually have seen the person who left the envelope containing the postcard on the corner of the counter while the station duty officer was out of the front office. It was addressed to CID, so naturally I brought it up here with me.'

Kate glared at him. 'And you're only telling me this now?'

He winced. 'I've been trying to get you on your own to tell you, but you've been tied up on this job at the church all morning—'

'A job, which it turns out, might actually be connected to the delivery of that very postcard!'

'I'm sorry, I didn't know that. I'm just the office manager. I'm not privy to your crime investigations.'

She took a deep breath and held up a hand to acknowledge his point. 'So what did this character look like?'

'I didn't see much of him, but he brushed past me as I came through the door from the street. I-I travel to work on a bike, you see, which I leave in the rack outside. All I saw was a tall, thin guy in a long black coat, wearing a black, floppy, wide-brimmed hat and tinted specs.'

'I suppose you didn't see his face?'

'Not much of it, no. His hat was pulled down low, but I thought he was wearing tinted specs.'

'Hair colour? Long, short, straight, curly?'

Singh shook his head. 'Short and grey, I think, though I only caught a glimpse.'

'What about his age?'

He thought for a second. 'Maybe forties, early fifties.'

'And how do you know that *he* left the envelope? If you were just coming into the foyer, you couldn't have seen him placing it on the counter.'

'I didn't, but he was the only one in there at the time.'

Kate frowned. 'Not much to help us there then, is there?' she observed ungraciously. 'It could have been someone else who left the envelope before his visit.'

Singh shook his head. 'The front desk at the nick is, as you know, always closed up at night due to shortage of staff. It opens each day at seven in the morning and closes again at eight in the evening. If a member of the public wants assistance they have to use the phone in the hatch outside. Tom Paxman, the civvy SDO, says he saw a man in a long black coat and floppy, black hat hanging about by the front door when he came on duty first thing and drove round the back to the yard. It was well before he opened up, but he thought no more about it as local people know our hours and are often queued up outside then.'

Kate's heart was beating faster now. 'You've spoken to Paxman about this then?'

'Only briefly. I was curious to know how the envelope was delivered.'

'Is Paxman still on duty?'

'I believe so. He should be in the canteen about now.'

Kate was on her way to the door when he called after her. 'There's one more thing, skip.'

She stopped and turned towards him. 'Which is?'

'The man I saw stepped to one side and turned away from me as we met in the doorway, and although, as I've just said, I didn't see much of his face, there was one thing I did notice. The lobe of his left ear was missing.'

For a moment Kate just stared at him, a new, more animated light dawning in her eyes. At last! At last she was in possession of a piece of real information about her target to add to the rather sketchy description Singh had already given her. Something tangible and visible, which Mr Anonymous couldn't easily hide. Okay, so it was only small, and it would only be of value if she were to confront him in some way. But as she well knew from her previous investigations, little items mattered, because eventually they could add up to a complete picture of someone. She now knew her man was tall and thin, possibly with short, grey hair and in his forties or early fifties. She also knew that he was last seen wearing a long, black coat, a black, floppy, wide-brimmed hat and tinted spectacles. It wasn't earth-shattering information. But by heaven, it was a start and suddenly it gave her new hope.

'You should be a detective, Singh,' she exclaimed as she strode out the door.

'Chance would be a fine thing,' he called after her.

* * *

Tom Paxman was of little help. He hardly looked up from his overfull plate in the canteen when Kate cornered him at his small table and said he could add nothing more to what he had told Singh. He had only seen the individual hanging about outside the police station for a moment and hadn't paid too much attention to him. A big, truculent man who had served in the force for twenty-two years before resigning on ill health grounds with a so-called bad back, Paxman made no real effort to try and remember anything else but shrugged the whole thing off. Kate formed the impression that he had probably been one of those officers who during his police service had avoided getting involved in anything. The type of useless policeman who would have been colloquially referred to by his colleagues as a 'uniform carrier'.

Now once more feeling angry and frustrated, she took her sour mood back to the office with her. She was not best pleased to run into one of the team en route as she started up the staircase to the first floor.

Detective Constable Danny Ferris was not one of her favourite colleagues. A big, heavily built ex-squaddie, with a coarse sense of humour and a foul mouth, he was the sort of tough, no-nonsense character every copper wants behind them when they are in a tight spot. He had a very short fuse and always reminded Kate of one of the old crime squad detectives portrayed on television in early seventies films. He was tactless, prone to insubordination and certainly one of the force's dinosaurs. He needed firm handling. But he was honest and courageous with two commendations for bravery to his credit, which made up for a lot.

'Can I have a word, skipper?' Ferris said, his bulk blocking her path.

'What, now?' she replied tersely. 'This is really not a good time. Will it wait?'

He rubbed the stubble on his chin with one large hand. 'Only take a minute, skip, honest. It's, er, sort of private.'

Kate sighed irritably, turning back down the stairs. 'Oh very well, one of the interview rooms should be free.'

In fact, both were marked as such and Kate went for the first one, swinging round to face Ferris after he had closed the door behind them.

'Well, what do you want to tell me?' she snapped, leaning back against the table in the centre of the room, curious in spite of her mood.

He took a deep breath and stared at her levelly. 'It's me what done it.'

'Done what?'

'Put that postcard up on the noticeboard and blew it up to A4 size on the photocopier.'

She treated him to a grim smile. 'I thought it might be. Proud of yourself now, are you?'

'No, I ain't. At the time I thought it were a bit of a laugh, but I don't no more, and I want to apologise.'

'Do you?' She couldn't help feeling just a smidgen of admiration for this big, clumsy ape of a man standing there like some recalcitrant child. It would have taken a lot for him to face her like this. He wasn't the type to bend his knee to anyone.

'Yeah, and if you want to take it further, I will take my punishment. I was stupid and I shouldn't have done it. I was talking to Singh when he opened the envelope at his desk and when I saw the pic I just couldn't resist doing what I done. I didn't think.'

'No,' she said, 'you didn't. But you rarely do, do you?' She paused for a second, then made her decision. 'Still, as far as I'm concerned, I have more important things to worry about than that. So let's forget it, shall we, and move on.'

His expression was one of total surprise. Then he breathed a perceptible sigh of relief. 'Well, thanks for that, Kate, I owe you one.'

'You certainly do,' she agreed, 'and you can be sure I will call in the favour first chance I get.'

'You got it, skipper. Whenever, okay?'

He half-turned for the door, then stopped and swung round again. 'The bloke what sent that postcard must've gone to a lot of bother making it up. It ain't an easy thing to do. What's his game d'ye reckon?'

'What do you mean?'

'Well, he didn't send it to you, did he? He made a point of sending it to the nick, knowing before he done it that it would be seen by everyone. Looks to me like he's trying to make you look small in front of people. You know, not just ruin your reputation, but make you lose confidence in yourself so you can't do your job properly no more. That's probably why he set you up by stiffing the vicar, then telling the press you'd missed finding the murder weapon at the scene.'

Her eyes narrowed. 'How did you know about all that?'

He grinned sheepishly. 'Word soon gets round this place, and I happened to hear the guv'nor talking to the DCI on the blower just now.'

'Listening at keyholes again, Danny?' she commented grimly.

He shrugged. 'Ain't that what detectives is supposed to do? Only way to find things out.'

'Maybe. But why would this character do what you are saying? I've never even had anything to do with him as far as I know.'

'It don't matter. Thing is, if he's got a screw loose, maybe he's latched on to you cause he feels you're better than him and he wants to put you down to show how much cleverer than you he is.'

She stared at him with a new kind of respect. It dawned on her that there was more to DC Danny Ferris than she had ever imagined. Studying his unshaven chin and the large beer belly bulging through a gap in his shirt, the saying immediately sprang to mind, *Never judge a book by its cover*.

'You seem to have hidden depths, Danny,' she said. 'A bit of a psychologist on the quiet, are you.'

He shrugged. 'Dunno about that. But I know a screwball when I sees one and it's obvious this one's got it in for you. He don't need a reason to do things and you gotta hang in there and play him at his own game. Everyone's rooting for you, so you're not on your own. I just wanted to say that.'

She smiled at him for the first time with genuine warmth. 'I'm glad you did, Danny,' she said quietly. 'I'm very glad you did.'

Heartened by what Ferris had said, Kate spent the rest of the afternoon at her desk, trying to concentrate on her paperwork again, but failing dismally. Her tortured mind kept returning to the same issue. Her sadistic tormentor and how to tackle the threat he posed. She was no longer officially part of the investigation, and she hadn't the faintest idea who he was and if and when he would strike again, so there didn't seem anything she could do. But there was one thing she *was* sure of. He was still out there somewhere on the Levels. While the police investigation was slowly getting underway, it was likely he would already have selected his next victim and be carefully planning his next atrocity.

CHAPTER 6

Wilf Carpenter had owned Summerdays Cider Farm for the best part of twenty-five years and had inherited the small business from his father, Josh. Although he had modernised much of the farm's cider-making equipment over time, he still used his father's ancient twelve-bore shotgun at the annual Wassailing Festival. This was when, in accordance with tradition, it was fired through the best apple tree in the orchard to protect the harvest for the next year and frighten away any evil spirits lurking among the branches. Summerdays Cider Farm was his life and he never tired of showing visitors around the place, including the barns containing its cider press and huge fermentation vats so tall that a ladder was required to get to the walkways at the top.

He was particularly pleased the morning the telephone call came through to the office from the reporter of a national beer and spirits periodical who was doing a feature on the cider trade.

'They want to do a piece on cider making, Wilf,' his young female assistant chirped excitedly as she handed him the phone. 'We'll be in the news.'

The visit had to be scheduled for the evening, seven o'clock the reporter said as it was the only time he could fit it in. But Carpenter didn't mind a bit. He had waited all these years for something like this and he wasn't about to turn it down just because it was after hours. Hazel, his assistant, offered to stay on too, 'to help out and make the coffee', she said, but he declined the offer. She was a bubbly, rather OTT youngster and prone to talking a little too much. He thought he would fare a lot better on his own. As for making the coffee, there was no way he was going to offer his visitor something like that when he had some prime vintage cider in his cellar.

The reporter was a tall, thin man, wearing dark glasses, a blue anorak and jeans who introduced himself as Tim Mayhew. He was quite charming, although Wilf found his gaze a bit disconcerting and formed the impression, without actually being able to see his visitor's eyes, that it was very intense, making him feel a little uncomfortable. Nevertheless, Carpenter was only too happy to show him around his domain if it meant Summerdays appearing in a national magazine read by thousands of potential customers and wholesalers in the beer and spirits trade.

Mayhew showed a keen interest in the farm's museum. Its old presses, cider barrels and other equipment, which Carpenter had picked up from various places on his travels over the years. He examined one particular exhibit in minute detail.

It was a curious and obviously ancient contraption. It consisted of two tall, upright posts bolted to the bottom of a large stone slab, one on each side. The slab had a groove running around its outer edge, which was intersected at the front by a channel cut into the stone, which had a wooden bucket placed beneath it. Above the slab a thick iron screw with a long handle at the top passed through a cross member fixed to the top of the tall uprights and was in turn fixed by more bolts to a heavy looking wooden plate.

'It's a very old cider screw press,' Carpenter explained, adding proudly, 'I salvaged it from a derelict farm in Devon and renovated it. In the old days a layer of cider apple pulp would have been spread out on the slab with a layer of straw on top to counter its wet consistency. Further layers of pulp and straw would have been placed on top of the first layer and so on and so forth. The stack that was formed was called "cheese". Two strong labourers would have turned the long handle at the top of the frame, forcing the top press plate downwards on the screw, crushing the pulp in the stack between it and the stone slab, and squeezing out the juice into the grooves. The juice would then have flowed along the grooves and out into the bucket placed in front of the press via the channel you can see cut into the slab. Ingenious when you think about it and so simple. This is only one of a whole variety of screw presses that were used over the centuries. I was lucky to get my hands on it.'

'Does it still work?' Mayhew asked politely.

'Course it does,' Carpenter said and gave him a quick demonstration with some crushed apples from an adjacent hopper. 'I keep these here to show the kids on school trips how things were done in those days. They're fascinated by it.'

'Well now,' Mayhew breathed from just behind him, 'it is certainly very impressive, and I think it will do nicely.'

Drawing a heavy spanner from inside his waistband, he struck Wilf twice over the back of the head and had the satisfaction of hearing the sound of his skull fracturing.

'There now,' murmured the man who called himself Mayhew, staring first at his victim lying in a heap at his feet and then at the long handle of the cider press. 'Time for some pressing I do believe.'

* * *

Hayden got home ahead of Kate that night and she noted his gleaming, red Mk II Jaguar already parked in the driveway. He was still in his morose, uncommunicative mood, and she guessed from previous experience that it would be a while before he chose to get off his high horse and come around again. The pair of them were so different in temperament that Kate sometimes wondered how they managed to stay together.

She was an extrovert. A direct, upfront kind of person who hated atmospheres, much preferring to get issues out of the way with a good row rather than sit brooding over things. Hayden on the other hand was just the opposite. A deeply sensitive introvert, he was easily offended and was quite capable of sulking for days on end over a particular grievance, imagined or otherwise. As one of his colleagues had once remarked, he could sulk for England when the mood took him.

But she had no intention of restarting their row this time. She had enough on her plate as it was and just couldn't be bothered. Instead, she ignored him slouched in a corner of the settee watching the television and went straight upstairs to take a shower. She heard him go out shortly afterwards and remembered it was the night he went to his regular vintage car club meeting, which meant he wouldn't be home until late. So she made herself a sandwich and a cup of coffee, then dog-tired after her early morning call and the traumatic events of the day, she made herself comfortable on the settee for the second night and promptly went out like a light.

It was past eight when she awoke the following morning and Hayden was already up and away for a change. That would be a first, she thought sourly. Then she remembered he was in Crown Court that morning as a witness in a case of GBH and would probably be there all day. But she could not help wondering if he had left her sleeping as a form of punishment, knowing she would be late in as a result, or because his kinder side felt she needed the sleep. She gave him the benefit of the doubt and presumed it was the latter.

Hurriedly dressing, she grabbed another cup of coffee and scooped up her car keys from the halfmoon table by the stairs before heading to her car in the driveway. She saw the note scrawled across her windscreen immediately. It was written in block capitals and looked as though a red crayon or lipstick had been used:

Fancy a cider, Kate? Try Summerdays Cider Farm. Nice and ripe.

Her skin prickled unpleasantly. 'Shit!' she mouthed, a horrible premonition gripping her chest like a cold, tight hand. 'What now?'

Singh was the only one in the CID general office when she arrived at Highbridge police station.

'Get the windscreen of my Mazda MX-5 in the yard checked out by SOCO and some photos taken,' she instructed the bewildered office manager. 'Some joker has scrawled all over it.' She threw a glance around the office. 'Where's everyone?'

'There's only Jamie Foster and Indrani Purewal on earlies this morning,' he replied. 'The others are either in court or on lates—'

'So where *are* Indrani and Jamie?'

Singh looked embarrassed again. 'With the DI down at the scene.'

'Scene? What scene?'

'No one's told you, skip? There's been another sus death. At a place called Summerdays Cider Farm. They're all down there with the new DS.'

Kate glared at him. 'New DS? What bloody new DS?'

'A skipper from Bridgwater,' he stammered. 'Sergeant Liam O'Sullivan. He was brought in to, er, give the team a hand.'

Kate's tone was harsh. 'Is that so? Well, you can give me the address of this cider farm right now.'

'I'm not sure if—'

'Singh,' she grated, 'just give me the address, will you? And don't piss me about.'

Two marked patrol cars were parked across the entrance to Summerdays Cider Farm, blocking the way completely. Kate abandoned the CID car she was driving and went ahead on foot, her fast-moving strides kicking up the loose gravel. She ran into a white-faced uniformed constable at the door of a large barn with a corrugated iron roof and he nodded in recognition when he saw her.

'Bloody dreadful, sarge,' he commented, and she detected the strong smell of vomit as she brushed against him in passing.

It wasn't too difficult to guess why he was standing out-side the barn, she thought grimly. Death wasn't something you ever really got used to and ripe corpses could be a particularly horrific sight. Especially if you were new to the job and had never seen what police officers called a 'stiff' before. She sensed that this one was going to be in that category and braced herself as she approached the line of police cordon tape that was in the process of being strung out across the barn by DCs Indrani Purewal and Jamie Foster. Charlie Woo was standing talking to a rotund, ginger-haired man dressed in a black leather coat just inside the doorway. Even from the back view, she rec-ognised Detective Sergeant Liam O'Sullivan whom she had worked with on a few occasions in the past.

O'Sullivan turned as she approached and nodded. 'Kate,' he said and smiled. 'Hope you have a strong stomach.'

Before she could respond, Charlie Woo quickly stepped forward.

'There's no need for you to be here, Kate,' he said quietly.

'Is that so, *sir*,' she snapped back, her eyes smouldering. 'Does this mean I am to be excluded from all violent death investigations from now on?'

He shook his head. 'Only ones that might be connected to the last one,' he said.

'So how do you know this one is connected?'

'I don't, but the killer seems to have left the same calling card behind. A dead crow, as before. In view of the circum-stances, I felt we should play it safe.'

'Then you're saying that this one is another murder?'

'Unless a man can commit suicide in the way this one did,' he said grimly. 'Why not take a look?'

She didn't need to go very far. The body had been con-cealed from the doors by a collection of heavy farm machin-ery. But standing at the edge of the tape, which had now been secured to both walls of the barn, it was clearly visible to her in all its horrific detail.

As a police officer, Kate had witnessed death in most of its gruesome forms during her service. Gassing, burning, shooting, hanging, poisoning, she thought she had seen it all. But she had never seen anything like this before. The man's corpse was lying on its back on the concrete floor in front of what she later learned to be an old cider press. His arms were folded across his chest as if in sleep. But there the similarity ended. His head was actually in the press itself. Or rather what remained it. This had been crushed between the upper wooden press plate with its central screw and the stone slab at the bottom. As a result, brains, tissue and shattered skull fragments had been forced out through the gaps between the two in a bloody pulped mash, which had draped itself over the edge of the stone slab and dropped on to the floor close to where the corpse of a big black crow was lying.

'Looks a bit like apple pomace, don't you think?' O'Sullivan commented behind her.

She closed her eyes tightly in disgust at the unfunny analogy. Then throwing him a contemptuous glance, she turned and joined Charlie Woo back out in the farmyard.

'You saw the crow there,' Woo said, more as an assumption than a question. 'Looks like its neck was broken. One hell of a coincidence if it isn't connected to the last murder.'

'It's my man again,' she breathed. 'It has to be.' She told him about the scrawl on her car's windscreen.

He frowned. 'So, he obviously means to go on with this then. The Rev Strange was not just a one-off. Supports the reasoning of the DCI and myself as to why you cannot be part of the investigation, doesn't it?'

Surprisingly, his comment failed to provoke a further emotional outburst from her. 'Who was the stiff?' she asked instead, as if she hadn't heard that remark.

'Owner of the place,' O'Sullivan answered for him and checked his notebook. 'A Wilf Carpenter. Bachelor. Lived on the premises. Well liked apparently. He was found by one of his workers first thing this morning. Looks like he's been there all night, but the forensic pathologist should be able to give us a more accurate time of death when they arrive.'

'DCI is setting up a major incident room at the nick,' Woo went on. 'I had a quick word with him yesterday and although you can't now be part of the actual inquiry team, he's okayed it for you to be involved on the sidelines. This character is bound to be contacting you again and you're our only link to him.'

She snorted. 'That's good of our Mr Ricketts! I'll have to kiss his boots later.'

Woo winced. 'Look Kate, you have to understand—'

But she cut him off. 'Presumably no one saw or heard a thing when Carpenter was killed?'

He made no effort to return to what he had been trying to say. 'Er, not really. All we have is a young office worker, named Hazel Drew. She apparently took a call from some guy yesterday afternoon claiming to be from a beer and spirits magazine. The guy allegedly said he wanted to interview her boss for a feature he was doing, and an appointment was made for him to see Carpenter at seven. Drew was in a hell of a state when we spoke to her and even after we'd finally calmed her down, all she was able to tell us was that the caller sounded quiet and smooth-talking and had a drawling 'posh' voice. Apparently when Carpenter spoke to him he gave his name as Tim Mayhew. Obviously false.'

'Sounds like the cool character from the plane who rang me to tell me about the Reverend Strange.'

'Plane? What plane?' O'Sullivan chimed in.

The DI shook his head. 'Forget that for now, Liam, I'll fill you in later.' Then he went on. 'But by all accounts, it seems that our man is a bit of an actor, maybe even a human chameleon.'

Kate shivered and not for the first time. 'Going by what he did to Carpenter and Strange, there's nothing human about this sadistic scumbag.' She glanced around the farmyard at the encircling trees. 'And I wouldn't be surprised if he's not out there now watching us.'

Both Woo and O'Sullivan followed the direction of her gaze. 'Why do you say that?' Sullivan asked.

'Well, he must have been watching us when we were at the scene of Strange's murder, otherwise how would he have known when it was the right time to nip up into the church tower and plant the alleged weapon for the press to find?'

Woo looked uncomfortable. '*If*, of course, he did plant it, Kate. You have to be realistic. Maybe you just, er, missed seeing it?'

Kate immediately flared. 'Is that the real reason you and the DCI have pulled me off the case? It's got nothing to do with personal involvement, has it? You both think I'm all washed up. Tell me, whenever have I missed something as obvious as that at a murder scene?'

'True, but there's always a first time and you *have* been ill.'

She shook her head bitterly. 'Is that what you think, Charlie? You know, poor old, nutty Kate must be losing it? Maybe we should dump her back in that loony bin of a clinic?'

'That's not what I meant, and you know it.'

'No? Well, think on this. If I missed the weapon, then so must Dick Cave have done since he was with me at the time. Maybe you've got two nutters instead of just one, eh? Must be catching.'

Then she turned her back on him and stormed off down the driveway to her car.

But if she thought her trials were over, she was sadly disappointed. The young woman with the spiky, pink hair was leaning against the driver's door of the CID car.

'Hi, Kate,' Debbie Moreton said. 'Bit of a domestic just then, was there? Sort of a falling-out among our finest?'

'Get your skinny arse off my car, Debbie,' Kate grated.

The reporter grinned and moved to one side. 'Did I hear right? That they've taken you off the case? Was it because of your last unfortunate cock-up?'

Kate threw open the car door. 'How did you know the police were here?' she said, ignoring her question.

Moreton popped a wad of gum in her mouth. 'My source likes to keep me informed of developments,' she replied. 'He rang me half an hour ago and claimed he'd committed a second murder. At the cider farm this time. Said something about someone getting their head mashed in a cider screw press. Nasty. Is that true?'

Kate paused as she was about to climb into the car. 'You're saying he contacted you again?'

The reporter studied the long green painted nails of one hand. 'He seems to want to confide in me. Sort of exclusive info. Doesn't think a lot of you, though—'

Kate studied her fixedly. 'You'd better be damned careful, Debbie,' she said, her tone harsh and uncompromising. 'You're playing a very dangerous game acting as a conduit for this guy's publicity. He's a cold-blooded killer and at the very least you could end up being charged with obstructing a major police inquiry or complicity in the commission of a serious crime—'

'And at the worst?'

'A corpse,' Kate replied. 'When your newfound "friend" decides you are surplus to requirements.'

Moreton laughed, but there was a slight edge to it. 'Just doing my public duty, Kate. Freedom of the press and all that.'

'Freedom of the press doesn't extend to aiding a murderer in publicising his crimes.'

Moreton feigned indignation. 'I only report the facts of a case as they come to light, you know that, and crime story revelations are very much in the public interest,' she said. 'It's not my fault if you won't agree to being interviewed about the case.' She produced a digital pocket recorder. 'So how about doing that now so my readers won't be spooked by rumours? It will only take a few minutes.'

Kate smiled without humour. 'What, so you can twist the facts to provide another sensationalist story of police incompetence, like the one I suspect is already on last night's front page of your rubbishy rag? No thanks.'

'What, you mean you haven't seen the story yet? Tush, tush. But you could at least set the record straight as to whether you are investigating another murder here as my source has claimed.'

'I've no comment to make.'

'Ah well, at least there won't be any risk of the murder weapon being overlooked this time, will there? I mean, a mashed head in a cider press is a bit difficult to miss, isn't it? Even for you.'

For reply, Kate slammed the car door and drove off, forcing Moreton to jump out of the way to avoid being run over.

CHAPTER 7

As if fate wanted to rub salt into her wounds, another nasty shock awaited Kate when she got back to the still empty CID office at Highbridge police station. A copy of Debbie Moreton's newspaper, The *Bridgwater Clarion*, had been placed in the middle of her desk, carrying the headline, *Murder Of Local Priest*.

'Latest edition,' Singh explained. 'But I thought you ought to see it PDQ. I snaffled this one from the briefing room. The other two copies are on the DI's desk and with the super. Front page is just plain news coverage of the death of the Reverend Strange. Nothing much to it, just the bald facts and a lot of ill-informed speculation by the paper who claim the killer actually rang their crime reporter, Debbie Moreton, confessing to the murder. Sounds a bit far-fetched to me. There's reference at the end to the suspect murder weapon being missed by police, then miraculously found by Moreton. But the editorial opinion piece inside, which was no doubt also written by Moreton anonymously, really gets stuck into the issue and you won't like it one little bit.'

That assessment turned out to be a mammoth under-statement on Singh's part. Kate inwardly cringed when he pointed to the piece on page two under the Opinion Page subheading *Keystone Cops*, which had been printed as a reverse block and seemed to jump right out at her. It got much worse as she read on.

Once again Highbridge police, our local 'Keystone Cops', have excelled themselves with their professional incompetence investigating the tragic incident we covered in our lead story. We can reveal that when the body of the man — we have been asked not to give out his name until after formal identification has taken place — was found at the foot of the church belltower, you would have thought that the investigating officer, our very own 'ace' detective sergeant, Kate Lewis, would have carried out a thorough examination of the scene before coming to a conclusion about the cause of the death. Not a bit of it. Poor old Kate, who we understand has only just been released from a special clinic after suffering a nervous breakdown, is obviously not the detective she once claimed to be. Instead of putting all that so-called professional expertise of hers to good use, she simply decided that the death was due to nothing more than a straightforward suicide, even though a bloodstained weapon believed to have been used in the commission of the crime was lying on the floor at the top of the tower in full view of anyone who happened along. It was only after our own crime reporter, Debbie Moreton, received an anonymous telephone tip-off from a man claiming to be the murderer himself, and raced to the scene, that the oversight came to light. Yet even when our reporter pointed our short-sighted sleuth in the direction of this crucial bit of evidence, instead of thanking her for her assistance, the embarrassed sergeant not only refused to comment, but used a rather unpleasant expletive we won't repeat here to tell our Debbie where to go. Unbelievable, wouldn't you say? So, come on, Kate, we know you've been ill, but for goodness' sake, get your act together and do what we pay you to do.

Kate's face was ashen, and it was evident that she was in a state of shock as her trembling hand reached for the mug of coffee she had just poured for herself. 'Well, that's my career down the toilet,' she said harshly. 'I might as well clear my desk right now.'

Singh frowned. 'With respect, Kate, I haven't been here very long, so I don't know you that well, but I didn't have you down as a quitter. Everyone knows the *Clarion* is anti-police. Are you going to let them drive you out of the job without a fight?'

She shook her head wearily and gave him a weak smile. 'Good try, Singh, but it won't just be the paper that does that. When the chief reads this, he'll go bananas and Ricketts will jump at the chance of getting rid of me.'

Singh smiled. 'Mahatma Gandhi once said, "The future depends on what we do in the present". You have had your setback today, but you can change what might happen tomorrow by catching the author of your misfortunes.'

She emitted a cynical laugh. 'Well might you say that, Singh, but I happen to have been struck off the inquiry so my chances of catching anything other than the common cold are pretty remote.'

'From what I hear, that sort of situation has not stopped you in the past.'

She nodded. 'Maybe you're right, but sometimes when everything's being thrown at you from all directions, you lose the will to fight anymore and just want a deep, dark hole to crawl into.'

He shrugged and turned back to his own desk. 'Your decision, skipper, but remember there is a danger in crawling into a hole. Sometimes you can't get out again and you simply stay buried.'

Kate thought about Singh's words after he had gone down to the canteen for lunch. She had never regarded the quiet, unassuming office manager as a philosopher, but like Danny Ferris earlier, he obviously had his own hidden depths, and what he'd said had certainly resonated with her. She had always been a fighter. Was she going to throw in the towel now just because the going had got tough? That would be exactly what Mr Anonymous wanted. It would mean he had won. Suddenly she felt angry. Angrier than she had felt for a long time. She involuntarily clenched her teeth until they made a cracking sound. Okay, so she was carrying a load of baggage after her near breakdown and treatment in the psychiatric clinic and it had hit her reputation hard. But things like breakdowns and PTSD could affect anyone. No one was immune. No matter how tough they thought they were. If her ruthless stalker believed he could wear her down to such an extent that she would fall apart, he was going to be disappointed. Throughout her career she had been nicknamed 'Go it Alone' and 'Maverick Kate' because of her tendency to do her own thing. Often in defiance of orders. Well, 'Go it Alone' Kate was back and the shitbag who had chosen to take her on was in for a bigger surprise than he could ever have imagined.

She downed the rest of her coffee with a grimace that had little to do with the fact that the coffee was cold and a lot more to do with the dawning of cold reality. Shaking off the destructive negativity, which had been dogging her for so long, and arming herself with a new resolve to fight on was certainly a big step in the right direction. But it didn't bring her any closer to tracking down the man Singh had almost poetically described as the 'author of her misfortune'. Okay, so her prime suspect was short of a left earlobe and the chances of there being more than one person living locally with such an affliction were remote. But finding him would be an impossible task without more substantial information to hand. Even if she eventually did get a breakthrough, there was no way she could prove that the voyeur who had dropped the revealing postcard of her into Highbridge police station and the ruthless killer who had so far despatched three people as part of some deranged game were one and the same person.

So she was back where she had started. Without a clue as to the identity of her adversary or what her next move should be. Totally stuffed in fact.

Lost once more in the doldrums, she would probably have stayed like that for the rest of the afternoon had not fate intervened and created a distraction that was totally unexpected.

The 'shout' blasted from her police radio as she was on the point of finally heading downstairs to the police canteen for a late bite to eat. 'Any units Soldier's Arms? Officers requiring assistance.' In a moment she had erupted from her chair and was streaking down the stairs to the yard.

The Soldier's Arms was a small, rundown public house buried in a maze of narrow streets between Highbridge and Burnham-On-Sea. It was the regular haunt of the local riff-raff and misfits. A place where the workshy could spend their ill-deserved dole money on hard liquor or illicit drugs while fencing stolen property.

Kate knew the pub well. It was one of the first places she and her colleagues visited when they were looking for one of their local villains and she had been to the dive many times before. The licensee, Alf Judd, was a former matelot, who was more often than not three sheets to the wind in the flat above while whoever he had been able to hire as a casual bar worker tried to run things downstairs under the jaundiced eye of Judd's foul-mouthed wife, Linda. Usually any trouble that broke out occurred at night around closing time, but Judd's disreputable clientele seemed to have got stuck in a few hours earlier this time.

She saw one of the windows had been shattered and broken glass glittered on the forecourt as she pulled up in front of the building behind a couple of marked police patrol cars and a protected Ford Transit. Two young constables were already struggling with a long-haired man in handcuffs on the pavement outside and as she scrambled out of her car, she saw them haul him to the Transit and dump him unceremoniously inside.

'Bit of a falling-out between pushers, skipper,' one of the constables explained with a grin as she strode past the open doors of the vehicle. 'The other one is away on his toes, but we'll find him.'

Leaving his colleague in the van with the prisoner, he followed her back inside the pub. The bar was a mess. It was covered in broken glass and overturned furniture. A group of half-a-dozen youths was sitting at a couple of tables in the far corner, corralled there by several uniformed police officers, one of whom was none other than Sergeant Dick Cave. A frightened, pasty-faced youngster was hovering in the internal doorway behind the bar counter and a buxom woman Kate recognised as Judd's wife, Linda, was leaning forward across the counter, glaring at the youths aggressively.

'I want that lot out, now!' she snarled, spittle forming on her over-painted red lips. 'They ain't nothin' but trouble.'

Cave nodded to Kate and turned towards the woman. 'Now, now, Linda,' he soothed. 'Don't go getting yourself all worked up. They're all leaving. Aren't you, lads?'

There was a reluctant murmur of assent and at the jerk of Cave's head towards the door the youngsters climbed slowly to their feet and slouched out of the room, grinning at the sergeant as they passed him.

'Usual thing,' Cave said to Kate. 'Pushing smack on someone else's turf. Bound to cause grief.'

'Nothing for me to do then?' she said, her eyes roving around the bar.

He shook his head. 'Not this time, Kate. I think we've got it all sorted.'

She nodded. 'Didn't expect to see you on again so soon, Dick,' she commented. 'Thought you were on nights.'

'Short straw job,' he replied ruefully. 'Brought back on early. Now twelve-hour shift, 2 p.m. to 2 a.m.'

She made a face. 'Nice one.'

Her gaze settled on a solitary male drinker ensconced in the snug on the other side of a low archway. She was surprised to see that he had stayed there with his pint despite the ruckus that had occurred next door. She glanced back at Cave with a questioning look.

'Not involved,' he said, seeing the direction of her gaze. 'Local wino. Kept out of it all and stuck to his beer. Wise man . . .'

His voice trailed off and he frowned suddenly, drawing her to one side and speaking in a low voice. 'Seen the local paper today, have you?'

For some reason, her gaze was still on the man in the snug. 'Er, yes. Just seen the story,' she replied, sounding distracted. 'Not good reading.'

He snorted. 'That bloody reporter's done us up like a couple of kippers.'

She refocused. 'It was me she was after, Dick. I don't think she mentioned you.'

'Maybe not, but I was with you, so I'll be in the shit too if there's an inquiry. Thing is, it's obvious we were set up.'

'I know that, and you know that, but I'm not sure the chief will believe it.'

'So what do we do?'

'Wait to see if we get forms saying we're under investigation and until then just carry on. Nothing else can we do.'

He made a face. 'That's reassuring! See you later then. Unless I get suspended first.'

She nodded a little absently, hardly noticing Cave and his crew leaving. Her attention had returned to the lone drinker in the snug. An unremarkable looking middle-aged man wearing tinted spectacles and dressed in a long, black coat that had also seen a lot better days. He looked to be the typical down-and-out Cave had dismissed him as. Probably just one of a handful of rough sleepers to be found on the street corners of the little seaside town begging for their beer money or next fix. He was already knocking back the last of his pint and throwing quick, furtive glances in her direction as he did so, evidently uneasy about her interest in him. Something within her stirred. A sixth sense perhaps. An indefinable 'itch' built up over years of experience as a police officer that told her something was not quite right. But even as she started towards the archway, he dumped his empty pint pot on the table and quickly hauled himself to his feet. She got to the snug a moment before he left through another door. Though not before she had got close enough to him to spot that he was missing the lobe of his left ear!

* * *

For a few critical moments Kate simply stared at the door of the snug through which 'missing earlobe' had left, making no immediate attempt to go after him. Completely out of the blue and in the most unlikely of places she had stumbled upon the very man who fitted Singh's description of the suspect she had been so desperate to trace. Okay, so he wasn't wearing the floppy black hat Singh had described, but the missing earlobe seemed more than a coincidence. Yet instead of being galvanised into immediate action, she had hesitated. Suddenly assailed by doubts. Her mind thrown into chaos.

A wino? Her suspect was a local wino? It seemed impossible. The rough looking down-and-out in his shabby black coat was nothing like the cold, calculating killer whose profile had already built itself up inside her head. A profile that conjured up the image of a clever, articulate individual with aspirations to be a writer who had the money and the acumen to book an expensive holiday in a sophisticated resort hotel in Mexico. A man with the single-minded determination to follow her all the way back to her home in Somerset for the express purpose of pitting his intellect against hers in a campaign of serial murder. Yet how likely was it that there could be two people in one small Somerset town with a missing left earlobe? Probably a million to one chance at the very least, and it was certainly true that looks could be deceptive. Maybe adopting the disguise of a down-and-out was the killer's way of avoiding detection. Furthermore, amid all the ifs and buts, one thing was clear. Spooked by her interest in him, her man had obviously no intention of hanging about long enough for her to probe his bone fides, which only served to confirm her suspicions that he was nursing a guilty secret of some sort.

Whatever that secret might be, it didn't look like she was going to be given any access to it either. When she finally snapped out of her semi-paralysis and stumbled from the bar on to the pub forecourt, her quarry was nowhere to be seen. He had completely vanished.

For a few moments she studied the street in both directions, willing him to materialise. Two cars passed her, heading back towards Highbridge, and on the opposite side of the road she caught sight of a young woman pushing a pram along the pavement. But otherwise, the street appeared to be deserted. Her heart sank. Her man had obviously legged it the moment he'd got outside, which only served to confirm her suspicions he'd had something to hide. Unfortunately it was a bit too late to draw any comfort from being proven right. In the words of the prophet, she was totally stuffed.

Furious with herself for allowing her quarry to slip away, she returned to the bar in a sour mood. Linda Judd was still behind the counter, cleaning a pint pot with a grubby looking tea towel like a character from a film set in a frontier town of the Wild West.

'The guy in the snug,' Kate snapped tactlessly. 'Who was he?'

The woman shrugged, her puffy eyes remaining focused on the glass in her hands. 'How should I know? I don't ask 'em for their names and addresses.'

'Is he a regular?'

'No idea.'

'You must know whether he's been in here before.'

'Ain't got a clue.'

'He looked like a rough sleeper.'

'Then maybe he was. We get all sorts in here.'

Kate bit her lip. Obviously the 'lovely' Linda was lying, but the woman was never going to tell her anything, so she was wasting her time. She was about to turn on her heel and leave when the pasty-faced youngster who had been behind the bar counter earlier reappeared.

'Gerry Thomas,' he blurted. 'His name is Gerry Thomas.'

Linda Judd swung on him. 'Shut your mouth,' she snarled.

The youngster ignored her. For the first time some colour had returned to his face and his expression was venomous.

'He's a bloody poofta,' he said. 'He's come on to me twice since I started here and he needs sortin'.'

Judd poked him in the chest. 'I said shut it!' she warned.

'He's dossin' in the old C & G factory in Signalman's Walk,' he went on defiantly. 'Word is, he's fresh out of a nut house in the Smoke.'

Judd was beside herself with rage now. 'You little bastard!' she shouted. 'That's it. You're fired!'

'Don't bother,' he retorted. 'After the crap that happened here today, you can stuff your job up your fat arse. I quit.'

Then tugging off his apron, he threw it at her and disappeared through a curtain at the back.

Judd's tirade of foul language followed Kate out of the bar, but it fell on deaf ears. She had more important things on her mind, and she sat for several minutes in her car, digesting what she had just learned. There was every chance she had been passed duff information. The lad could have been as anti-police as Judd and had been giving her the runaround. But somehow she didn't think so and what would he have got out of it anyway? Furthermore, it was logical that a down-and-out like Gerry Thomas, if that was his real name, would choose somewhere like Signalman's Walk as a doss.

Once home to a number of small engineering companies, the cul-de-sac had been given its curious name in recognition of the town's proud links to the old Somerset and Dorset Railway, which several of the firms who had set up there had supported through the supply of specialised machined components. But over time these firms had either folded or had simply moved away, leaving their factories empty and boarded up. Inevitably, the places had fallen into disrepair, attracting a twilight-zone mix of rough sleepers and down-and-outs seeking somewhere to doss, as well as youthful drug addicts looking for a place to 'shoot up' on heroin to satisfy their craving. As a result, the street had earned an unenviable reputation for itself, and it had become the first port of call for the local police when they were looking for missing persons, runaways and criminals wanted for questioning. Kate had been into several of the factories before, though always 'mob-handed' on an organised raid with plenty of backup.

To be fair, she had found the vast majority of those inhabiting this twilight world of flitting shadows to be pathetic addicts, alcoholics or people who through no fault of their own had fallen on hard times and been rendered homeless. Harmless inadequates who lived from day to day and were keen to avoid any contact with the police. But she was also conscious of the fact that there would be some with a long history of violence who could present a real danger to a woman venturing into their domain on her own, even if she did happen to be a police officer, and if the man with the missing earlobe *was* one of those, she could actually be gifting herself to him.

The sensible course was to call for backup before going anywhere near the Cane & Grove factory. But she dismissed that as a non-starter straight away. After all, what reason would she give the control room? That she was in pursuit of a man she suspected of dropping a topless postcard of her into the nick? That would go down a real treat as an assistance call, wouldn't it? Especially as she could provide no actual evidence of a connection between him and the murderer they were looking for. Giving up on the pursuit was not an option either. Now that she had finally traced her suspect, she was not about to call it a day simply because of the risks involved. Okay, so she was on her own, but this wasn't the first time and it certainly wouldn't be the last. Returning to her car, she pulled away from the pub, heading back towards the main road and Signalman's Walk.

CHAPTER 8

The old C & G factory was an ugly, two-storey building with a flat roof. Its boarded-up windows reminded Kate of eyes, which like the rest of the derelict properties in the street, peered blindly at the bowed, chain-link fence separating it from the road like those of a distressed, caged animal in a zoo. Much of the building was covered in ivy and other climbing parasites and an air of gloom and despair hung over the whole site. Not much of an incentive for a visitor, she thought grimly.

Leaving the CID car parked by the padlocked main gate, she ducked through a hole in the fence. She then made her way across a concrete strip sprouting a forest of calf-high weeds to the gaping rectangle, which had once been the main door. She remembered from a previous visit that the door itself had been kicked in by someone a while ago, replaced and kicked in again. So it had been left where it was lying on the floor just inside. But somewhat incongruously, the sign screwed to the wall alongside the entrance bearing the words 'Reception' in bold black lettering was still intact and in pristine condition. Flicking on her torch, she stepped carefully over the threshold and felt broken glass crunch beneath her feet. There was a wooden counter on her right, its glass top shattered. A couple of steel-framed chairs, which must have taken some effort to destroy, lay in bits in a corner. Otherwise the room was bare.

Initially, the familiar disagreeable smell of damp and decay that in her experience always seemed to seep from the walls and timbers of derelict buildings rushed to greet her arrival. But as she advanced a few more steps into the room, she became aware of another even stronger ammonia-like stench that made her want to gag. It seemed to emanate from nearby, but she didn't need to investigate more closely. The foul stench, the dark stains on the wall and the pile of screwed-up newspapers in the corner told its own story. Regrettably, dossers didn't have the luxury of flushing toilets.

Beyond the alcove, which she quickly bypassed, she went through another doorless opening into a large square hallway into which the slowly diminishing afternoon light still found its way through a number of high-level windows. Evidence of rough sleepers was everywhere. Pieces of old carpet. Ripped sleeping bags. Tattered blankets and plastic bin bags stuffed with newspaper. But for the time being the place was empty. The 'tenants' had either fled at her approach or were still out in the town begging on street corners. That suited her well. There was only one dosser she was interested in and he was certainly not here.

She crossed the room to a broad wooden staircase at the far end, intending to check out the old offices, which from past experience she knew to be on the upper level. But with one foot on the first tread, she stopped dead. The loud clang had been quite distinct, and it seemed to have come from somewhere on the other side of a pair of steel doors behind her. The factory itself. Someone was moving about inside. She frowned. What the hell would anyone be doing in there? From memory, it was the old factory floor containing just the leftovers of engineering installations and hardly the place for a doss.

Ignoring the stairs, she swung round and made her way back across the room. The doors proved to be intact for a change. Steel was a match even for the most destructive vandal. Pulling one door open, she stuck her head inside. What had once been a busy machine shop was now just a windowless mausoleum of abandoned wood and steel. Its windows were boarded up like the rest of the property, which reduced the light filtering through the cracks to just a trickle. It left much of the place in a creepy, shadowy gloom. Here and there the beam of her torch picked out the gaunt remains of massive girders, abandoned benches and the skeletal metal frames and racks that had once held or supported the different precision tools with which the place had been equipped: the lathes, the grinding and milling machines and the drill presses that had cut, shaped, bored, polished and burnished the many metal parts required by the company's industrial and commercial customers. But the machines were long gone and only the ghosts of the operators remained to mourn their passing. The ghosts and whoever else was lurking there in the darkness.

She hesitated. Go on or give up? What was it to be? Going on in such circumstances was risky and foolhardy and it occurred to her that her quarry could have been aware that she was following him and be luring her into a trap. But giving up meant losing any chance of getting to the bottom of what was going on and probably ever finding her suspect again. The choice was hers and as far as she was concerned it was a no-brainer. She was here now and she had no intention of throwing in the towel after having got so close to finding answers. Taking a deep breath, she partially masked the torch in her hand to reduce the strength of the beam and avoid advertising her exact position unnecessarily and stepped through the doorway.

It was the smell of oil, paint and other chemicals instead of raw urine and excrement that assailed her nostrils this time, Despite the passage of the years the heavy odour was still present. Pungent. Bitter. Earthy. Nauseous. It reminded her of a newly opened grave. She moved on cautiously with the torch directed at the concrete floor. Unable to see more than a couple of feet in front of her. Several times she tripped on big metal bolts and raised plates left in situ when the key machinery had been hastily stripped out of the factory by the departing bankrupted owners. Then there were the dead electric cables hanging down from the roof in places like giant strands of liquorice, which she found herself brushing against.

All the while the little voice in her head was mocking her. Asking her what she hoped to achieve. She had no idea who was lurking in the gloom around her. It could be her quarry. But on the other hand, it could be anyone. Maybe a dosser completely unconnected with her investigation. A dangerous criminal with a nasty agenda of his own. Even if it *was* her man, what was she supposed to do if she succeeded in confronting him? Ask him politely to come quietly? She had been totally stupid. Allowed her fixation on catching the killer to get in the way of basic common sense. It was time to pull out while she still could. Sink her pride and get some help. But that proved not so easy to do.

Ahead of her, double doors with aluminium panels suddenly reflected the beam of her torch. She knew that they led to the old warehouse and the loading bays for the lorries, which meant she was on the wrong side of the machine shop. At the same moment she heard a loud 'clonk' and glimpsed what was just the fuzzy outline of a figure as it flashed across the doors on the edge of the narrowed beam. She abandoned stealth and swung the torch in the direction it had gone but saw only more cables and the yawning interior of a large, empty, metal cabinet. Another loud 'clonk' behind her. Instinctively she spun round to face whoever might be creeping up on her. She saw no one.

More noises, this time to her right. It seemed like there was more than one of them. Her heart began making heavy squishing noises like an electric fan on the blink. She backed slowly towards where she thought the exit doors were. Feeling her way with her heel. One hand extended behind her.

She brushed against something which caught on her sleeve. There was a ripping sound when she tugged her arm free, and the beam of the torch shook in her hand. Then her heel clipped what she guessed was a projecting bolt or some sort of raised metal plate and she tried to guide her foot around it. Only to stop dead a second later when she found herself up against what her questing hand told her was a bench of some kind.

Scuffling sounds in front of her and there was another loud 'clang'. She edged slowly to her left following the bench along. Then she caught the sound of boots scraping on a gritty floor directly in front of her. Too close for comfort. The damned torch. The light was giving away her position. She switched it off and taking a chance, crept blindly away from the bench in another direction altogether. But her eyes failed to adjust to the pitch blackness around her after relying on the beam of the torch. She collided with coils of electric cable, moved to one side to avoid them and walked straight into a wall. Before she could turn round a heavy body had slammed her back into it, holding her there with her face pressed up against the cold, rough surface.

'What's your game, girl?' a voice demanded in her ear, the speaker's foul breath enveloping her. 'Why you followin' me?'

The tone was coarse and rasping and had what sounded like an East London accent. Nothing like the cold metallic tones of Mr Anonymous. Her confidence in her deductive reasoning took an even steeper nosedive.

'You know why,' she grated through clenched teeth, trying to stick to her guns. 'So don't try to deny it.'

'Deny what?'

'That you are a callous murdering thug.'

'I ain't stiffed nobody. What you on about?'

She tried to twist herself free, but her captor didn't budge, and she could feel powerful hands now gripping both her shoulders.

'You're hurting me.'

'I'll hurt you a bleedin' sight more less you tell me what this is all about.'

'You were spotted at Highbridge nick.'

'Don't know what you're talkin' about.'

'When you dropped that envelope in.'

He said nothing for a moment but didn't argue the point. 'What's that got to do with anythin'?'

'It ties you into all three murders.'

'I told you I ain't murdered nobody. Okay, so I did drop the envelope into the cop shop, but only cause this geezer paid me to do it for him on the quiet like.'

'What geezer?' There was discernible contempt in her tone. 'I don't believe you.'

'I don't give a shit what you believe. He come up to me when I was on the seafront and give me a "pony" to deliver an envelope. Why wouldn't anyone do that? It ain't a crime?'

'And you didn't ask him why?'

'That was his business. I done the job while he waited nearby. Then he give me the money and that was it.'

'Twenty-five quid isn't much.'

'It is when you're skint.'

'So what did this guy look like.'

'Why should I tell you that? Just sod off and leave me alone.'

Quite abruptly the hold on her relaxed and even as she came off the wall and turned round to face him, she heard his heavy clomping footsteps receding into the gloom.

For a few moments she just stood there, leaning against the wall with one hand as she waited for her pounding heart to return to something like its normal rhythm. That had certainly been a close call and she was still shaking after it. She had been totally helpless. He could have done anything to her he wanted, and she couldn't have stopped him. Instead, he had simply walked away, leaving her completely unscathed. How lucky was that? One thing was pretty obvious, though. Gerry Thomas wasn't her man. He was just a messenger. She was right back where she had started. Again.

Rummaging around on the floor for her torch, which she had dropped, she found it and tested the beam. To her relief, it worked. Now all she had to do was get out of this place before one of the other denizens took an interest in her.

No longer having to worry about giving her position away, she kept the torch fully on and followed the wall along to the end. Moving carefully to avoid colliding with anything else, she was through the double doors and into the square hall with its still empty sleeping bags and crumpled blankets in a couple of minutes. But her intention to put as much distance as she could between herself and the C & G building received a major setback.

The much more subdued, grey afternoon light that stole into the hall through its high-level windows left shadows in the corners. But it was impossible to miss the figure lying on its back across the lower treads of the staircase. He was violently convulsing as if in a fit. But Kate's former suspect, Gerry Thomas, was not having a fit. The blood still pumping from his severed carotid arteries was adequate testimony to the fact. In the time it had taken Kate to find her way back out of the machine shop, someone had slit Thomas's throat and left him collapsed on the stairs, jerking and shaking in his last bubbling, choking gasps of breath.

* * *

At first sight, it looked as if some mad artist had run amok with red spray paint. Part of the staircase and an adjacent wall were gruesomely plastered with the dead man's blood, which also saturated his clothing and formed a thick mucus-streaked pool on the floor between his legs.

'The heart is quite a powerful organ,' the police surgeon commented cheerfully after surveying the scene. 'It will continue to pump until there is nothing left *to* pump. It can have quite some force behind it too, and as this poor fellow struggled to contain the haemorrhage, it would have performed a bit like a high-pressure hose. Do you know, I have seen—'

'Yes, thank you, Doc,' Charlie Woo cut in quickly. 'Any idea what kind of weapon was used.'

The medical man shrugged. 'Something with a long broad blade, I would imagine, going by the breadth of the wound inflicted. Cut through the arteries in a single sweep.'

'Left or right-handed assailant?'

'Oh, I think I'll leave that assessment to your forensic pathologist. Not really my bag, that sort of thing. I'm just a humble police surgeon. Goodnight.'

Woo followed the rotund, bespectacled figure as he disappeared through the door to Reception, then turned to DS O'Sullivan with a grimace.

The sergeant answered his question before he asked it. 'Pathologist and SOCO on their way as we speak, guv.'

'And where's Kate?'

'I left her sitting in her car. She's pretty shook up.'

'Not surprised. I'd better have a word with her before the shit hits the fan.'

Kate was sitting behind the wheel staring straight ahead. White-faced and unseeing. Woo eased into the passenger seat beside her.

'You okay?' he asked.

She turned slowly to face him and flicked her eyebrows as an alternative to a shrug. 'What do you think, Charlie?'

'Do you reckon the killer was your man?'

'Had to be. He must have followed me to the factory and lay in wait for that poor devil when he came out of the machine room.'

He sighed. 'Recapping on what you told me when I first arrived, why didn't you tell me before about this guy with the missing earlobe? It's the second time in this inquiry that you've not passed on critical info. We could probably have prevented what's happened here if you'd followed procedure.'

'I didn't know about it myself until after I got back to the nick from seeing you at the last murder scene, and it was pure luck that I happened to spot him when I responded to the assistance call at the Soldiers. I had no choice but to follow the job through or I would have lost him, and Cave and his crew had left by then.'

'You had a radio. You could have called up and got them back.'

She gave a short, cynical laugh. 'With what I had to tell them? Do me a favour. I think I've suffered enough humiliation from that topless postcard, don't you?'

He grunted. 'Well, you've certainly done it this time. And on top of the business at the church too.'

He turned his head sharply as she slapped her warrant card on top of the dashboard in front of him.

'You might as well take that now. It will save time later.'

He snorted and tossed it back into her lap. 'Don't be a bloody exhibitionist. Just go home.'

'What again?'

'You're not in the right mindset to carry on today. Also, the DCI is on his way here as a prelude to a full major incident investigation being set up over these murders and it's best you're not here when he arrives.'

She nodded and followed him with her eyes as he climbed out of the car and shut the door behind him.

'Take it easy, and have a proper rest,' he said, turning round briefly to stare at her through the open passenger window. 'I'll see you in the morning and we'll discuss what's to be done then.'

'And the incident report to HQ?'

'You leave that with me. It won't have to be a detailed essay. Just the basics. Leaving out superfluous information like who you told or didn't tell, what and when. Capiche?'

Then he winked and headed back towards the now open gate in the factory fence.

CHAPTER 9

Kate heard Hayden's Jaguar churning up the gravel in the sideway when she was in the shower. Seconds later she heard the front door of their cottage crash back against the wall as it was clumsily thrown open. She closed her eyes briefly in resignation. Another lecture coming up, she mused, thinking that she was just not in the mood for it at that precise moment.

Then her husband was charging up the stairs, calling her name. She met him on the landing, a big fluffy towel wrapped around herself, ready for the anticipated outburst. Instead, to her astonishment he grabbed her in an enormous bearhug and crushed her against him while she dripped on to the landing carpet.

'Gordon Bennett,' he gasped, raising one arm to stroke her wet hair. 'I just heard on the QT. Are you okay?'

She gently prised herself free. 'I'm fine, Hayd,' she replied. 'Just a bit pissed off, that's all.'

'But when they said you'd been sent home, I thought . . .'

She eased past him. 'I'm okay, really I am.'

He followed her into the bedroom, frowning as he watched her dry herself. His blurted censure came a few minutes later.

106

'Whatever made you go after him into that place? I mean, you should have known better. Anything could have happened to you. It was reckless and stupid.'

She didn't deny it but smiled into her towel. Relieved that if this was to be the extent of the lecture, she had got off lightly and secretly delighted at his obvious concern for her safety. It suggested the postcard issue was no longer burning indignant holes in his fevered brain. Nevertheless, she couldn't stop herself putting that to the test.

'Am I now forgiven for the holiday snap then?' she asked innocently.

He scowled. 'Don't push it,' he growled but propped himself on a corner of the bed and patted the coverlet, adding, 'Now you'd better tell me all about this business. I was worried sick.'

Not for the first time, she thought, remembering other occasions when she had raised his anxiety levels over what he had called her 'hair-brained go-it-alone stunts'. She had certainly tried his patience over the years, and it was a wonder he had continued to endure her cliffhanging approach to life instead of just walking away.

She gave up on drying her long, auburn hair and draped the towel around her shoulders. Then dropping on to the bed beside him, she gave him the full story, leaving nothing out.

'The killer must have been waiting for Thomas when he left the machine shop,' he commented. 'Plainly, he wanted to shut him up before he passed on any useful information to you.'

'He was a bit late then. Thomas had already confronted me by then, so anything he wanted to say would already have been said.'

'Maybe your man didn't realise you'd already had your little chat and he decided it was time to tidy up before you did?'

'Hell of a way to do that. Cutting someone's throat practically from ear to ear.'

'Pretty effective, though, don't you think? It also means he must have followed you all the way from the Soldier's

Arms. Maybe even from the nick. Which indicates he's keeping close tabs on you.'

'I think that's been apparent from the very start of this business,' she said with heavy sarcasm. 'His infatuation with me appears to know no bounds.'

'This is not funny, Kate. I believe you are at great personal risk from this creature. He is not simply some vicious no-account thug, slaughtering for the sheer joy of it, or because he's a sadistic sexual pervert. There is a method in everything he does. Plainly, he has some sort of misogynistic phobia and because you are a woman, he resents the fact that you are a successful police detective. He is not only seeking to prove he is intellectually superior to you, with the ability to outwit you at every stage by winning his macabre game. He aims to ruin your reputation in the process and destroy you as a person, using gaslighting tactics to achieve his goal.'

'And what the hell is "gaslighting" when it's at home?'

He looked surprised. 'You've never heard of it?'

'Why don't you enlighten me?'

'It is a quite ruthless underhand technique to undermine a person's personal perceptions of reality by making them second-guess their judgements and their confidence in themselves. The term stems from the remake of a Patrick Hamilton play in a 1940s Alfred Hitchcock film called *Gaslight*. In the film a chap plays malicious, psychological tricks on his wife, like dimming the gaslights at home, then telling her she is imagining things, so that she starts to think she is losing her mind. Psychologists later officially adopted gaslighting as a recognised form of manipulative, controlling behaviour, carried out by an abuser with a mental personality disorder, such as narcissism, to exert power over their victim. It is usually found in romantic settings or within the family, but it can also happen elsewhere. In your case, I believe this character has deliberately created a relationship with you, not only to gain power over you, but to prove his superiority by ultimately bringing you down.'

Kate stared at him for a moment without speaking, plainly astonished by what he had come out with. She knew

Hayden was perceptive, highly intelligent and very well read, even if his practical abilities as a copper appeared questionable at times, but the breadth and depth of his knowledge never failed to amaze her.

'Well, who's just swallowed a trick cyclist's workbook,' she commented finally.

He shrugged. 'Thought you would have been aware of the term,' he replied pompously. 'Maybe you should get out more.'

'Maybe I should. So my man is a gaslighter, is he? I'll remember that. But where does all this get us? We still have no idea as to this nutter's identity, or even the slightest idea of what he looks like. Whether he's in his thirties, middle-aged or a pensioner. Is tall or short. Fat or thin. Has dark or fair hair. A beard, moustache or is clean-shaven. We have absolutely nothing to go on.'

'That's bound to come in time.'

'So is Christmas! In the meantime, while everyone is faffing about in the dark, looking for this scumbag, there's every chance I'll be served with discip forms for a "rubber-heel" investigation into my catalogue of so-called transgressions, which could ultimately cost me my rank, or, even worse, my job.'

There was a mischievous glint in his eyes. 'At least if it does come to that you'll be able to embark on the new career as a crime writer you've been thinking about.'

She scowled. 'Not funny, Hayden, not funny at all.'

He made a self-deprecating face. 'Sorry. No it's not, is it? But you were jumping the gun a bit there, weren't you? There's no certainty you will be investigated, and in the meantime it's in your own interests to keep a low profile.'

She eyed him steadily. 'You mean just sit back, do nothing and let this filthy bastard get away with cold-blooded murder?'

'What happens to him is not your responsibility. When I left the nick just now, moves were already afoot to reopen the incident room upstairs, so a major crime inquiry is obviously being set up. From now on, whatever happens in this awful business, it will be down to whoever is appointed senior investigating officer to sort it. The local CID team here will take their cue from the new SIO, and you will be well out of it.'

'There's no way I can just sit on my hands while all this is going on.'

He released his breath in an explosive, exasperated snort. 'You've got no choice. Kate! You're in enough trouble as it is. You have to stay out of this case altogether, or you'll bring more heat down on yourself.'

She turned away from him to pull on the clean clothes she had laid out on the bed.

'Do you hear me?' he said sharply.

She nodded. 'Every word, Hayd, every word.' She pulled on a T-shirt and turned back to face him. 'But what if Mr Anonymous won't let that happen? What then?'

'I don't see how he can do anything about it. You've got to stop letting him get inside your head. That's what gaslighters do. That's how they win.' He glanced at his watch. 'Now, do you mind if I nip out for a couple of hours? There's a classic car club gathering down the road at eight and I should be there.'

'What about dinner?'

'I'll get something at the pub. I won't be back late.'

She nodded. 'No problem. I'll probably watch a film on Sky anyway.'

He frowned again. 'If anything happens, you will ring me on my mobile, won't you?'

She forced a smile. 'Don't fret, Hayd, I'll be fine. I'm a big girl now, you know.'

He gave her a searching glance. 'Sometimes I wonder about that,' he replied.

Ten minutes later she heard his Jaguar pull out of the driveway, its throaty growl quickly fading into the marshy countryside. She was left with a strangely unsettling stillness broken only by the creaks and groans of the old cottage as it flexed its aged limbs. Pausing briefly in the act of pulling the living room curtains across, she stared into the gathering dusk, only vaguely aware of the bats wheeling through the light splashed across the patio by the security lamps fixed to each corner of the cottage. He was out there somewhere on the marsh, she felt certain. She could sense his presence. Watching her standing at the window. He'd probably seen Hayden leave. What would he do? She was overdue a call after what had happened that afternoon, so she guessed that's what it would be. She waited for the bleep of her mobile, knowing it would come soon. It did, just minutes later.

She spoke before the caller could say a word. 'Another burner?' she commented drily. 'You must be made of money.'

'Oh, I have several of them, Kate,' the cold, drawling voice replied. 'Suffice to say, this one will be at the bottom of a rhyne after this call. By the way, did you enjoy your trip to the cider farm? I thought I achieved a rather artistic result there, though I don't think Wilf Carpenter appreciated it.'

'Enjoy killing, do you?' she retorted. 'Three innocent people slaughtered for no reason other than to satisfy your sadistic ego. You really do have a screw loose.'

He made a tutting sound. 'You seem rather worked up today, Kate? Problem with the old time of the month issue, is it? Or is Hayden not giving you one as often as you would like? But you shouldn't get over excited about things after your recent time in the nut clinic. It could get you sent back there. I must admit, though, I was quite surprised to read about your brush with mental instability. And there was me thinking you were so "with it" and controlled. Just goes to show, you can't judge a book by its cover, doesn't it? And you have the nerve to suggest *I* have a screw loose. Tut-tut, a bit hypocritical that, isn't it?'

Kate refused to bite and he released a loud theatrical sigh.

'Oh incidentally, I must apologise for the mess I had to leave behind at the factory. But I'm sure you will appreciate that I had to act rather quickly. On the hoof so to speak. I

111

couldn't risk poor Mr Thomas having second thoughts about things and giving my description to one of your colleagues later.'

'Well, you're too late. He and I had already had a chat before you butchered him, and I now have all the info I need.'

A deep sigh. 'And you are a very poor liar, Detective Sergeant. I am quite sure he told you nothing. In fact, he couldn't have done anyway, because he didn't know anything. He only saw me once and I was wearing a scarf over the lower part of my face then. So what was there to tell?'

Kate was on a loser with this and she knew it, so she changed tack. Anything to keep him talking in the hope that he would give something away about himself. 'So I suppose you tailed me from the pub to the C & G factory? Sitting outside, were you?'

'Oh, I've tailed you, as you so eloquently put it, quite a lot, my dear. But I have to admit you are quite a live wire, aren't you? You must be exhausting to work with. Still, a worthy opponent for me in this little game of ours.'

'Well I hate to disappoint you, but you overdid it trying to rubbish my reputation and I've now been taken off the case altogether, so I won't be playing anymore. Sorry about that, but you'll have to manage without me.'

A hard laugh. 'Oh, I am well aware that your superiors have decided to pull you off the crime inquiry, Sergeant. The trees have ears as well as walls, you see. You should remember that. But it makes no difference. The game goes on and you will continue to play, I assure you.'

Kate's mind flashed back to the crime scene at the cider farm and her outburst to Woo about the inquiry. She'd sensed at the time that the killer was watching from among the trees, and now it seemed, listening too. Even if he hadn't picked up on the full drift of what was being said, he would almost certainly have heard the loud voice of Debbie Moreton, the reporter from the *Clarion*, asking about her removal from the team.

'Eavesdropping part of your repertoire then, is it?' she snapped.

'Of course. Don't you police officers often boast about keeping an ear close to the ground? Why shouldn't I do the same thing?'

'Well, you've wasted your time. I'm no longer on the team and that's it. Nothing you can do about it.'

'Oh, I wouldn't be so sure about that. I have invested too much time, money and effort in setting things up to allow the plug to be pulled now. Too much is at stake. So I strongly suggest you ring your DI tonight and advise him to reinstate you as lead investigator forthwith or suffer the consequences. I will expect nothing less.'

Kate laughed. '*You* will expect nothing less? Well, it may come as a surprise to you to learn that the police tend not to take the views of pathetic inadequates like you into consideration when they are making operational decisions.'

There was a sharp hiss in response. 'Is that so? Then on your head be it.'

The phone went dead.

* * *

Kate passed another uneasy night, with Hayden snoring fit to burst beside her. She had told her husband about the phone call and also called the DI on his mobile to make him aware. Both seemed to have shrugged it off as merely something to bear in mind. An idle threat, just that, and it was true that nothing could be done about it at that time in the evening anyway. Especially as the call had been made on a burner once again, which could not be traced.

The killer's last words dominated her own thoughts, though. *Then on your head be it.* What did he mean? What was he going to do? She regretted taunting him now. Winding him up. Calling him a pathetic inadequate. If, as Hayden had indicated, gaslighters had narcissistic tendencies, then the insult would have really got to him. She had checked on the subject of narcissism through the internet once her husband had gone to bed, so as not to reveal her lamentable ignorance of the mental condition after his own highbrow references to gaslighting. She had learned that narcissism itself amounted to an inflated sense of a person's own importance and delusions of grandeur. Narcissists, it was said, basked in the glow of excessive attention, thriving on admiration and praise, which suggested that being treated dismissively or with contempt was perhaps the worst thing they could encounter. Because of what she had said to Mr Anonymous, she imagined all sorts of carnage he might wreak to make his point. Doubling his murder count, for example? Carrying out some sort of 'spectacular' and making use of his tame reporter, Debbie Moreton, to publicise his message? She felt once again that she had handled things poorly and anything bad that now happened would be her fault. She had caused it to happen through her own clumsy stupidity.

Or was she just falling into the very trap Hayden had warned her about? Allowed the gaslighter to get inside her head and influence her perceptions of herself?

Confused and bewildered, she finally got up and went downstairs to make herself a coffee. She was sitting there, shivering in the cold, when she heard the familiar 'clang' of a sprung metal plate. Jumping to her feet and knocking her coffee mug over in the process, she ran back into the living room. The piece of paper was sticking out of the letterbox in the front door and at two o'clock in the morning it was much too early for the post. With trembling fingers she pulled it out and held it up in the light.

The note was short and to the point. It read quite simply:

RIP DS O'Sullivan.

CHAPTER 10

The road outside the cottage was deserted. He had disappeared back into the night. Kate re-closed the front door and bolted it before snatching up the telephone and dialling the police control room at Highbridge.

They seemed to take forever to answer. Then abruptly the operator was on the other end. 'Ring DS Sullivan at his home and tell him to get out of the place now,' she rapped, 'and send a car to that address immediately. He's under immediate threat.'

'Who is this, please?' the male voice at the other end asked patiently.

'DS Lewis. My number will have already come up on your screen if you care to look.'

There was a brief pause. 'Why is he in danger, Sergeant?'

'No time to explain. Just get it done.'

'But I need to know—'

Suddenly Kate knew how members of the public must feel when trying to get an immediate response in an emergency. She wished she had dialled three nines.

'For heaven's sake, get a car round there now,' she blazed. 'I'm on my way.'

Slamming the phone back down, she raced up the stairs, grabbed the glass of water by her bedside and threw it over Hayden's face. He awoke with a yell to see her pulling on her clothes.

'Get up, fat man!' she shouted. 'I need you with me now.'

Her tone must have communicated the urgency of the situation to him. For once in his life he didn't protest or ask questions but scrambled out of bed and bent down to retrieve his trousers from the floor.

Kate explained what was going on as they raced out to her car and within minutes they were hurtling through Burtle village and across the Levels towards the village of Mark.

Kate was aware that O'Sullivan lived in an old farmhouse on a back road across the moor connecting Mark to the A38. They arrived at the same time as a marked police patrol car with its strobes flashing. Kate was out of the Mazda even as she braked to a stop. She hammered on the front door and the two uniformed officers ran round the back. There was no answer.

'We'll have to break the door down,' she said to Hayden breathlessly. 'He could be lying seriously injured in there.'

But before she or Hayden could do anything, they were interrupted by a shout from one of the uniformed officers, who had emerged from the back of the house and was waving frantically. 'Hold it, skipper,' he shouted. 'You'd better come round the back.'

Kate felt her stomach muscles tighten in dreadful anticipation, and she started towards him, at a run with Hayden stumbling along behind.

'Why, what is it?' she exclaimed when she got to him.

'You won't like it,' he panted.

That proved to be a gross understatement. There was a garage and a wide gravel hardstanding behind the house, accessed by a separate entranceway. A blue Ford Galaxy was parked in front of the garage with its lights full on and one of the rear doors hanging open. Kate recognised the car as

O'Sullivan's. The second uniformed officer was bent over a few feet from the driver's side of the car, vomiting into some bushes, and Kate knew before she even got to the vehicle what to expect.

Liam O'Sullivan was still in the car. In fact, it was obvious he had never got out of it again after pulling up in front of his garage. He was sitting behind the wheel, with his head leaning against it as if asleep or drunk. But he was neither, as the heavy deposits of blood caking the windscreen and dashboard revealed. Someone had cut his throat and a black crow lay dead on the passenger seat beside him.

* * *

There were uniformed officers everywhere and blue-and-white police perimeter tapes sealed off both entrances to the property. Kate stood with the DI a few paces from the Ford Galaxy, on the other side of yellow tapes, bearing the words *Police Line. Do Not Cross.*

'Police surgeon's on his way,' Kate said as Woo reread the chilling note that had been put through her letterbox and was now secure inside a plastic evidence bag. 'And we've also called out the forensic pathologist and SOCO. No doubt about this one being murder either. Slashed across the throat with what must have been quite a long blade. Looks like it cut through both arteries in one go. Poor devil never stood a chance.'

Woo nodded grimly. 'I'll get this note checked out by SOCO, but I don't expect them to find anything on it. As this guy has already shown, he's much too with it to leave any traces behind—'

'Apart from another bloody crow, that is,' Kate retorted. 'He was obviously keen to let us know this was his handiwork again and killing Liam was his way of telling us I should not have been taken off the case.'

'Except that it's apparently not a crow,' he corrected. 'Indrani Purewal, who was at the last crime scene, is apparently a keen twitcher in her spare time, and she told me the bird left beside the cider press was not a crow but a rook, even though rooks are of the crow family. This one looks the same as the others. It seems carrion crows are not quite so common, and they are solitary birds, whereas rooks congregate together in large numbers and would be easier to get hold of. So our man is perhaps not as clever as he thinks he is.'

'For the purposes of these murders, I think we're talking semantics here. Whether it's a crow or a rook, is irrelevant. It's the same sort of calling card anyway. Furthermore, whether he knows his rooks from his crows, he has proved himself a lot cleverer than us so far anyway.'

He frowned and studied her white face. 'You okay?'

'Just about. This isn't something I haven't seen before, but Liam *was* a colleague, which makes it a lot worse.'

He nodded sympathetically. 'Bad business. D'ye reckon he'd been here long?'

'I'm no forensic expert, but I'd say several hours, going by the partial solidification of some of the blood spatter. Probably happened just after he drove home from the nick. The rear nearside passenger door was left wide open, so it looks like the killer was in the back of the car behind him and decamped from there.'

Woo grimaced. 'Well, I left Liam at the cider farm murder scene to liaise with SOCO after the forensic pathologist had left around four, and he didn't get back to the nick until well after seven. We had a pint and a wad in the pub down the road and then he returned to the nick on foot to collect his car to go home.'

'And since I doubt whether Liam would have picked up any hitchhikers on the way, the killer must have hid himself in the back of it before he left the nick—'

'Which means it was left unlocked, presenting the swine with a golden opportunity.'

She shrugged bitterly. 'Yeah, but why would anyone need to lock their car in a bloody police station yard?'

'We can see why now, but it's a bit too late. Funny O'Sullivan never saw anyone there when he first got in, though.'

'Not if he left after dark and he was tired. No doubt he just wanted to get home after a long day. Also the car's full of junk and the back seats are down, so there were plenty of places to hide. Then the killer obviously crept up behind his seat and reached over to do the business. I don't suppose Liam even realised what was happening until it was too late.'

Woo glanced around the garden, which was largely enclosed within high hedging. 'No neighbours, I see, so no possible witnesses?'

'Not out here. This is the back of beyond.'

'And obviously no one at the nick saw anyone getting into Liam's car either or something would have been said. Incredible that someone could just walk into the car park of a police station and climb into one of the cars just like that.'

She shrugged. 'Skeleton crew at night, with most of them out on patrol, I would think. No camera surveillance, which I hear they are only just thinking about, because of the cost. No one to see.'

'I wonder how this swine knew the Galaxy was O'Sullivan's car in the first place?'

'He'd probably seen him getting into it before when he was watching the nick or even at the last murder scene. I saw his car there when I arrived.'

'Yeah, he was on a mileage allowance like you and me, so he often used his own car on duty commitments. I suppose it all saves the force the astronomical cost of diesel, but it would have been a dead giveaway for anyone watching.'

'We'll have to inform the poor devil's next of kin?'

'I don't believe he was married, and I think his relatives are all in Ireland. Details should be on his personal file any-way. Rotten job coming up for someone in the Garda.'

'Rotten job all round.' She nodded towards the main entrance. 'Looks like the police surgeon's car has arrived . . .'

Hayden wandered over to her as the DI went to meet the doctor in the road outside.

'We should be heading back home. If you can't be involved in the investigation, there's no point your being here.'

She shook her head. 'I can't just leave, can I? This happened because of me.'

'How so?'

'Well, it's all down to me, isn't it? These murders are only being committed because I went to Cancun.'

'Don't be ridiculous. You can't blame yourself because you took a holiday and some psycho latched on to you. '

'But he obviously murdered O'Sullivan to try and force the DCI to reinstate me on the team.'

Hayden clicked his tongue irritably. 'Maybe he did, and who took you *off* the team in the first place, eh? Charlie and the DCI. You might as well blame them too. Kate, the only person responsible for all this carnage is the perp himself. No one else. Remember what I told you. As well as a murderer, this swine is also an accomplished gaslighter, and he's trying to make you doubt everything about yourself. That's his strategy. You have to shake him off. Otherwise, you'll end up back in the clinic or worse.'

'Gaslighter?' Woo commented as he rejoined them. 'What the devil's a gaslighter?'

Kate gave a wan smile. 'I'm glad I'm not the only one to ask that question,' she said. 'If you're very lucky, guv, Hayd will be only too pleased to tell you.'

* * *

The mood in the DI's office at Highbridge police station was sombre. There were three of them in the small, glass-panelled room. Kate sat in front of the DI's desk beside Charlie Woo and DCI Toby Ricketts occupied the swivel chair behind it. There were no buzzing flies in the office this time and a pregnant silence reigned while Ricketts devoted his attention to the report in front of him summarising the developments of the last few days, which Woo had updated in the last hour.

For her part, Kate felt cold and dispirited after her lack of sleep and she was unable to repress a yawn, which did not go unnoticed by the DCI despite his apparent preoccupation with the report.

Raising his head with a sneer on his youthful face, he said, 'Not keeping you up, Sergeant, are we?'

'Sorry, sir,' she said without meaning it. 'Didn't sleep much last night.'

She was not surprised by his jibe, though it was uncalled for and in pretty poor taste in view of what had just happened to one of their close colleagues. For some unknown reason Ricketts had never bothered to conceal his antipathy towards Kate and he never missed an opportunity to try and humiliate her. Maybe he was also a gaslighter, she thought, and she studied him for a moment with an expression of undisguised contempt.

A dapper well-groomed man in his thirties, with a head of silky, blond hair and a matching luxuriant moustache, he liked, as now, to dress to impress in expensive Italian-style suits. He had joined the force as an ex university graduate through the fast-track entry scheme and had devoted his energies to impressing those in high places. In so doing, he had made an unenviable name for himself as a sycophantic governor's man. He had risen quickly through the ranks as a result. But something had gone wrong on the way so that the blue-eyed whizz-kid seemed to have lost his 'whizz' and had come to an abrupt stop. Like a tram which suddenly runs out of electricity. Desperate to get back in favour with the top hierarchy, he was known to have no allegiance to anyone save himself and the next rung on the ladder and as such, few of those he worked with had any respect for him.

'Well, try and pay attention if you can,' he went on sarcastically. 'After all, it seems DS O'Sullivan lost his life because of this madman's infatuation with you. So it would be reasonable for us to expect you to show some interest.'

The barb struck home with painful force and Kate blinked hard to prevent herself from dissolving into tears.

Then the next instant her face coloured up as the fury rose like molten lava from deep within her. But perhaps sensing she was about to lose it big time, Woo cut in sharply.

'Sorry, guv, but I have to say that was well out of order.'

Ricketts turned angrily on him, but met by an unflinching gaze, he changed tack and simply shrugged.

'In any event, I note from this report that you think O'Sullivan may have been killed in an attempt to force our hand to reinstate DS Lewis on the murder inquiry,' he said, ignoring the censure and continuing as if Kate wasn't there. 'Hence the killer's reason for leaving his calling card at the scene. But that is not going to happen. We will not be intimidated by this thug. It was obvious to me from the start that Sergeant Lewis was much too personally involved in this affair to play an active part in the investigation, though I agreed that she should remain available to us as a possible future link to the man. Therefore my decision to remove her from the inquiry while keeping her on hand to assist where necessary still stands.

'As you will know a major crime inquiry is now being set up in the incident room upstairs, which I expect to be active with effect from 9 a.m. today. This means the whole thing is now out of our hands and a dedicated team under an independent SIO will carry things forward. But before that actually happens, I need to know where we are with the inquiries we have already set in motion so that I can brief Detective Superintendent Hennessey properly when she arrives.'

'Deidrie Hennessey?' Kate blurted before she could stop herself.

Ricketts raised an eyebrow. 'I didn't realise you were on first-name terms with her, Sergeant,' he said drily.

Kate didn't reply, and looked down at her feet, feeling suddenly embarrassed. But inside herself she felt a sense of relief. At last things were looking up. She knew Deidrie Hennessey well and had worked under her on a number of crime inquiries. Hailing from Northern Ireland, the blonde-haired senior detective had a practical no-nonsense approach to the job and a keen analytical mind that missed very little. She could be sharp and impatient, especially with procrastinators. But she also had a dry sense of humour and was a pleasure to work with. She would eat Ricketts for breakfast, Kate mused with malicious satisfaction. Even more important, with Hennessey as SIO maybe, just maybe, she herself would find a listening ear for once.

Woo cleared his throat, conscious of the tense atmosphere that had developed in the room. 'As I've said in my report,' he said quickly, keen to cool things down, 'inquiries have so far failed to turn up any witnesses to the crimes, and no prints or other forensic evidence pointing to the identity of the killer has been found at either of the first two crime scenes. You will be aware that SOCO are still in the process of examining DS O'Sullivan's car and we await their findings. None of the other forensic material submitted for examination, including the murder weapon from the Strange murder scene and the notes sent by the killer to Kate, have yielded anything of evidential value. It has been confirmed, however, that the blood on the candlestick found at the top of the church tower is that of Strange. An examination of Kate's car has also been carried out after the message regarding the cider farm killing was scrawled across the windscreen, but that has also proved negative.'

'Negatives all the way, it seems,' Ricketts sniped. 'Any further news yet on DS Lewis's mobile phone the technical unit have been tasked to interrogate?'

'We're still waiting for a result there too, but I understand it is doubtful whether the geeks will be able to come up with anything anyway as a burner was used, which is likely to be untraceable.'

'Have we considered putting a tap on her present mobile? After all, I would have thought that that would have been a key step. Her replacement phone carries the same number, does it not?'

'It's not that simple, sir. It's not like this man is ringing a static phone, and if it were possible to set that up, the calls would need round the clock monitoring since he could call at any time of the day or night. But in any event, as I've already said in the report, he is using a cheap, old-style burner, so trying to track him would be a pointless exercise.'

'What about this reporter woman, Debbie something or other? Have you thought about putting a tap on her static office phone or setting up some form of liaison with the paper? Your report indicates that this man seems to ring her on a regular basis. That presents us with a golden opportunity for some meaningful cooperation.'

Woo shook his head. 'I did speak to the editor on the blower and suggested we had a meeting. But I got pretty short shrift from him. As you will know, the *Bridgwater Clarion* is rabidly anti-police. Maybe that's why matey chose them as a point of contact in the first place. They will never cooperate with the authorities on the lame excuse of maintaining their public credibility and impartiality. It's bollocks, but we can't force them to cooperate.'

Ricketts seemed determined to continue picking holes in the investigation. 'And I gather even the post-mortem results on the Reverend Strange haven't arrived, but are still in the pipeline?'

'No, but I did attend the PM and based on what the pathologist told me, I expect the report to say that although Strange died from massive trauma consistent with a high-level fall, there are indications that he received a heavy blow to the back of the head pre-mortem, which ties in with what the killer has claimed. As for Wilfred Carpenter, his PM is still to be carried out, but I don't think there is much doubt as to how he died anyway.'

'Hmm. What about the passenger manifest that was to be obtained from the airline re the flight from Cancun?'

'Still waiting for that too, sir. The airline has to get approval from the top before they can send it. Something about privacy and data protection.'

The DCI referred to the report in front of him. 'And the Villa Ambrose where the sergeant was staying? I assumed we would be contacting them for a list of those on the course at the time.'

'We have done that, but unfortunately the course director, a Mr Martin Keogh, absolutely refuses to supply the information on the grounds of confidentiality. He said many of those on the course would not want their attendance to be communicated to anyone else. We can't force him to provide the information without a messy inquiry through the Cancun police. Even if we did eventually get the info, it's not likely to be of much help to us anyway as it will amount to just a list of names and addresses, which would tell us nothing.'

'I disagree. We could then at least carry out checks on each guest, as I would expect us to do with the passengers listed in the airline manifest when it is provided. That would tell us if any of them have previous criminal convictions.'

Woo stared at him for a moment, disbelief written all over his face that a DCI could come out with such a crass statement. 'I am sure you would appreciate that such a massive sweep would be seen as simply a fishing exercise and considered out of the question, sir. If only on a privacy and human rights basis. Furthermore, even if we could do it and there were some positive results, that would not prove anything in so far as this case is concerned, coupled with which, I don't know how many hundreds of names would be involved for a large passenger jet, many of them not even connected with the Villa Ambrose.'

'And the sergeant's suspicions about the death of the woman at the Villa Ambrose, have we done anything about that, or is it also too difficult to do?'

'We have already passed Kate's suspicions about the incident to the police in Mexico, but so far we have had no response, although it is early days yet.'

'So, yet more negatives, eh? In essence, everything about this investigation so far appears to be negative and we've got absolutely nowhere with it. That will really impress Detective Superintendent Hennessey, won't it? This thug is running rings around us, and the local media seem more intent on illustrating our incompetence than anything else.'

He dumped two copies of the *Bridgwater Clarion* on the edge of the desk in front of them.

'In fact, our detective sergeant here seems to dominate the rubbish they are putting out rather than the facts about the crimes themselves and the appeal for witnesses. The control room has received numerous calls from the national media, all anxious to get in on the act. When news of Sergeant O'Sullivan's death gets out, doubtless they will all be descending on us like a swarm of locusts. Well done, Sergeant Lewis. You have finally made the fifteen minutes of fame the American pop artist, Andy Warhol, once claimed everyone would briefly enjoy. Though removing you from the case may at least prevent anymore PR disasters.'

Kate couldn't let that pass. 'With respect, sir,' she responded in a tone of pure ice, 'your decision to take me off the case may actually turn out to be the biggest disaster of the lot. As you said just now, Detective Sergeant O'Sullivan may have died as a result of this killer's infatuation with me, but my removal from the investigation seems to have been his primary motive.'

For a moment Ricketts's face went white and his blue eyes flashed dangerously. Then perhaps realising he had asked for all he'd got, instead of giving vent to his feelings, he abruptly recovered his composure and continued on another tack.

'Well, tell me this, Sergeant, how did this ruthless individual come to know Sergeant O'Sullivan had replaced you in the first place. You didn't inadvertently reveal this in your chat on the phone, did you?'

Kate tensed. The way he had put the question seemed to suggest she had some sort of convivial relationship with Mr Anonymous. She could see where this was going, despite his inclusion of the word 'inadvertently', and she wasn't about to give him the rope he was trying to hang her with.

'I never mentioned Liam O'Sullivan to him at all, sir, and I didn't have to anyway. He disclosed that he already knew I had been replaced on the inquiry, though he never mentioned Sergeant O'Sullivan by name.'

She could tell by the look on Rickett's face that he didn't believe her. 'And how on earth did he manage to find that out?'

'Quite simple really. When I met up with Detective Inspector Woo and Liam O'Sullivan at the cider farm crime scene, I had a feeling the killer was hiding nearby, watching and listening to us. I actually mentioned this to the DI at the time. Plainly, I was right, because the man boasted to me on the phone that trees had ears as well as walls. Furthermore, even if he hadn't picked up on our conversation, which included a discussion on my present situation, he would have heard questions being asked about it by Debbie Moreton, the local reporter, who buttonholed me as I was leaving and loudly asked about my removal from the team.'

Ricketts smoothed his moustache with his index finger seemingly to convey the impression he was considering her explanation as a plausible answer. But the twist of his thin lips gave him away. 'Hmm, well suffice to say that the chief constable will not be at all happy about the problems that have dogged this inquiry so far any more than I am. We need results and fast. Hopefully, with the additional resources Detective Superintendent Hennessey will have at her disposal, we can look forward to greater success in the future.'

Here we go, Kate thought. Making excuses already to protect your own reputation, as usual, but she couldn't be bothered to make further comment.

He turned on Kate again, still determined to have his pound of flesh. 'Pity your pursuit of the vagrant ended in his murder too, isn't it, Sergeant? But since the circumstances there will undoubtedly be the subject of an internal inquiry in due course, together with your faux pas over the murder weapon at the church, it would be inappropriate for me to go into that any further. Nevertheless, I would like to know why you think this killer chose you to pursue out of all the other students on your so-called writing course.'

Kate glanced across at Woo. The DI frowned a warning, and she picked up on the unspoken message. So despite half the nick at Highbridge being aware of the postcard, Ricketts was still in the dark, it seemed. Seeing as how unpopular he was, that certainly didn't surprise her. Probably no one talked to him anyway.

'I think it was due to the fact that I admitted to being a serving police officer, sir,' she replied. 'This character sees himself as a future crime novelist and obviously resents my aspirations.'

He grunted. 'Well, maybe he has a point. You can't be both a police officer and a novelist. The two things don't go together and I'm not sure the chief would approve anyway.' He smirked again. 'Unless, of course, you are thinking of leaving the force and becoming a crime novelist instead.'

Her returning smile was tight, and she was delighted to see the disappointment in his expression when she replied. 'I've no such plans, sir. I love my job here far too much to even think of leaving before my normal retirement date in around fifteen years at the earliest.'

Woo closed the office door as soon as the DCI had left, and his grin practically split his face in half, despite the tragic reason for the impromptu briefing.

'That last riposte of yours was a masterstroke, Kate,' he said, waving her back to her chair. 'Did you see his face?'

She nodded and managed another of her small smiles. 'Thanks for not reporting the postcard issue. He was obviously unaware of it, though he's bound to find out eventually.'

'What if he does? Going topless on a beach is hardly a crime, is it? I go topless all the time on my beach vacations.'

She gave a short laugh. 'But your assets in that respect are not quite the same as mine.'

'Agreed, and unfortunately for you, it was your assets that seem to have attracted this killer in the first place.'

She shook her head firmly. 'My boobs had nothing to do with it, as I've said before. I'm convinced this man isn't motivated by some kind of sexual hang-up. He's not that kind of deviant. Hayden put it pretty succinctly to me a short time ago. He said that the bastard's on a twisted mission to prove his own intellectual superiority and to satisfy some misogynistic phobia by rubbishing my reputation as a professional female detective in the process. Like Hayden, I believe this business is about fulfilling narcissistic fantasies and he is probably inadequate sexually, which only adds to his sense of frustration.'

'Accepting all that psychological claptrap, has this arsehole ever indicated to you how he sees this so-called game of his concluding? After all, every game ends with a result and a winner and a loser, so how will he decide when that point is reached? By means of a timescale of a month, two months or whatever? Or when he has reached his predetermined target of "X" number of victims? He must have something in mind.'

'If he has, he's never told me.'

'Then perhaps you should ask him the next time he rings?'

'I will, but that's if he'll tell me.'

'Let's hope vanity will out and he can't resist the temptation. But in the meantime, how do we go about nailing him?'

'I haven't a clue unless we get some sort of a lead. Maybe Deidrie Hennessey will come up with something when she arrives.'

'Well, someone needs to before the local mortuaries run out of fridges.'

CHAPTER 11

He went cold in the hot shower. The long cut he'd found on his right thigh when he got up in the morning had not yet crusted over, which meant that it had not long dried up. It also meant he must have cut himself crawling through the rubbish in the back of the copper's Ford Galaxy. He remembered feeling his trouser leg catching on something sharp at the time but hadn't been able to see what it was in the dark and he couldn't remember scraping against anything anywhere else. But spilled blood, however small, could pose a serious problem. If he had left a trace somewhere in or on the car, there was a real risk the police SOCOs could find it and come up with a match on the National DNA Database. Shit! Shit! Shit!

His mind flashed back to that stupid incident so many years ago when, as a lad in his twenties, he had lost his temper at the local pub after being called a poof and had been arrested for cutting one of those taunting him with a broken bottle after having had the same done to him. He had got off lightly for the offence as the charge should have been one of Grievous Bodily Harm. But his brief had managed to do a deal and it had been reduced to the lesser offence of Assault Occasioning Actual Bodily Harm. He'd escaped a custodial sentence on the grounds of provocation, coupled with the nasty injuries inflicted on him by the violent group of tearaways he'd confronted, and had been given a two-year suspended sentence instead. But the police had nevertheless insisted on taking a blood sample from him as well as his fingerprints because of the nature of the charge. That sample would still be on the database with all the other criminal profiles held there.

So, one stupid mistake in the past, which had now come back to haunt him. It was so unfair. It was all due to the need to divert from his carefully planned operation to deal with an unforeseen hiccup. Up until now, he had been scrupulous about the precautions he had taken to ensure he'd left no incriminating evidence at the scenes of the previous three murders. But this time he had not given as much thought to the execution of it all. He had rushed things. Been too clumsy. He could only hope he had not left any blood traces for Old Bill to find this time, or if he had, that the forensic team would miss them. But he was worried. The long tear in his trousers indicated that the wound had been caused by something very sharp, possibly a nail or a screw, so the blood leaking from it could have got on to anything or dripped on to the floor.

For a moment he seriously considered quitting his game altogether. Getting away while he had the chance. But then he cursed himself for thinking like a quitter. There was no way he could abandon his 'pet project' now. Not after all the planning and hard work that had gone into it. Especially as that detective bitch would then be able to claim she had won and had frightened him off. So he had stiffed a copper, which meant the heat on him would be intense from now on. But that was no reason to give up. He would just have to be more careful in future and keep a keen eye and ear on developments. What was done was done. So patch up his injury, burn the torn trousers in case any tell-tale fibres had attached themselves to anything, and return to the programme he had devised before Old Bill had time to regroup after recovering from the shock of losing one of their own.

Which reminded him, he needed to talk to his tame reporter again. To update her about his latest achievements for the next edition of her newspaper and also to take her to task over the tone of her latest piece he had read on the cider farm murder. Its derogatory references to him as a psychopath and a maniac had rather displeased him. After that, it might be a good idea to take some additional precautions to cover his tracks, just in case Kate and her cronies got lucky.

* * *

The news seemed to blast from Kate's mobile as she was dressing. SOCO had found something at the O'Sullivan murder scene.

'Don't get too excited,' Woo told her, though she could hear the excitement in his own voice. 'It may turn out to be nothing, but there was an old, battered tea chest in the back of the Galaxy. It seems O'Sullivan had only recently moved into his present address, and he'd obviously not yet cleared his car out completely. The team found what looks like blood. Part of it on the plywood and part on a metal reinforcing strip around the bottom of the tea chest, which had somehow got pulled away at the corner and twisted into a jagged point. They found a couple more splashes on the rear door sill. If it *is* blood, it could just be O'Sullivan's from an earlier accident while handling the tea chest. But they said it looked fresh, so here's hoping. Thought you'd like to know so you're kept in the loop.'

Kate was on an adrenalin rush as she drove to work a lot earlier than she had originally intended, skipping breakfast and leaving Hayden confused and still half-asleep in bed on a rostered day off after she had woken him to tell him about the call. At last it appeared that the killer may have made a mistake. Almost as if O'Sullivan had reached out from the mortuary to implicate him. At last it looked like the lead they had been hoping for had presented itself. At last there was a chance that an arrest could be on the cards. It gave her the lift she needed. Okay, so she wasn't on the team now, but she could still feel the sense of elation Woo must have felt when he'd heard. She just prayed that the hopes of both of them wouldn't suddenly be dashed, as was frequently the case in police major investigations.

Highbridge police station seemed to be under siege when she drove into the rear yard. The press were everywhere, and flash bulbs were popping in rapid succession as she eased her car carefully through the crowd of reporters and camera crews blocking the entrance. So many were there that she couldn't help wondering if there were any left to cover stories elsewhere.

She ran into Charlie Woo as she went into the station via the back door. He was just about to climb the stairs to the next floor, a newspaper under his arm. He turned quickly when he saw her and nodded towards the corridor leading to the canteen. She followed him into one of the vacant interview rooms and he closed the door behind her.

He looked tense as he spread the newspaper out on the interview-room table. 'You'd better read that,' he said.

Bending over the table, she saw that it was a copy of the *Bridgwater Clarion*. The headline made her wince: *Levels Bogeyman Kills Again*.

She speed-read the piece on the front page, unsurprised by the graphic portrayal of Wilf Carpenter's murder or the frequent references to the killer as 'the Somerset Psycho' and 'the maniac Bogeyman'.

'Now take a look inside at the editorial opinion piece,' Woo said.

Kate did so and screwed up her eyes for a second. The subheading read: *Police Investigator Chopped*. She read the first paragraph with a sense of despair.

> *We understand that incompetent Highbridge detective sergeant, Kate Lewis, has finally been sacked from the inquiry into the bloodthirsty killings that have been recently committed on the Somerset Levels. Calamity Kate has now been relegated to other routine crime inquiries but will probably*

excel at investigating cases involving bicycle theft and shop-lifting. Not before time, we say . . .

She pushed the newspaper away, unable to read any-more, and straightened up, shaking her head.

'You could always sue,' Woo pointed out. 'I mean, the language is well OTT.'

Kate sighed. 'No point, Charlie,' she replied tightly. 'It wouldn't get anywhere, and it would only make things worse publicity-wise.'

He seemed to agree. 'Well, at least the paper seems to have missed out on the murders of Liam O'Sullivan and that vagrant at C & G for the moment, so their bitch reporter isn't as much on the ball as she thought she was.'

Kate shrugged. 'I bet it will be in the next edition instead, and when Moreton gets hold of the facts on Gerry Thomas, she will have even more ammunition to fire at me in her bloody editorial opinion column.'

He clapped her on the shoulder. 'There you are then, you've got something to look forward to for a change,' he joked, 'so cheer up. As the DCI pointed out, you're famous at last.'

She shot him a daggers glance. 'I'd prefer to remain in obscurity, thanks.' Then she took a deep breath and abruptly changed the subject. 'Good news about the blood found at the O'Sullivan crime scene examination, though, isn't it?'

He nodded. 'Potentially, yes, but as I said on the phone, we shouldn't get overexcited about it at this stage. As you well know, even were the captured blood trace to actually be from the killer, if he has not committed a previous crime and none of his DNA is held on the National DNA Database, it would be of little value as an identification tool.'

'We can but hope.'

'Agreed, and in the meantime, have you had breakfast?'

'I don't want any.'

'Well, I'm buying. Egg and bacon do, will it?'

* * *

Debbie Moreton got the call just as she walked into the office, half an hour early for a change.

'I have a bone to pick with you, Debbie,' the voice said quietly.

She felt a momentary surge of excitement. She recognised who it was at once. It was her contact again. The man who had given her journalistic career the biggest boost it had ever received.

'How's that?'

'The words you use to describe me on your front page are, quite frankly, insulting. I am not a maniac bogeyman or a psycho and I don't like being referred to as such. I am simply an intellectual radical who has set out to challenge the investigative skills of your local police force. Particularly those of Detective Sergeant Lewis, who so far has turned out to be sorely lacking in her professional competence. So, you will stop denigrating me and continue to highlight Lewis's incompetence instead. Do you understand?'

She felt suddenly angry. 'You don't tell me what I can write, mister. That's my business. You should be grateful to me for giving you the publicity.'

'Grateful?' the voice purred. 'Is that what I should be? Well, sadly I'm not and I strongly advise you to tone down the rhetoric about me. Concentrate on the crimes I have committed and on the inadequacies of Sergeant Lewis, then we'll remain friends.'

Moreton put a brake on her acid tongue. 'Well, Sergeant Lewis is out of the picture now anyway. She's been thrown off the inquiry.'

'So I hear, Debbie, so I hear. But I assure you it won't be for long, and I am confident that I will have her reinstated shortly.'

'I don't understand. If you feel she is so incompetent, surely you have proved your point by highlighting the fact and forcing her superiors to take her off the major inquiry team? So why would you want to see her reinstated?'

'I didn't force her superiors to do any such thing, my dear, and it was not in the interests of my little game for that to happen anyway—'

'Game?' Moreton interjected. 'What are you talking about?'

There was an irritable hiss in response to the interruption. 'The intellectual game I have devised for Kate and myself, Debbie. It's a sort of challenge. I provide her with a corpse and she has to try and outsmart me by using her so-called detective skills to, I believe the term is "feel my collar", before I am compelled to provide her with another one. It's quite a simple arrangement really.'

'Arrangement? You mean you are killing innocent people as part of some obscene contest?'

'Game, dear, not contest, and so far my official tally is two, which means there are another four to go before we decide on the winner. I don't count those I am forced to eliminate to further the interests of the game, you see. I throw those in for free. Intriguing, isn't it? I have already selected Kate as my key opponent in the game, so obviously I can't have her taken out before the end, and I have provided her superiors with a compelling inducement to reinstate her.'

'What inducement?'

'If you want an answer to that, perhaps you should take a look at the crime scene at Juniper Farm in Mark where the investigators are still trying to come to terms with the punishment I have meted out to them for defying me. Oh yes, and you might also want to look into an earlier rather grisly death at the old C & G factory in Signalman's Walk. Sergeant Lewis made another of her serious errors of judgement there, which forced me to take rather drastic remedial action.'

Moreton set her freshly poured coffee back on her desk, her hand trembling with excitement. 'What do you mean by remedial action?'

'You're supposed to be an investigative reporter, my dear, so investigate. But remember, no more insulting language in your write-ups. Don't offend my sensibilities. That would be a big mistake.'

The phone line reverted to the dialling tone again.

'A big mistake, eh?' Moreton breathed, grabbing her car keys from the desktop. 'Well, have I got news for you, dickhead. As I said, no one tells me what to write.'

* * *

Deidrie Hennessey was waiting in Woo's office when he and Kate returned to the department. Seeing her through the glass partition, Kate abruptly stopped off at her own desk, leaving the DI free to join the senior detective for what was no doubt going to be a confidential meeting. But moments later she found herself summoned by an imperious knock on the glass partition.

Hennessey was wearing one of her neat trouser suits, fawn this time, and her short blonde hair seemed to shine in the sunlight now streaming through the single external window. She was sitting to one side of the DI's desk. Unlike the DCI before her, she had ignored Woo's vacant chair, and now waved him to it instead. Kate wasn't surprised by the gesture. Hennessey had never stood on ceremony, which was one of the reasons she respected her so much. But although the face of the attractive forty-something wore a smile, there was a firmness in the set of her jawline and a discomforting sharpness in the blue eyes that carried a 'not to be trifled with' warning.

'Morning,' she said after introducing herself, more as a formality than anything else. 'I won't say "good", so I won't. But I thought that before we held the official briefing upstairs, it would be helpful for me to get the full SP on things. I mean *full* SP too, without anything being left out in relation to this banjaxed inquiry.'

She fastened her gaze on Kate. 'You first, Sergeant. As I understand it, this whole business revolves around you, so take me back to the very beginning, would you.'

After a moment's hesitation to collect her thoughts, Kate did just that and to her own surprise she found herself coming clean on everything that had happened, including the postcard incident and her pursuit of the vagrant. It was as if she had been given some sort of truth drug and was left with no choice but to be totally honest, despite the likelihood that this would work against her.

When she had finished, Hennessey turned to the DI without comment and raised an eyebrow for him to top and tail all that Kate had said. For several minutes after that she sat there scanning a thick file in her lap, while Woo and Kate waited nervously for a response. It came abruptly and completely surprised them both.

'Sure, that's grand,' Hennessey said, her smile back again. 'At least I now know what I'm getting into, and it's a desperate mess, so it is. One thing is clear, though. I can see why it was decided to pull you off the team, Kate. You're not only personally involved in this business as a victim but are also the focal point for this gobshite's actions. It might be argued that if you were retained on the major inquiry team, that might provide some encouragement to him to resume his killing spree. Equally, though, there is the other risk, illustrated by Detective Sergeant O'Sullivan's murder, that keeping you off it could inflame him further to commit even more atrocious acts.'

She shook her head and frowned. 'Whatever we do, it will be a case of damned if we do, damned if we don't. So I suggest we play for time. But you must let us know immediately if he phones you again, day or night. If I'm not available, Detective Inspector Don Tappin on the inquiry team will handle things on my behalf. Have you got that, Kate? Immediately, and I mean immediately.'

* * *

The initial briefing of the major crime inquiry unit took place at three that afternoon and Kate was placed at the back of the room with strict instructions only to answer questions from those present through Hennessey to ensure that the information given out was carefully controlled on a need-to-know basis for the purposes of the investigation. This suited her perfectly because it meant that some of the more embarrassing personal material was kept under wraps. As it turned out, numerous questions came from the assembled detectives and uniformed officers who had been drafted in from neighbouring areas to form the major inquiry team, but she was not put on the spot by any of them. She left afterwards with a brief smile of satisfaction directed her way from Hennessey.

She was not invited to attend the early evening press conference managed by the force press officer who had raced down to Highbridge from headquarters. That came as more of a relief to her rather than anything else. A forensic public scrutiny in front of a dozen or so cameras was something she had been dreading. Especially as she knew Debbie Moreton from the *Clarion* would be almost certain to attend. Fortunately Hennessey had obviously seen the wisdom of keeping her safely out of harm's way, so she was able to go for a much-needed mug of canteen coffee instead just before it closed for the day.

But if she'd expected a quiet afternoon, she was disappointed. Her office phone rang just as she was once more settling back behind her desk.

'Call for you, skipper,' the woman on the control room switchboard said. 'Asked for you personally.'

A click and then another, younger female voice was on the line.

'Is that CID?' the voice asked in a rush.

Kate frowned. 'Detective Sergeant Kate Lewis,' she replied. 'Can I help you?'

There was silence for a moment and Kate picked up the sound of heavy breathing.

She waited patiently.

'You the copper what was looking for Gerry Thomas?'

'I was, yes.'

'He was my friend and now he's dead.'

'I know and I'm sorry.'

'He looked after me, you know. So who's going to do that now?'

'I can help you if you want me to.'

'I saw the bastard what did him.'

Kate felt a sudden adrenalin surge. 'You saw him?'

'I was hiding under the stairs.'

'Can you tell me your name?'

'Sally.'

'Sally who?'

'Sally will have to do. Meet me in the rattrap next door and come alone or I'll be gone.'

'Wait. I need to know your full name.'

'You got five minutes. Your choice.'

The caller rang off.

Kate knew that the 'rattrap' the woman had referred to was the derelict shop that occupied the land beside the police station. It was accessible from a narrow alleyway that ran down the side of the rear yard where the police vehicles were parked, so it was almost within spitting distance of where she was sitting. But she hesitated, thinking of the past occasions when she had unwisely responded to similar 'invitations' and put herself in danger. Okay, so the place this time was right next door, but it might just as well have been the C & G factory several miles away. No one in the nick would know where she had gone, and no one would be in a position to help her if she got into trouble. She had no idea who the mystery woman was or her motive for contacting her. She could be walking into a carefully prepared trap.

She bit her lip and glanced pointlessly around the empty office. The DI was at the press conference with Deidrie Hennessey and the force press officer. The rest of her colleagues were conspicuous by their absence. As it was just after five, even the office manager, Ajeet Singh, had gone home. There was no time to get a message to anyone. If she went to the meet, she was likely to face criticism, if nothing else, for going it alone again. If she didn't, it could mean missing out on crucial information. 'Your choice', the caller had said. She had just seconds to make up her mind. But as far as she was concerned, it was a no-brainer.

'Maverick Kate strikes again!' she muttered grimly to herself, and grabbing her radio, she erupted from her chair and raced from the office. Not for the first time, taking the stairs to the ground floor two at a time.

CHAPTER 12

Kate felt a strong sense of déjà vu as she stood in the lane outside the derelict Victorian end terrace. Once a popular local shop, it was now just a grim frowning shell, with half-boarded windows that, as usual in the case of derelict properties, always reminded her of baleful eyes. She well remembered her last visit to the place all those years ago in the manhunt for the psychopathic undertaker, nicknamed Twister, who had concealed recording apparatus inside to eavesdrop on the police investigative strategy next door. Twister was long gone, but his malevolent presence still seemed to hang over the place and she felt she could sense him standing inside on the upper floor, studying her through the bare branches of the trees, which had sprung up along the perimeter fence.

Shaking off the chilling feeling, she ducked through a familiar hole in the wooden slats and made her way along a path someone had recently forced through the overgrown garden to the half-open backdoor.

The foul, cloying smell of the old derelict building assailed her nostrils as she stepped over the threshold, and she peered carefully into the large, square room beyond, which ran the full length of the property to the boarded-up front windows. There was a screened-off area to her right with a long counter standing in front of it. To her left an open doorway revealed a staircase dropping away to some sort of basement, and just beyond it, another staircase climbed to the upper level. The floor was littered with rubbish and the street poets had been busy on the walls with the usual obscene slogans, but there was no sign of anyone.

Her mouth tightened. So where the hell was the mysterious Sally? Hiding upstairs or in the basement maybe? Surely she hadn't already given up on her and gone?

'Sally?' she called. 'It's Kate. Where are you?'

There was a loud rustling and a mouse streaked across the room in front of her and disappeared into a hole in the rotten floorboards. Kate ignored it. Mice were fine. It was spiders that freaked her out. Outside, a heavy goods lorry thundered past on the main road, followed by a motorcycle. Then a brief lull before more vehicles went past. In the shop nothing else moved.

'Sally, I'm not playing silly games with you,' she called a little louder. 'Either you show yourself or I'm going back to the nick.'

In response, there was a clumping sound and a figure emerged suddenly from the doorway to the basement and stood there for a moment studying her. Kate turned quickly to face her.

Pale and emaciated, with matted, shoulder-length, black hair and a slightly crooked mouth, the young woman had to be in her early teens and was dressed in a torn donkey jacket and Doc Marten type boots. She snuffled constantly as she stood there, wiping her runny nose on the back of one grimy hand as if she had a heavy cold. The cracked sunglasses she had obviously been wearing outside were now pushed up on top of her head, exposing heavily bloodshot eyes and large, dilated pupils. She had no doubt been a pretty girl once, but cocaine had left its unmistakable mark on her. It was obviously only a question of time before the cruel addiction destroyed her completely.

'I need a fix,' she blurted. 'But I got no dosh.'

Kate frowned, wondering if that was the only reason Sally had contacted her, which meant this could all be a con.

143

'Tell me what you know about the man who killed Gerry, and I'll give you some money,' she said, inwardly wincing when she thought about what she had just promised. The informants' fund was a tightly controlled resource and Charlie Woo would take a dim view of her claiming back cash she had handed over without permission. She had been criticised for doing that by her old DI a few cases back, so she knew that expediency would not be accepted as a reasonable excuse.

'How much you gonna give me?'

'Enough. But we're wasting time. Info first. Dosh second. Now it's *your* choice.'

Silence for a moment as the young woman thought about it. Kate saw that she was shivering and there were beads of perspiration forming on her face. Her craving was obviously growing.

'I was waiting for Gerry,' she said abruptly. 'Then I saw this geezer coming towards the front door from the road, so I hid under the stairs.' She shuddered. 'He — he pulled out a blade and slashed Gerry across the throat right there and then. There was blood everywhere and—'

Kate could scarcely control her impatience. 'What did he look like, this man?'

Something, possibly the mouse again, made a scrabbling sound close by. Sally turned her head quickly and would have fled in panic if Kate had not blocked the doorway.

'Take it easy. You're quite safe with me.'

'He could be out there.'

'He doesn't know anything about you, so why would he be out there? Now, if you want us to catch him, you've got to help us. What did he look like?'

Sally shivered. 'Tall and thin. Wearing an anorak and a baseball cap.'

'What else?'

She shook her head. 'Couldn't see his face properly. The baseball cap was pulled down low and he had the collar of his anorak turned up.'

'How old do you think he was?'

She shrugged. 'Forties, fifties, I don't know. Can I have my dosh now?'

'Did he say anything?'

She shook her head. 'He — he just walked right up to Gerry and done him in front of me. It were horrible.'

'Is there anything else you can tell me about this man? Anything at all? It's very important.'

'I seen him once before. Few days ago. Same anorak and cap. Got out of a big black car with a white roof in Burnham.'

'Did you get the number?'

'Do me a favour. What do you think I am? A sodding traffic warden?'

'Anything else you can remember about it? Stickers on the windows? Dents or scratches?'

'Well, there was a lot of mud on the wheels and wings, but that's all I can remember.'

'Where did the man go?'

'Into one of them places that sells houses. I tried to touch him for a couple of quid, but he just barged me out the way and went in.'

'What was this place called?'

'Corbin's Letting Agency. It's down a back street near an old chapel I used when I needed somewhere else to doss. Look, you said you'd give me some dosh.'

Kate nodded and pulled her wallet out of the back pocket of her jeans. 'Would you know this man if you saw him again?'

The gaze fastened on the wallet was like that of someone contemplating a five-course meal. 'Not a chance.'

Kate hadn't expected any other answer. Sally wouldn't pick him out in a line-up even if she recognised him. Dwellers in her twilight world didn't help the police unless there was a handout and after what she had seen, she would be too terrified to do it again anyway.

The way the woman snatched the money Kate held out to her practically left burn marks on her fingers.

'It's all you're getting,' Kate replied. 'Unless you come up with any more info, in which case, you know where I am.'

'Stingy bitch,' Sally snapped back ungratefully and pushed past her through the doorway.

Kate watched her stumbling off along the garden path, knowing full well that she couldn't expect any further contact from her. Sally would probably be dead within a few weeks anyway. It was so tragic and unnecessary. But she had seen it all before so many times. She knew there was nothing she could do for that wasted young life. It was too late. The die was cast. But at least she could make use of the information Sally had given her to try and track down a ruthless killer and save other innocent lives.

She glanced at her watch and headed quickly back towards the lane. If the killer had visited an estate agents', it could mean only one thing. He was looking for a roof over his head while he was in Somerset. Accommodation was a basic necessity, and she should have considered this avenue of inquiry right at the start of the business, never mind wasting time trying to trace his mobile phone or turn up a witness to his crimes. The most likely arrangement he would have been looking for had to be a property let where he could be on his own to pursue his murderous game without attracting attention, which meant the key to feeling his collar could be a recent contract held in the records at Corbin's. All she needed was an address and her quarry was in her sights. But time was not on her side. Everywhere in the seaside resort would soon be closed at this time of year. Passing on what she had so far discovered to Charlie Woo and Deidrie Hennessey would have to wait. She would just have to risk the 'wrath of the gods' afterwards. It would not be a new experience for her after all.

* * *

It looked as though Corbin's Letting Agency had finished early when Kate pulled up in her Mazda a short distance from the premises in the Burnham backstreet. The blinds were down over the windows and the front door was locked when she tried it. Yet the 'Open' sign was still displayed on the glass panel in the door and the opening times printed on a yellow card beneath it gave the business hours: *Monday to Friday 9 a.m. to 6 p.m.* Frowning, she checked her watch. It was just five-forty. Strange that they had decided to shut up shop twenty minutes ahead of normal closing time. Maybe they were out visiting prospective customers. Frustrated that the place would have to be closed on the very day she needed it, she turned round and returned to her car, resigned to trying again the following day. But she had only gone a couple of steps when she heard a loud bang, which seemed to come from the back of the premises. There was a narrow alleyway scarcely the width of her shoulders down the side of the building and she quickly retraced her steps to take a look, thinking that perhaps a member of staff was still in the process of clearing up before going home.

The alleyway ended in a small walled yard with an opening in one corner, presumably accessing a rear exit of some sort. An unattended Mercedes car was parked in the yard alongside the right-hand perimeter wall, facing towards the exit. Its presence there suggested that someone was still on the premises, as she had hoped, and to her relief she found that the back door of the building was unlocked.

Calling out to whoever might be inside, she opened the door and found herself in a small kitchen or tearoom, complete with a sink, kettle and some mugs, but not much else, except a narrow door bearing the words WC. There was another normal-size door opposite, which was closed, and crossing the carpeted floor, she called out a polite, 'Hello' as she pulled it open.

It was as far as she got. The familiar stench hit her first. Even as it registered and the alert in her brain screamed the warning, she was bowled over by a figure bursting through the doorway. Backlit by a massive conflagration. The flames leaped gleefully up the walls and across the ceiling of the kitchen. In seconds the whole room was ablaze.

'Stupid, interfering cow!' a voice shouted at her. Partially dazed, she was conscious of being dragged backwards through choking smoke. Of being dumped on a hard concrete surface, then rolling over on to her stomach and coughing up her insides.

Behind her the whole building was a raging inferno of collapsing timbers and exploding glass. The searing heat reached out across the yard in fiery fingers that seemed to be blindly searching for more combustible material to ignite. She had the presence of mind to drag herself through the opening she had spotted on her arrival. In the relative safety of a short gravel driveway connecting with another backstreet, she propped herself up against a wall. Just as a door slammed and a car pulled away from a kerb further along the street with a screech of tyres. A black Volvo SUV with a white roof. Him! She tried to pick out the registration number. But her eyes were filled with tears, and it was gone before she could properly focus on the index plate. It was then that the realisation dawned on her. The ruthless killer she had been so desperately trying to track down must have been the one who had just dragged her to safety and saved her life. Obviously he had other plans for her, and she dreaded to think what they might be.

* * *

'Maverick actions forgiven this time then?' Hayden asked, bending over Kate to refill her empty brandy glass before returning to his armchair.

Curled up on the settee at home, dressed in a white towelling robe, Kate threw him an old-fashioned glance. It was a good four hours since she had returned home from the scene of the fire after liaising with Deidrie Hennessey and Charlie Woo and briefing them on all that had happened. After over two hours in the shower scrubbing off the filth from the blaze and restoring her hair to something like its usual coppery lustre, she looked and felt an entirely different person. But she knew she would never forget the sight of the twisted, blackened corpse the fire service had pulled from the smoking ruin of the letting agency after they had extinguished the fire. The wire binding the wrists still partially attached. The gaping hole in the ruin of what had once been a human face stretched wide in the final agonies of living cremation. The eyes just empty sockets still faintly smoking from the inside. The hands almost completely devoid of flesh twisted into naked claws, like those of some tortured animal.

She shook her head several times and screwed up her eyes to try and clear her mind of the nightmare memory. 'Hennessey and Woo were surprisingly pragmatic about it,' she replied. 'They acknowledged that I'd had no option this time but to use my initiative in pursuing the inquiry. The informant, Sally, would not have waited while I faffed around, and I couldn't have been expected to anticipate the killer targeting the letting agency.'

He nodded. 'Do we know the ID of the corpse?'

'Not absolutely. But we think it was the owner of the agency, Terry Corbin. The plod from the local neighbourhood policing team, Giles Tennyson, said he was a bit of a one-man band and had been running the business single-handedly since his wife died. Apparently the place was a tea-spot for patrols, and on one of his visits Corbin had told Tennyson that he was giving it another six months, then packing up the business altogether.'

'Well, it looks like the arsonist packed it up for him,' Hayden replied drily. 'I believe you said there was some evidence that he had been tied up before his death.'

'It looked as though his wrists had been bound with wire, yes.'

'Which means he was burned alive?'

She shuddered. 'Don't remind me. What kind of sadistic scum does that to another human being?'

'A very dangerous psychopath,' he replied, 'and one who has his gaze firmly set on you.'

'Yet, as I said to you earlier, he must have been the man who saved me from the fire. If he hates me so much, why on earth did he do that?'

'Maybe because you are an integral element in his so-called game. That's why he murdered Liam O'Sullivan. Nothing must interfere with your participation in the game.'

'And by destroying Corbin and his property records, he frustrated any immediate opportunity we could have had of tracing his whereabouts. Do you think he may have somehow found out about Sally approaching me and resorted to the arson as a result?'

'I don't see how he could have done, bearing in mind that he must have paid his visit to Corbin at about the same time as she was talking to you. It's more likely in my view that it was a spur of the moment thing, which suggests he's now feeling more vulnerable because he wasted a copper, and he knows the heat on him will be turned up. It probably dawned on him that sooner or later we might try to trace his whereabouts through checks on accommodation providers. Hence the precautionary action he took. I'm just surprised not only that he didn't do it at the start, but that this avenue of inquiry didn't occur to us before.'

'He must know he will be caught eventually.'

'He probably does. I suspect that that recognition of this fact was built into his plan from the start. He expects to be caught one day, but not before he ends the game with a successful victory over the police in general and you in particular. He wants notoriety and a prominent place in criminal history.'

She whistled. 'I've said it before and I'll say it again, you should be a bloody psychologist.'

He shrugged. 'I do but try,' he said with false modesty.

'Then let's just hope the DNA check on the blood trace achieves a positive hit,' she said. 'And soon.'

'And if it doesn't?'

'We're up shit creek without a paddle.'

'Delightfully put, as usual,' he said drily. 'Why don't you say what you really mean?'

CHAPTER 13

He could still smell the smoke on him from the previous day's fire when he got up again in the morning, and he took another long shower. Standing under the rejuvenating hot jets, he reflected on the previous day's work. He had to admit it had been a close-run thing. Once again a last-minute decision. Once again too rushed for proper planning. Just like the hit on the police detective. As a result, once again a near foul-up. He scowled. He knew he had panicked into torching the letting agency after his blunder stiffing the cop. He'd had no reason to believe that the police were imminently going to carry out inquiries at local letting agencies as a means of trying to trace his whereabouts. But he'd reasoned that it would be the logical thing for them to do and as it had turned out, he couldn't have been more right. After all, why else would Kate Lewis have been visiting a backstreet letting agency? Hardly because she was looking for somewhere to live. Unless, of course, she and that dipstick husband of hers had fallen out.

It struck him as quite ironic, though, that she had been the one to be making the inquiry and on the very day he had chosen to give old man Corbin the Guy Fawkes treatment. But he was glad he had still been there when the building actually went up. The silly bitch may never have survived the blaze if he hadn't been on hand to pull her to safety. That really would have been a disaster after he'd only just managed to get his game back on track. Still, at least it meant she must have been reinstated on the case, otherwise someone else would have attended. That really was excellent news, and it made the killing of the copper well worthwhile.

But his sense of satisfaction at the way things had finally turned out only lasted until he went downstairs to make himself a coffee. The paper boy from the newsagents in Street had been and the latest edition of the *Bridgwater Clarion* was lying on his front door mat. He frowned as soon as he glanced at the front page.

The headline ran: *Rabid Cluedo Killer Slays Cop.*

'Rabid?' he murmured to himself and studied the story as he waited for the percolator to go through its gurgling motions.

The rabid killer terrorising our local area has struck again! This time, it seems, he has added not only a helpless rough sleeper to his tally of slaughtered victims, but a local police officer as well. A police spokesman declined to release the identity of the cop until his relatives had been informed, or to say how he died. But an anonymous source close to the inquiry has disclosed to us that he was a member of the very team investigating the current murders and that it is believed he was killed at his home near the village of Mark in the early hours of yesterday morning or late the previous night. Inquiries into the brutal murder of the unidentified rough sleeper, who was evidently killed the previous afternoon, are also continuing. The police have refused to say whether they are linking both murders to the sick killer we have nicknamed the Bogeyman.

But to add to this ongoing drama, the Clarion has been able to clarify the situation for them! A man we firmly believe to be the killer himself has once more reached out to this newspaper's crime reporter, Debbie Moreton, as he did after the original two murders, claiming responsibility for the crime. At the same time he made the significant and terrifying boast that there are still four more murders to go. During his chilling phone call, he provided our reporter with a terrifying insight into the sadistic, twisted mind of a psychopath. He revealed that his brutal attacks on innocent people have been carried out as part of a sick 'CLUEDO' like game, giving him the opportunity to pit his wits against Highbridge police station and in particular none other than Detective Sergeant Kate Lewis, who, our readers will know, has only just been sacked from the inquiry following allegations of incompetence. He claimed Sergeant Lewis was a 'key player' in his obscene game and that he had killed her unfortunate colleague to punish the police hierarchy for taking her off it in the first place. It remains to be seen whether Calamity Kate would actually welcome his support or regard his description of her as his key player rather less than a compliment! The plot certainly thickens, as they say in all the best crime dramas. The worrying thing is if the claims of this sick thug are true and he plans to slaughter four more innocent members of the Levels community, is the local cop shop playing Monopoly with people's lives in order to crack their case? Worse still, if they are incapable of protecting their own against this mindless thug, how on earth can they expect to protect the rest of us?

He quite liked the tone of the story, but the continued derogatory references to him as rabid, sadistic and psychopathic tended to spoil it. Obviously Debbie Moreton was getting a bit too big for her pretty little boots despite his warning. He couldn't have that. He would have to punish her. But first he had other fish to fry.

The back pages of the thick newspaper carried a multitude of advertisements and close to the bottom of one page was a reverse block, bearing the main heading: *Magic Hands Therapy* followed by the subheading: *Sensuous Massages. All tastes catered for*. It invited potential clients to ring Tina for information and provided a mobile telephone number. Just what he was looking for, he mused with a grim smile, and scribbled down the details before attending to the alarm of the coffee percolator.

* * *

'So, this gobshite's working on the rule of six, is he?' Deidrie Hennessey said, leaning forward on the edge of her desk.

In the corner by the window a man in a suit sat quietly listening and taking notes, his eyes flicking occasionally around the room to fasten briefly on either Charlie Woo or Kate, as if he was assessing their body language.

Detective Inspector Don Tappin, Hennessey's bag carrier, was an almost perfectly bald, thickset copper in his forties, with pale blue eyes and a penetrating gaze that missed very little. With his heavy jowls, florid face and hands like meat hooks, he looked more like a farmer than anything else. But he was known to be a very experienced detective and was well respected throughout the force. Plain speaking and often unorthodox in his approach to the job, he was a 'doer' rather than a talker. Kate knew him well from her time on the drug squad in Bristol. She couldn't have been more pleased to see him on the major investigation team. Confident that with him as Hennessey's number two, things would get done and unnecessary red tape dispensed with.

The incident room outside seemed to be a hive of activity. Through the glass partition a number of plainclothes officers could be seen talking animatedly on their phones or studying computer screens. A couple of coffee machines, considered essential equipment by incident room staff, were being set up in a corner. A bespectacled technician was crouched under a desk connecting cables to a portable photocopier and a uniformed woman constable was attaching notes and photographs to a couple of whiteboards suspended from one wall.

Charlie Woo sighed and, half rising from his chair, placed the newspaper Hennessey had given him to read back on the desk beside her. 'Well, according to the *Clarion* here, that's what he plans.'

'Aye, so I saw,' Hennessey grated, 'and they should have told us about this phone call earlier. I've been on to the editor again, but the wee skitter refuses to cooperate with us, except by agreeing to pass on any info he sees as relevant, and I stress what *he sees* as relevant. The force press officer has also been leaning on him, but it's made no difference. All he wants is dramatic headlines. He hasn't an ounce of interest in the substance behind them.'

'Well, it was bloody stupid and irresponsible publishing the killer's boast about killing more people,' Kate snapped. 'It will cause panic.'

Hennessey nodded. 'The nationals will be full of it today, and ACC Ops has already been on to me this morning, bending my ear about the progress of the inquiry. I have an appointment to see him at the "big house" this afternoon.'

'What does the man expect?' Woo commented drily. 'Miracles?'

She gave a short laugh. 'Probably. But they're in short supply at the moment, so they are.'

'Then we'd better get hold of a magic wand,' Woo retorted. 'Or just hope that in the meantime this bastard bleeds to death from the wound he got in the back of O'Sullivan's car.'

'Not that that is likely to happen,' Kate said ruefully. 'The devil always looks after his own.'

* * *

The modern, detached house was one of a number of similar properties standing within a neatly tarmacked half-circle bordering a small lake. All eminently respectable with pseudo-Georgian windows, lush green lawns and expensive cars parked in the driveways. He sat on one of the seats provided in the adjoining recreation area close to the stubby entrance to Camomile Close, half-hidden by the encroaching trees of the encircling copse. He watched the comings and goings for at least an hour while munching on a couple of sandwiches over his newspaper. Close to the lake a young woman with a terrier dog was helping a small boy feed the ducks in the fragile sunlight. On the far side of the green a man in a suit and unzipped anorak drank from a can, his briefcase on the seat beside him. An idyllic scene in a pleasant part of the town within easy reach of the shops. He guessed a lot of shop workers came here for their lunch, so he was confident that his presence during the lunch period would attract little interest.

He was determined to plan properly this time. Not just rush into things, as he had with the copper and the vagrant. Part of that planning meant carrying out a careful scrutiny of the area. Ways in. Ways out. Any cameras on the houses or the lamp standards. Children likely to be playing.

The appointment he had made on the phone was for the evening, when it was unlikely many people would be about. Going by the class of housing, most would-be businesspeople, commuters of some sort or retired professionals. It was not the time of year to be cutting lawns and it got dark fairly early, so by the time he arrived they were likely to be indoors watching television or enjoying a late meal.

From the outside, the target property looked as eminently respectable as the rest. He had no idea whether Tina's neighbours knew what she did for a living. But he doubted it very much. She had told him on the phone after a polite but intense grilling, that the brass plate on the front door said: *Marianne Dawson, Physiotherapist*, with lots of post numerals after it. No doubt that was the regular job her neighbours knew her for, and her normal home telephone number would almost certainly differ from the one he had rung for the masseuse. Sensuous massages were obviously not in Marianne's official prospectus. But it definitely would pay a lot more. The sort of fees she had outlined to him were like a mortgage, so she was obviously used to very well-heeled clients who would keep their mouths shut for their own good as much as hers.

'Lovely day, isn't it?'

The voice cut into him with razor-sharp force and his gaze automatically flicked up. The woman with the small child was standing a few feet away smiling at him. He hadn't heard her leave the lakeside to retrieve the tennis ball the child must have thrown his way for the dog.

He had no option but to respond. He forced a smile and nodded. 'Lovely,' he agreed. 'Still, must get back to the office.'

He folded his paper and rose to his feet as nonchalantly as he could. It was then that the dog began to snarl at him, raising its hackles and showing its teeth. The little boy giggled and wiped his nose on the back of his hand. The woman looked shocked by the dog's aggression and stared quickly at the animal before grabbing it irritably by the collar and attaching a lead.

'I'm awfully sorry,' she said, plainly embarrassed. 'Billy isn't usually like this. He loves people.'

He glanced at the dog again and it lurched forward, barking at him. He forced another smile.

'No problem. He can probably smell my dog. I'll get out of his way.'

'Really, you don't have to . . .'

But he was already walking towards the entrance to the cul-de-sac with what he hoped was a courteous wave of one hand, trying hard not to quicken his pace at the same time. He glanced quickly behind him when he reached the main road to see her following him with her eyes. Damn! Damn! Damn! He shouldn't have done that. It made him look suspicious. 'You bloody fool,' he grated to himself when he got back to his car. 'She could be a witness. She can ID you now.' Well he couldn't kill everyone, could he?

Maybe he should call it all off? The second time he had thought like that in the last few hours. For a moment he sat there drumming his fingers on the steering wheel, staring unseeing in the rear view mirror. But no, the target was exactly right, and the location was ideal. He had no intention of scotching everything now. He was just overreacting.

Why should she be suspicious of him more than anyone else? What about the other guy with his briefcase on the far side of the green? Okay, so the dog hadn't liked him. So what? That didn't prove anything. Dogs had likes and dislikes the same as human beings. He was getting paranoid after the hit on the copper. Just calm down and stick to the plan. He gave another of his thin humourless smiles, remembering the familiar phrase of the late prime minister, Margaret Thatcher, and adapting it. 'This man is not for turning,' he murmured. He started the engine . . .

* * *

He saw the camera above the front door when he rang the bell. It was angled towards him, and a green light flicked on below the lens seconds later.

'Yes?' a soft female voice asked.

'Douglas Matthews,' he drawled in his most cultured tones. 'I telephoned you this afternoon. I have an appointment.'

There was a pause and he felt as if he was being X-rayed. It was practically dark. Lights glowed behind the windows of the other houses in the row. A cat wandered past the front doorstep, stopped to give him the once-over, then sauntered off across the lawn towards the lake. He was about to ring the bell again when he heard a distinctive buzz and the front door swung open.

Beyond lay a softly lighted square hall. It was tastefully furnished with a thick blue carpet and white-painted doors opening off on three sides. The door directly in front of him was signed *Private* while those on each side, *Treatment Room 1* and *Treatment Room 2*. There was a white-painted desk positioned at an angle across the far right-hand corner and an attractive brunette in a white coat aged about thirty was standing behind it studying him.

'Mr Matthews,' she said, her heavily made-up face creasing into a welcoming smile, 'I am delighted to meet you. Just a few admin queries before we begin the treatment you are seeking.'

He inclined his head in acknowledgement. There followed another rigorous series of questions, prefaced by the undertaking that everything he provided would remain absolutely confidential. Could he supply his full name, address and date of birth? Could he provide his credit card details? Where did he hear about her 'salon'? Had he used such services anywhere else before? She was obviously a very cautious lady. Finally she asked him to confirm the type of treatment he was looking for and proffered a printed sheet of A4 paper with a list of individually priced options that would have made a docker's hair curl. Dirty bitch, he thought, and smiled back at her as he returned the sheet after ticking his selection.

'Would you like to come through then?' she said and indicated the door signed *Treatment Room 2* on the left of the hallway.

Inside, lay a small, softly lit room, smelling strongly of some kind of sweet perfume and decorated in a seductive shade of pink. It was equipped with the usual kind of massage table with a padded, vinyl covered mattress. A side table carrying an assortment of stubby jars, bottles and boxes of wipes stood on one side of it. But the open doors of a cupboard standing against one wall revealed a range of curious devices held in racks or suspended on pegs. Whips. Bamboo canes. Handcuffs and ligatures and halters. None of which had anything whatsoever to do with standard therapeutic practice. What particularly interested him was a tall metal frame attached to one wall and the handcuffs hanging from the topmost bar. He studied it thoughtfully before turning his dark eyes on the young woman. Just for a second she seemed taken aback by the intensity of his stare and there was a flicker of doubt in her expression. But the next instant she recovered and treated him to a coquettish smile that was plainly manufactured as part of her act.

'Why don't you take off all your clothes and lie on the table,' she said in a low, husky voice. 'There are hooks on the wall for you to use over there. I will be back in a minute.'

Then she disappeared through another door at the far end of the room and closed it behind her.

Had she remained in the room, she would have been surprised to see that he made no attempt to take anything off. Instead, he donned a pair of black leather gloves and lounged against the wall, waiting patiently for her to return. When she did, shortly afterwards, she no longer wore her respectable white coat, but was dressed in just a black thong and a miniscule bra that left little to the imagination.

His gaze roved over the shapely figure and pale skin. He noted with a sardonic smile the hummingbird tattoo on the upper curve of her left breast and the glittering stud and chain dangling from her navel. But he felt no excitement, no palpitations or tightness of the chest. No sense of arousal. He never did. Neither female nor male nudity had any effect on him. Since puberty he had been dead from the waist down. He'd long had to accept that he was a freak of nature. For him there could be none of the heady enjoyment of sex that most other men experienced. He got his kicks another way.

'Not shy, are you then, Douglas?' Tina said in almost a whisper and sauntered suggestively towards him. 'Maybe I should help you out of those clothes, eh?'

'Oh, I don't think that will be necessary,' he drawled, and her lascivious grin faded when she read the cold, hard look in his eyes. 'I have a much better idea.'

He didn't leave the house immediately after he killed her. Instead, he searched for the DVD recording equipment to which not only the doorstep camera, but tiny cameras he had also spotted in the hall and treatment room were connected. He found it in the tiny box-like room next door. Quite a sophisticated bit of kit too. But it was a simple enough job extracting the discs and slipping them into his pocket. Then he removed the hard drive, using a small leather case of tools he had brought with him. He slipped it into his pocket before attending to the laptop computer in the hallway on which she had recorded his personal details.

Deliberately leaving the front door open behind him, he stood for a moment in the cover of the porch studying the cul-de-sac on either side and drawing in great lungfuls of clean night air. Then peeling off his gloves, he strode briskly back across the lawn that encircled the lake and disappeared into the shadows beyond the reach of the streetlights. Mission accomplished.

CHAPTER 14

Mavis Talbot had been a cleaner for over five years and was paid well by the wealthy clients she had managed to secure. She had a word-of-mouth reputation for being efficient, reliable and discreet and she made sure she met the individual requirements of those who engaged her without question. That put her head and shoulders above the vast majority of her competitors. Marianne Dawson was one of her favourite customers. She was a real lady. Nice to deal with and meticulous about paying on time. Not that Mavis saw much of the respected physiotherapist, except on payday Fridays as Miss Dawson liked to sleep in late weekday mornings as most of her client bookings were in the afternoon and evening. She had a beautiful house too and in fairness, there wasn't much for a cleaner to do there as it was always kept clean and tidy. There were only two stipulations in the cleaning arrangements. First, always finish by one o'clock. Second, of the rooms at the front of the house, only clean Treatment Room 1. Treatment Room 2 was apparently never used, and the door was always kept locked. Mavis had no problem with this, and it never occurred to her that there was anything odd about the locked room. Not until the one fateful day when her cleaning contract was abruptly terminated through the most shocking of unforeseen circumstances.

Her first surprise was to find the front door wide open when she arrived at eleven as usual. Miss Dawson was always so scrupulous about security. She was even more surprised to find that the door of Treatment Room 2 was open too, which had never happened before. Ordinarily she would never have disobeyed Miss Dawson and looked inside, but after calling her name and getting no reply, she was tempted just to take a quick peep. Immediately she wished she hadn't and the next second she was running out into the street screaming her head off.

*　*　*

It was like an invasion. Camomile Close was choked with police vehicles. Patrol cars, a dog van and several unmarked cars that obviously belonged to the detective department. The cat who could possibly have provided the best witness evidence of all regarding the crime that had been committed at number sixteen sauntered through it all with a look of disdain, which he could afford to do since he couldn't speak anyway.

In the neighbouring houses residents peered through curtains as a couple of uniformed officers started to reel out blue-and-white perimeter tape across the entrance to the cul-de-sac. At the same time, the police dog handler slowly led his charge around the edge of the lake and tried not to look too embarrassed when the animal stopped frequently to relieve itself on tufts of grass liberally adorned with duck excrement.

In the pink room of number sixteen the woman known to her disreputable clientele as Tina had no interest in what the dog or anyone else was doing. She was obviously dead and therefore past caring about anything anymore. Dressed in just her miniscule bra and thong, she was hanging from the top bar of a metal frame attached to the wall. Her wrists were cruelly secured by steel handcuffs to the topmost bar with another pair securing her ankles to the bottom. The plastic bag that had been pulled over her head and tied under her chin had been ripped open and now formed a tattered skin-like frame around her face. The hideous contorted expression and bulging eyes of her death mask were horrific testimony to the agony she must have suffered in her last moments of suffocation. But as if her sadistic murder wasn't enough for the warped mind of the perpetrator, a dead crow had been suspended around her neck on a length of cord. In addition, the word WHORE had been scrawled in thick block capitals across her stomach with what looked like red lipstick.

Standing together in the hallway dressed in their protective nylon suits, Charlie Woo and Kate Lewis stared into the room with world-weary despair.

'So, yet another one,' Woo commented. 'The press will just love this when they get hold of it.'

'Cleaner found her hanging from the bars when she came in at eleven this morning,' Kate said. 'Fled screaming to the house next door, and the old boy living there dialled three nines after taking a peek. We got the request for CID assistance via Control from Jane Rafferty, the first plod at the scene, about half eleven and Jamie Foster attended with me.'

'So who ripped the plastic bag apart?'

'Rafferty, but the woman was plainly dead by then. Rigor mortis had already set in. Police surgeon's been and gone, but he reckoned that as a very rough guestimate, she's probably been dead since late yesterday evening. We'll be able to get a more accurate assessment when the forensic pathologist arrives.'

'And no one has thought of actually trying to get the poor woman down from that frame?'

'We tried, but you've seen the handcuffs on her wrists and ankles and there's no trace of any keys. The killer obviously took those with him just to make our lives more difficult. Bolt cutters are soon to be provided by the Support Group. But since the woman is already dead, there is no urgency now. We might as well leave her in situ for SOCO who are already on their way. Then we can do the business afterwards when the pathologist gets here. I gather we're talking a couple of hours.'

Woo grunted. 'The cleaner who found her. Eleven was a bit late in the day for her to do her cleaning job, wasn't it?' He glanced at his watch. 'I thought cleaners did their work first thing in the morning. You know, cracked on before the business of the day began.'

'Yeah, but it seems this particular client of hers kept unusual hours and liked to have a lie-in until midday.'

Woo's gaze fastened on the cupboard set against the opposite wall. The two doors were wide open, a key on a ring still in the lock. The assortment of sexual paraphernalia on the hooks inside was clearly visible. 'I can see why,' he said. 'Did most of her business in the late hours, I would think, when the creepy-crawlies are about. Maybe her services didn't quite come up to scratch for her last client.'

'I don't think our killer came here to sample her services.' Kate pointed at the dead crow hanging round the dead woman's neck. 'He left his usual calling card just to make sure there was no doubt who had stiffed her.'

'So who was his victim?'

'Marianne Dawson, a registered physio and masseuse.'

'What? You mean she really was a pukka physio?'

'Apparently so, though it appears she didn't work for the NHS. Strictly private. Elderly man next door told me he had received treatment from her for his arthritic joints. He said she was very skilled and well respected locally, though predictably, not cheap. Her place was apparently adapted for business use when she moved in about two years ago. The door you can see at the end of the hallway accesses her private quarters. I checked. The area at the front here is restricted to her business and the room opposite this one is kitted out in the manner you'd expect of a legitimate physiotherapist.'

'So she led a double life?'

'Looks like it. Probably made more dosh in the sex industry than she did as a professional physio.'

'And do you think the cleaner knew what shady practices she was involved in?'

Kate shook her head. 'The dodgy treatment room was off-limits and the old girl was told there was no need for her to clean in there. It was always kept locked anyway. Until today, that is.'

'The killer obviously wanted her to be found. He must have watched the place before and seen the cleaner arrive at eleven.'

'Or he just took a chance on his victim being found by a client or a neighbour. Seems he left the front door open too, so it would have been an open invitation to any nosy plonker who happened along.'

'No husband or family living here then?'

'Divorced and no kids according to the elderly neighbour who called the police. Apparently lived alone.'

'Any possible witnesses?'

'Not yet. I've got a couple of the lads doing preliminary door-to-door inquiries at the moment, but knowing how our man operates, I don't hold out much hope.'

'I saw a CCTV camera over the front door when I came in. Any chance that there's a nice video or DVD recording of his visit?'

Kate grimaced. 'There might have been, yeah, but it looks like the killer took the evidence with him, including the hard drives.'

'Came prepared then? Clever cookie.' He sighed. 'Well, you certainly worked quickly setting things up. Even if, er, by rights you shouldn't have been dealing with this when you're supposed to be off the current inquiry.'

She turned on him angrily, her sensitivity to her current position erupting. 'And how the hell was I to know this would be another hit by the same scumbag? All I got when I turned up was a report of a woman found hanging in her home. I took it as a potential suicide. What was I supposed to say to Control. "Oh sorry, I'm banned from attending

incidents like this now, so you'd better call someone else."
That would have gone down a treat, wouldn't it?'

He threw her a quick, boyish grin. 'Okay, okay, don't
go getting all waspish on me. Just mentioning it, that's all.
The DCI is likely to say a lot more on the subject when he
hears about it.'

'Sod the bloody DCI. The man's a cretin.'

He winced. 'Whatever you think of him, he's still the
DCI, never forget that. Anyway, I have to apologise that I
didn't get here sooner. I was at Wilf Carpenter's post-mortem, and Deidrie Hennessey is still at her meeting with ACC
Ops. But I understand her bag carrier, DI Don Tappin, is on
his way here and he can take over from me.'

'Anything useful from the PM?'

He shrugged. 'Not a lot more than the pathologist found
at the scene.' He grinned again, a little guiltily this time for
what he was about to add. 'What else can you say about a
mashed head? I just love the way these people describe violent deaths the way they do. You know, massive trauma and
haemorrhaging somehow doesn't seem to cover it.'

Kate made a face and threw another glance at the corpse
hanging from the metal frame. 'When you think what this
madman has done to all these perfectly innocent people and
all he's likely to face as a punishment is a nice comfy room
at the funny farm, you can't help wondering about so-called
British justice.'

He shrugged. 'You've omitted one minor detail. We've
got to catch him first.'

* * *

It is often said that murderers have a habit of returning to
the scenes of their crimes. Either out of some form of morbid
compulsion, or simply to gloat over what they have done. For
the Bogeyman killer, as Debbie Moreton had called him, it
was more to do with intelligence gathering than anything
else. He'd needed to establish whether his victim had been

found and to check on the police response to the crime, though his ego was certainly given a real boost by the stir he had created.

It would have been impossible to have missed the knot of what looked like reporters and camera crews gathered on the roadside at the entrance to Camomile Close. After doing a slow drive past, he parked his car in a side street further along the main road and walked back to the scene to mingle with the crowd. The blue-and-white cordon tape drawn across the entrance to the cul-de-sac was reinforced by the presence of two capable looking coppers. A well-proportioned woman sergeant and an equally muscular male constable. The cul-de-sac itself was crammed with a large number of what were obviously police cars. Some liveried. Others unmarked. He glimpsed the strip of yellow crime scene tape stretched across the front door of number sixteen and couldn't help feeling a sense of elation over the drama unfolding in front of him. It was all for him. He had caused this. No longer could he be called inadequate. Now he was somebody to be reckoned with. He strained his eyes for sight of Kate Lewis, but he couldn't see her. She was probably inside the house studying his handiwork. He would have to ring her later to find out what she thought of it all. He also looked for Debbie Moreton among the febrile, jostling crowd, but she was not there. Pity. He reproached himself for not giving her the heads up on the murder he had planned, as he had his other accomplishments.

Then abruptly he forgot all about Kate Lewis and Debbie Moreton. Some inexplicable sixth sense had alerted him to the fact that someone was staring at him. Turning his head quickly, he met the curious gaze of an attractive young woman. She was standing on the edge of the crowd with a little boy holding on to one hand and a terrier on a lead on the other. He instantly recognised her. It was the same woman who had approached him as he'd sat on the seat by the lake the previous day. The last person he had expected or wanted to see.

Reacting in the only way he could think of under the circumstances, he turned away from her and pushed his way back through the crowd. He risked a glance over his shoulder when he reached the pavement on the other side of the main road and saw his worst fears realised. The woman had made no attempt to go after him. Instead, she was talking to one of the uniformed police officers reinforcing the cordon and was plainly gesticulating in his direction. He felt the muscles in his stomach knot. The interfering cow could only be telling the copper about him. It was time to be gone.

Back in his car in the side street further down the road, he sat there for a moment hammering the steering wheel with the palms of his hands and cursing his arrogant stupidity in so brazenly returning to the crime scene so soon after the murder.

'Bloody idiot!' he snarled at himself in the rear-view mirror. The woman was bound to have left her name and address with the police as a possible witness. There was a real risk that she could identify him in any future line-up. Things were starting to stack up against him. First cutting his leg and maybe leaving DNA traces in the back of the dead copper's car. Then facing near disaster when Kate Lewis had almost caught him as he'd torched Corbin's Letting Agency. Now the million to one chance that the same stupid bitch he had run into while giving the prossie's house the once-over had happened along to the murder scene at the very moment he had chosen to return to it.

It wasn't that he was terrified of being caught. He'd known all along that that was likely to be the eventual outcome. But it had to be on his terms and only after he had actually won the game and destroyed that cocky little bitch Kate Lewis in the process. Then he would have proved his intellectual superiority over her and established a top place for himself in the annals of criminal history as one of the most successful serial killers since Jack the Ripper and Ted Bundy.

Further remedial action was called for if he was to reduce the odds building up against him still more. He had to find and eliminate the woman with the dog before she could do any real damage to him and running away was certainly not the answer. But first he had to find out where she lived. With a bit of luck, the copper on the cordon had only taken her name and address for future interview and she was now on her way home along the main road. All he had to do was spot the bitch and follow her. That meant going back to the scene yet again, which was a further risk in itself. Sometimes, though, risks were justified to achieve an overall goal. As far as he knew the police had no idea what sort of car he was driving, and people tended to be anonymous behind the wheel, didn't they?

Checking his rear-view mirror, he turned round in the entrance to a private house and headed back the way he had come at a virtual crawl.

* * *

Kate was in a foul mood when she finally left the crime scene shortly after briefing the DI. Though complimenting her on her initial handling of the incident, Woo was adamant that he would have to take it over from her. 'Sorry, Kate, but now that we can be certain this is another hit by the same killer and not a completely unconnected crime, you know you cannot officially remain as an investigator. So just be patient and remember the old saying, "all things come to those who wait".'

Although she had expected this to happen, the patronising advice on top of it all really rankled and her mood was not improved when she received the radio call about a potential witness. Only to find after making her way to the police perimeter cordon that the witness was no longer there.

Drawing the young constable to one side out of earshot of the reporters, she glared at him. 'And you let her go?' she fumed, noting the woman's address from his pocketbook.

'She wouldn't wait, skipper,' he replied, his embarrassment plain. 'Said she had to get back to let her kid have his afternoon nap. What else could I have done? I had no grounds to detain her.'

Kate released her breath in a sharp exasperated hiss, but she reluctantly accepted his explanation. 'Okay, okay, what's done is done. But did we get any description of the man she said she saw?'

He shook his head. 'She was in a rush, though she did say she was happy for someone to call and see her this afternoon. Should be home in half an hour apparently.'

'So to recap, she said she had spotted the same suspicious looking man she'd seen sitting on the seat by the lake yesterday hanging about in the crowd just now?'

'That's about it, yes. She said the first time she saw him she thought there was something weird about the guy and that her normally placid dog then went for him. Something he'd never done to anyone before.'

'Did she point out the man to you?'

He shook his head. 'She waved an arm towards the main road and said he had already made off through the crowd.'

'Did you see him?'

'No, sorry.'

Kate's frown deepened as a worrying thought occurred to her. 'But he must have realised she'd clocked him, otherwise why would he suddenly scarper?'

'Must've done, I reckon.'

'Which means she could be in real danger.'

He gulped. 'Shall I get Control to send a car round to her home?'

She was already turning away from him. 'No time for that,' she snapped irritably over her shoulder. 'I'm closest. Just get Control to send some backup just in case.'

Within minutes she was back behind the wheel of her car. Nosing her way through the reporters out on to the main road.

* * *

He'd lost her and he swore viciously. He'd followed the road all the way along to a small roundabout, but she was nowhere in sight. He couldn't understand it. There was no way she could have got so far in the time with a small boy. She must have turned off somewhere. He wrenched the wheel around and went back the way he had come. Once more at a crawl and ignoring the cars blasting him as they pulled out from behind and raced past him.

Then suddenly he saw her. She was emerging from a shop on the opposite side of the road, peeling back the paper from what looked like an ice lolly and handing it to the child. He drove on, turned round in the mouth of a side street and sat there in the entrance for a little while before pulling out again to follow her slowly at a distance. Someone honked at him for driving so slowly and he saw her glance round quickly. But she was quite a way ahead and didn't seem to notice him.

A few minutes later she turned into another side street lined with smart modern houses and led him right to her front door. He drove past a short distance, reversed round in another driveway, and pulled into a layby conveniently screened by conifers a few yards from the detached house she had entered.

He had already noted the tall bushy shrubs between her house and the properties on both sides, plus the gate to the back garden. He'd also observed the rails on each side of the front doorstep of the next property nearest to him. It suggested that at least one of the residents was elderly or infirm. Couldn't be better. No risk there. The only real problem was the bloody dog. After a moment's thought, he got out, went round to the boot and extracted a business-like wheel brace. He tested it against his palm and smiled. Just the job, he mused. In fact he might be able to finish them both off with it, even if it did make a bit of a mess. It would be a novel mode of despatch.

CHAPTER 15

Julia Thorogood heard the sound of her dog barking in the garden and pulled back the vertical blinds across the kitchen window to peer out. She had just put her son, Daniel, down for his afternoon sleep and she wasn't best pleased with the noise. She could not see the dog anywhere. Opening the window, she called out sharply. 'Quiet, Billy! Stop that!' There was a whimper, then silence. She raised her eyebrows in surprise. An obedient response? That was a first for the terrier.

She finished tipping the rest of her chopped vegetables into the saucepan for the evening meal, wiped her hands down her apron and crept to Daniel's bedroom to check that he was still asleep. Peering round the edge of the door, she saw that he was well out. She crept into the room to bend over the little bed and carefully placed two fingers over his chest. She knew it was stupid. But she had a phobia about always checking to make sure he was breathing okay ever since her husband, Tom, had died suddenly from an unexpected heart attack a month after Daniel was born.

Withdrawing again on tiptoe, she was heading back to the kitchen to finish her other chores, when she heard what sounded like the patio door sliding back. Frowning, she about-turned and made for the lounge. Only to freeze in the doorway as soon as she stepped into the room. The patio door had been pulled right back, but there was no one there. Just a bloodstained grey bundle lying on the flagstones outside.

'Billy?' she exclaimed and running out into the garden, she bent down beside the little terrier. The animal was plainly dead. His skull had been smashed in and was still haemorrhaging blood.

'Oh Billy,' she choked, sobbing into the palms of both hands and rocking backwards and forwards on her heels. Unable to comprehend how such a thing could have happened to her beloved dog. Then suddenly, shock turning to fear, she stumbled quickly to her feet, and stared around the small garden. The side gate was still shut. Daniel's half empty plastic pool, with the boats floating among the leaves, and the garden rake she had been using the day before to rake the lawn, were all still there. But nothing else was in evidence. Yet someone must have come into the garden and done this to Billy. There was no other plausible explanation. But why? She knew a couple of the neighbours had complained about his yapping, but surely no one would have resorted to such awful measures to silence him? It was beyond belief.

And it was at that moment that another even worse thought occurred to her. Was the intruder still there? Was he now actually in the house? 'Daniel!' she gasped.

Whirling round, she raced back through the patio doorway, heading for her son's bedroom. The little boy was still fast asleep and snoring. She breathed a sigh of relief and returned to the hallway, closing his door behind her.

A noisy, backfiring motorcycle roared down the main road and faded into nothing. Silence. She could hear the sonorous ticking of the hall clock, but little else.

She walked slowly down the hallway, her heart thumping and her knees trembling. She wiped the tears from her eyes and checked the main bedroom and the downstairs toilet. Both were empty. She glanced up the staircase, listening intently. A rafter cracked. Otherwise, just a heavy stillness.

She retraced her steps to the kitchen where she remembered leaving her mobile phone on the worksurface by the sink. Poor little Billy may have only been a dog, but it was still a job for the police, and she was determined to make someone pay for what they had done to him.

She got the sixth-sense warning too late. He was hiding behind the door and his arm was locked round her neck even before she could turn.

'Remember me, sweetheart,' he said and tightened his grip, shutting off her air supply.

But if he expected her just to flake out and allow him to finish her off with the wheel brace, like the dog, he got a big surprise. Instead of bending forward in an effort to break his grip, she threw herself backwards, crashing him into the wall. Before he could recover his balance, the heel of her hard leather shoe found his shin and viciously raked it from top to bottom, making him cry out in pain. As his grip on her neck relaxed slightly, she jabbed her elbow back into his diaphragm with all her strength, breaking free of his hold completely as he went into a desperate gasping fit.

He was a tough cookie, though, and his incapacity only lasted a couple of seconds. He got to her again even as she went for the rack of carving knives on the worksurface. Snarling like an animal, he seized her by the throat. Then with one powerful hand, he forced her right back over the edge of the cooker until it seemed as though her spine would snap. His grip was like a steel clamp. Neither of her clawing hands could break it and he studied her with an intense, unwavering stare as he slowly squeezed the life out of her.

It was at this moment that fate decided to change the dynamics of the situation. Suddenly she felt the burning pain of erupting steam through her blouse. Despite the red mist of fading consciousness, she remembered the vegetable soup she had put on the cooker before going out into the garden. Allowing her left hand to drop away from his wrist as if in capitulation, she groped for the handle. Then with a sudden twist of her hips, she heaved the small saucepan off the cooker and swung it sideways and upwards. It was a clumsy desperate manoeuvre and some of the liquid splashed over her own body as the utensil flew from her hand and bounced away across the floor. But most of it found her assailant. His screams of agony must have been heard all the way down the street. As he staggered back from her, clawing the sticky liquid off his face and neck, she made the most of the opportunity. Stumbling past him out into the hallway, she tore open the front door, shouting for help, and ran straight into the arms of Kate Lewis.

* * *

With hindsight, Kate realised later that she should have gone for the side gate on her arrival, not the front door. It was only after she had raced past the distressed woman into the house and found her assailant gone that she heard the gate slam back. By the time she got back out to the street, it was to see the big Volvo fishtailing towards the main road and away. To her frustration she wasn't quick enough to get even part of the registration number.

The ambulance she called arrived at the same time as two marked police patrol cars. Sending them off on what she knew would be a fruitless search for the Volvo, she sat with the injured woman while the ambulance crew attended to her burns, which fortunately were not serious, and bounced her little boy on one knee.

After the crew had gone, Kate gently questioned the woman about her ordeal and her previous contacts with her assailant and was able to build up a reasonably good description.

'Hopefully his burns are so serious that he will have to seek hospital treatment,' Kate said. 'I will make sure all the hospitals and GP surgeries in the area are alerted just in case he tries to get help.'

'Do you think he'll come back here?' the woman said. 'I'm worried about Daniel.'

Kate shook her head. 'I very much doubt it,' she replied. 'I will arrange for a police officer to be stationed outside for twenty-four hours anyway.'

Thorogood nodded, making a funny face at her son. 'Thank you,' she said. 'But I think I will go away with Daniel to my mother's place in Hull for a few days.'

Kate stood up. 'Fine, but please leave us the address in case we need to contact you. I assume you would be prepared to attend an identification parade if and when we bring this man in?'

The pretty face twisted into a hard vindictive smile. 'Wild horses wouldn't keep me away from identifying that swine,' she said. 'What do you think he will get as a punishment?'

Kate compressed her lips into a tight line. 'With a bit of luck a full life term,' she said. Though she felt like adding what was more likely to happen, 'Maybe a cosy room in Broadmoor and a pound out of the poor box when he's released a few years later to kill again.' But she kept these words to herself for now.

* * *

The initial pain had been excruciating. Fortunately, the wraparound sunglasses and baseball cap he had been wearing had saved him from more severe injury. Only one side of his face and part of his neck had suffered. He had also had the good sense to pull over on to some waste ground when he was clear of the scene to douse his face in cold water from the litre bottle he always kept in the car. He had followed this up when he got back to his cottage by submerging his face in a bowl of cold water, keeping it there until his breath ran out, then repeating the process. This had had the effect of taking some of the heat out of the scalds, though his face continued to hurt like hell and the affected areas were badly inflamed.

By rights, he should have sought immediate medical treatment, but that was just what the police would have expected him to do. Having alerted all the hospitals and GP surgeries in the area, they would have pounced on him the moment he put in an appearance. No, suffering in silence was his only option and after treating the scalds himself with a thin layer of the petroleum jelly he always carried in his toilet bag, he swallowed some strong painkillers and washed them down with a large glass of malt whisky.

Then he sat in an armchair in his cottage kitchen, trying to ignore the burning tremors coursing through his wounds as he stared out of the window at the mist now rising from the flat, marshy fields, and plotted his next move.

So another unprofessional, bungled job, he mused bitterly. Again, one that had not been planned properly and had nearly ended in disaster for him. When would he learn?

Revenge was uppermost in his mind. It was burning through him almost as much as the scalds he had sustained. Returning to the scene and subjecting that bitch to a slow, agonising death was what he wanted most of all. It would be a just payback for what she had done to him. But he knew it was out of the question. She was bound to have police protection by now. He wouldn't get anywhere near her. He would simply end up in handcuffs in the back of a police van. His game plan in tatters. His hopes of becoming the most successful serial killer since Jack the Ripper and Ted Bundy dashed for ever. He had to put it behind him and move on. He couldn't afford another cock-up. He already had his next target lined up, so he should concentrate on that. Still, he could at least allow himself one small indulgence before that. He held his last gulp of whisky in his mouth for a few thoughtful seconds to savour the taste as well as the thought, before pouring himself another.

* * *

The DCI was waiting for Kate when she got back from an extended lunchbreak in the police station where she had been talking over her feelings with Hayden. Ricketts looked ashen and his eyes bored into her when she walked into the general CID office.

'Sergeant!' he snapped. 'With me, now.'

Walking into the DI's empty office and closing the door, he turned on her like an icy blast. 'I've just been down to the latest murder scene, and what do I find?' he snapped. 'A certain DS Lewis had actually been supervising the police response in direct contravention of my instruction that she was no longer to participate in this major inquiry.'

Kate met his gaze without flinching, musing that he obviously hadn't stayed at the scene very long.

'I had no choice, sir—' she began, but before she could try and explain he was at her again, his voice harsh and uncompromising.

'I will not be defied, Sergeant,' he blazed. 'If you think you can ignore my instructions and just carry on as before, you are badly mistaken. This was disobedience to a lawful order, which is a disciplinary offence.'

It was plain that either he had not listened properly to the briefing he had been given or was determined to ignore the full facts of the matter so he could pursue his own prejudiced agenda.

'And what about this incident at the home of a key witness? You should not have been there in the first place. There were enough other officers at the scene who could have attended.'

'If I hadn't got there when I did she would be dead by now,' Kate retorted angrily. 'Then you wouldn't have a bloody witness at all.'

'What did you say?' he choked, and his eyes were like organ stops. 'That is downright insolence. You are already likely to be the subject of a discipline inquiry over your past misdemeanours and with this on top of it all, it will be a miracle if you are still in the force afterwards, let alone a detective sergeant on CID!'

'Holy Mary, what is going on in here?'

Neither Kate nor Ricketts had heard the door open behind them. But as she was facing the door, Kate had the advantage over the DCI of seeing Deidrie Hennessey first. It was plain from the expression on her face that the detective superintendent was far from happy.

Ricketts took a deep breath. 'The sergeant here has once again blatantly disobeyed my instructions to stay off this major inquiry,' he blurted. 'It is a breach of discipline.'

Hennessey sighed heavily. She looked pale and drawn. 'Aha, but you can forget all that now, Chief Inspector,' she cut in. 'I've just been with ACC Ops and he agrees with me that Sergeant Lewis has been the victim of a deliberate conspiracy against her and that there will be no further action by the force in this respect. That means she's back on the team, so she is, which I feel sure you'll agree is a blessed relief to us all.'

For a moment it looked as though Ricketts had been struck dumb and he just stared at Hennessey in open-mouthed disbelief.

'This is not acceptable,' he protested suddenly. 'She is out of control.'

Hennessey sighed again. 'It is neither the time nor the place to discuss this, Mr Ricketts,' she said sharply. 'A decision has been made, so I suggest we drop the subject.'

'But — but she was insubordinate. I will not have it.'

Hennessey's eyes narrowed dangerously. 'Leave us, Sergeant, will you,' she said quietly, 'and close the door behind you.'

Back in the general office, Hayden and Danny Ferris, who were sitting at their desks, threw Kate quizzical looks. But she frowned warningly and went straight past them to her desk. Even as she sat down, she could hear voices raised in the glass-panelled office she had just left, but the altercation didn't last long. Minutes later Ricketts emerged with a look of thunder on his face. Then he marched past them all without looking left or right and disappeared through the double doors at the end, slamming one of them behind him.

'Sergeant Lewis?' Hennessey called moments later and when Kate went back into the office, she found the detective superintendent perched on the edge of her desk with a tired smile on her face.

'Welcome back, Kate,' she said. 'At least you're in the clear now.'

Kate made a grimace. 'Sorry I caused you all the hassle with the DCI,' she said. 'I did try to explain to him that I had no idea that the latest incident was connected to the major inquiry when I attended initially, but he just wouldn't listen.'

She waved a dismissive hand being too discreet to comment on the row between the two senior officers or to say what she really thought of Ricketts.

'Ach, just a wee difference of opinion, that's all. Now it would be grand if you could fill me in on the latest developments in this case of ours, so it would.'

* * *

Hennessey listened attentively to Kate for the next hour, throwing in questions as and when she felt it was necessary to clarify a point or clear up what she saw as an ambiguity, and when the briefing had been concluded, the Ulsterwoman nodded and stood up from the edge of the desk to stretch her legs.

'We'll get a public appeal out for any dash-cam footage other drivers might have caught of the Volvo car near either of the two crime scenes,' she said. 'We can also check to see if there's any street CCTV coverage that could have picked him up. But even if we strike lucky, which I doubt, it will take time for anything to come in. Any other thoughts you want to share?'

Kate frowned. 'There are actually,' she replied. 'I've been thinking about the sort of people the killer has targeted so far. We can forget Gerry Thomas, DS O'Sullivan, Terry Corbin and Julia Thorogood, all of whom he appears to have gone for at the last minute through force of circumstance. But what prompted him to choose his other three victims. A cleric, the proprietor of a cider farm and a high-class prostitute. Why them?'

Hennessey shrugged. 'Probably selected at random.'

Kate shook her head. 'I don't buy that. Those three killings had to have been carefully planned, not on-the-hoof jobs like the others.'

'So what are you saying?'

'That there has to be some kind of connection between the three, and if we could establish that, maybe we could be closer to determining his next victim.'

'A very long shot, and what could a cleric, the owner of a cider farm and a prostitute possibly have in common anyway? There's no obvious link.'

Kate bit her lip in thought. 'Well, two of them are supposed to be sinful professions to some Christians, aren't they? Alcohol and lust. Even if alcohol isn't one of the seven deadly sins in the Bible, could they have been killed perhaps by someone with a moral hang-up?'

'But that doesn't explain why a man of God was also selected. Not unless you're saying the killings could be related to sectarian terrorism, which would be a whole different ball game.'

Kate shook her head. 'No, I'm not saying that at all. I think this character is suffering from some kind of psychosis and is delusional, but I am satisfied that although he is obviously a ruthless serial killer, he has no political bent. I get the feeling, though, that his victims are linked by some common denominator and that there's a message amongst it all that he's teasing us with. Okay, I know I'm sounding a bit weird, but I'm sure I am right.'

Hennessey emitted a low whistle and shook her head. 'Wee bit deep for me right now. But the idea is worth exploring.'

She brushed imaginary crumbs off her trousers, then straightened up. 'Maybe you should talk to that husband of yours. From what I hear, Hayden is into all this wacky psychological stuff. In the meantime, I have an incident room briefing to attend and now you're officially back on the team, you can't escape being there.'

CHAPTER 16

Debbie Moreton was working into the evening again after making the scene of the Camomile Close murder a lot later that afternoon than she would have wanted. She had only found out about what was going on after a call from one of the newspaper's part-time, freelance reporters, or 'stringers', and she was furious that she had not picked up on things much earlier. Maybe she had upset her homicidal inform- ant after their last conversation because he certainly hadn't bothered to ring her this time. Well, sod him if that was the reason. She had still managed to get the SP by twisting the ear of one very indiscreet copper and the story had turned out to be a real juicy one.

A respectable physiotherapist on the game in a quiet suburban backwater? Murdered by one of her own clients? A client who police believed to be the Bogeyman killer again? What could be better? Scandals attached to serious crimes always provided a thrilling draw for the *Clarion*'s readers over breakfast. Especially when a serial killer was involved. But she'd needed to write it up PDQ, so it made the front page for the following day.

She finally left the office after filing copy around eight o'clock in the evening, determined to have a long hot shower and a nice bottle of white wine. But unbeknown to her as she tripped down the stone stairs to the *Clarion*'s basement car park, someone else had planned a different sort of evening for her.

She saw that most of the day staff had already gone home by the time she pushed through the heavy basement door and the car park only boasted about half a dozen vehicles. She was conscious, as she always was when finishing late, of the shadows cloaking some of the bays where the overhead lighting had fused, and the echoes raised by her heels on the concrete floor seemed unnaturally loud as she walked quickly from the stairway door to where she had parked her old BMW at the far end of the large, pillared garage.

She already had her bunch of keys in her hand well before she reached her car and felt reassured when she pressed the button on the fob and saw the four-way flashers flick twice in greeting. But her confidence was short-lived. She was just a couple of feet from the driver's door and reaching for the handle when she heard the strange, unnerving sound like a throaty growl emanating from somewhere close by. Even as she turned quickly in the direction of the sound, she caught the blur of sudden movement. Something moving very fast. Something coming straight at her. The next moment a dark shape erupted from the gloom. She caught a glimpse of a snarling face and wild, staring eyes and staggered backwards with a sharp cry, hardly aware of her keys flying from her hand and skating across the floor as she slammed into the concrete pillar behind her.

But then almost immediately she was laughing out loud. Her scary attacker had been nothing more than a big black moggy. The feral cat that had been haunting the car park for weeks. It must have been asleep on the bonnet of her car and had been startled by her arrival. She caught a final glimpse of the animal as it streaked away from her and disappeared into another patch of shadow on the other side of the car park.

Still chuckling at her own stupidity, she dropped down on to her hands and knees to check the floor around her for her bunch of keys. But she never found them. Instead, her gaze fell on a pair of black shoes, which had suddenly stepped into view in front of her. Slowly lifting her head, she found herself staring up at the tall figure of a man dressed in an anorak and baseball cap. Much of the man's face was in shadow, but the glow thrown across the car park from a nearby security light was enough to catch the wicked gleam of the long-bladed knife he clasped in one black-gloved hand.

'Hello, Debbie,' a familiar voice said harshly. 'You've been a naughty girl, you know.'

* * *

'A link?' Hayden looked up from his laptop screen and frowned. 'What do you mean, a link?'

Kate had spent over an hour and a half at the incident-room briefing and a further hour discussing the latest murder investigation with Charlie Woo on his return to the police station from the crime scene. Hayden had already gone home by the time she'd left work, and she found him in the armchair with his laptop computer on his lap and a glass of red wine on the coffee table in front of him.

Kate dumped her ignition keys on the halfmoon table by the stairs. 'I think there's a connection somehow between the victims in three of our murders,' she said to clarify her opener. 'I don't reckon they were killed at random, but specifically selected.'

He set his laptop down on the coffee table and poured some red wine from the bottle on the floor beside him into a second glass. She took it from him gratefully and perched herself on the edge of the settee opposite.

'Stretching it a bit to find a commonalty between a prostitute, the owner of a cider farm and a cleric, don't you think? Hardly the sort to share a friendship,' he said.

She acknowledged his point with a shrug, then said, 'That's more or less what the boss said when I told her about my theory. Give it some thought anyway, will you?' She grinned. 'Deidrie Hennessey thinks you're the ideal man to puzzle out wacky stuff like that.'

He grunted. 'Not sure that's a compliment, but I will focus my magnificent brain on the issue in due course.'

She acknowledged the offer with a nod, then stared at the laptop he had put down. 'So what's with that?' she asked drily. 'Checking the runners and riders for Saturday's races, or just researching the latest football scores?'

'Neither, old girl. I was actually working on something much more important.'

He reached forward and turned the laptop round so she had a full view of the screen. She was astonished to see that it was displaying a coloured page of properties to rent.

She whistled. 'Not thinking of moving, are we, Hayd?' she exclaimed. 'I thought you were happy here?'

He tutted irritably. 'I'm not and I am,' he snapped. 'This is about work.'

She chortled. 'Work? At home? Off duty? That must be a first.'

He threw her a sour look but chose to ignore the jibe.

'When Corbin's Letting Agency was destroyed in the fire,' he went on, 'so were all his records, right? Which means we thought we had lost our chance of finding out what property he may have let to our killer—'

'Thought?'

'Precisely. You see, it dawned on me that as our felon seems to have popped in to see Corbin as soon as he arrived in the area, it is very likely he had already contacted him before his arrival, possibly through a phone call, after seeing the sort of property he wanted to rent advertised. Since he would probably have been abroad at the time, the likelihood is that he saw the property—'

Kate cut in excitedly. 'On the net.'

'Bingo!' he said drily. 'You win the prize. The thing is, properties tend to be advertised for a set period and contracts renewed or cancelled when that period expires. This suggests that if our man saw the property just before he arrived in this country, it is very likely it will still be present on the agency's property pages, even if it is no longer available, as Corbin wouldn't have had time to have it taken down before he died. It occurred to me that all we have to do is to scour those pages for rentals advertised by Corbin's Letting Agency and draw up a list of properties which might have attracted the killer's interest.'

'Okay in theory, but that could mean checking on possibly hundreds of properties, and how the hell could we know which ones he would have gone for anyway?'

'We draw up a list of his likely requirements based on logic and experience.'

'Such as?'

'Well, to start with, a place that is fully furnished and isolated as much as possible from human contact, enabling him to come and go as he pleases without attracting the attention of nosy neighbours. So maybe an old farm or a rural cottage. Second, somewhere with good access to a main road and with a further exit in case he needs to leave in a hurry and can't use the front entrance. Third, somewhere reasonably proximate to Highbridge so he can keep tabs on you, which is obviously his main focus. Finally, somewhere he can keep his car out of sight, just in case it has been spotted at any of the murder scenes.'

He snapped his fingers as another thought occurred to him. 'Oh yes, and don't forget the rooks.'

'The rooks?'

'Of course. For him to be able to leave such a calling card at the majority of the crime scenes means he must have a natural resource, like a rookery, close by, and the means to capture and slaughter them. This in itself would be an indication that we are on the right track with any property we checked out. The presence of the Volvo XC40 on top of this would clinch it for us.'

'The whole thing sounds a bit barmy to me.'

'Maybe it does, but it could work, and we would lose nothing by trying. The only thing against it where we are concerned is the fact that we are not now part of the MIT inquiry, so that leaves us out on a bit of a limb with the powers that be.'

She smiled and shook her head. 'Not any more it doesn't. I forgot to tell you, I was reinstated today, much to the DCI's fury, so I am back to being a legitimate team member.'

'But I'm not.'

'Think of yourself as seconded.'

He brightened. 'Then you feel we should go ahead with my idea?'

She shrugged. 'Why not? As you say, we would lose nothing by trying.' She stood up. 'So, let's get cracking, shall we?'

His jaw dropped. 'What, er, right now?'

Inwardly Kate chuckled, knowing full well the almost legendary importance Hayden attached to filling his belly.

'Of course. You seem to have already started and the sooner we get done with the elimination work, the sooner we can finish. I can then put our findings to the boss first thing in the morning.'

'But — but dinner first, surely? I mean, we need some sustenance to maintain our concentration.'

'Oh, I think a round of cheese sandwiches would do that well enough.' She picked up the bottle of wine and headed for the kitchen. 'And I'll make us some coffee instead of this to help that concentration you're so worried about.'

'Me and my big mouth,' he muttered under his breath and reluctantly turned his laptop round to face him again.

* * *

Debbie Moreton was terrified. Lying in the boot of a car she had been dumped into somewhere close to the *Clarion* building, she knew only that she was in the process of being driven somewhere. Blindfolded, gagged, with her wrists handcuffed behind her and some sort of tape binding her ankles together, she had no idea where they were going or what fate her abductor had in mind for her. But knowing what he had done to his other victims only served to wind her fears up to fever pitch, and she was sobbing hysterically when the car finally stopped again.

She sensed moonlight blazing in her face. The next moment she was being hauled out of the car and hoisted over his shoulder. His breathing sounded harsh and laboured and he emitted several sharp exclamations as if he was in pain. There followed a short walk, during which she could actually feel his breath on her neck. Then there was the sound of a heavy door, like that of a barn, sliding back and she was dumped unceremoniously on what seemed to be a pile of evil-smelling sacks. She heard his footsteps fade, followed by the crash of a door being pulled shut. Then silence. She had been left in the dark heaven knew where. But she wasn't alone. The scampering of tiny feet soon became audible all around her and moments later what felt like wet fur brushed the back of her hand. Inside her head she screamed and screamed . . .

* * *

It was after midnight before Kate and Hayden finished their task and Kate stretched back in the settee beside her husband with a yawn.

'So, what have we got?' she asked, even though she knew the answer already.

Hayden laid out the five properties they had printed off the laptop on the coffee table and both leaned forward to study each of them again.

'White Bridge Farm Cottage out at Blackford,' he said. 'Faradays, a cottage in Yarrow, Bentley's Halt, Ashcott, Walnut Cottage near Catcott and Wainrights at Westonzoyland. All possibles and all fit the criteria.'

Kate made a clucking sound with her tongue, then said, 'I reckon we can knock out White Bridge Farm. It's got five bedrooms, a study, two toilets and a stable block. Bit big for his needs, I would have thought. Also it's accessed via quite a long driveway shared with another farm, albeit some distance away.'

'So that leaves us with just the four properties.'

She nodded. 'That's if the boss goes with your idea.'

He snorted. 'She'd better. I had to sacrifice a nice steak in the fridge to get us to this point.'

'My heart bleeds for you. Let's just hope that if she does go with it, one of the addresses hits the mark or I'll have even more egg on my face than I've got at the moment.'

* * *

Debbie heard the footsteps returning what must have been several hours later, though she had no idea of the time as she couldn't see her watch. The rats had gone as soon as they had realised she was still very much alive. But there were other creatures in the barn. Spiders, bugs and flying things that didn't care whether she was alive or dead, as long as they could crawl all over her with impunity. And crawl they did.

'Hello again, Debbie,' he said. Bending over her, he carefully removed her gag and blindfold and straightened up. 'Had a nice rest?'

She could now see a little of her surroundings partially revealed by shards of moonlight filtering into the place from high-level windows and through cracks in the slatted wooden walls. It was a barn all right, but it looked as though it had been abandoned. Piles of rotting straw lay everywhere. There was an old wooden cart on its side in a corner and bits of rusted machinery poked up through the straw. She was sitting on wet hessian sacks with a wooden pillar supporting the roof a few feet behind her.

Her captor was wearing a full hood now, like a member of the Ku Klux Klan, and she could just catch the glint of his eyes through the slits. The fact that he had taken the trouble to conceal his face completely at least gave her reason to hope that he was not going to kill her. But she knew that death was not the only thing she had to fear at the hands of this twisted killer. She dreaded to think what else he might have in mind for her.

'Had time to reflect, have you?' he said, and his voice sounded harsh and strained, nothing like that of the smooth, assured man who had rung her several times at the offices of the *Clarion*.

She found herself starting to hyperventilate. 'What are you going to do to me?' she whispered.

'Do?' he retorted. 'What do you think I should do?'

'I-I don't know. Are you going to—?'

'Rape you?' he finished for her. 'Don't kid yourself, girlie, I have no interest in your pitiful body.'

He bent over her again and cupping one hand around her chin, held it in an over-tight grip. She could feel his sour breath on her cheek as he bent closer. 'You defied me,' he rasped. 'I told you to tone down the defamatory rhetoric on me in your rubbishy paper, but you thought you could ignore my instructions. What is it you called me in the last edition? A mindless thug. Rabid. Sadistic. Psychotic. Sick. Not very nice descriptions, are they?'

She tried not to think about the words she had used to describe him in the copy she had filed just that night. 'I-I'm sorry, I really am. It — it's what the editor wanted.'

There was a derisive snort. 'Well, I don't like it, and it will stop. Do you understand?'

She could hardly find her voice and finally blurted, 'I won't do it again, honest, but — but please don't hurt me.'

A long pause as he seemed to consider her apology. When he finally replied, it was certainly not what she wanted to hear. 'Sadly, everything we do in life has consequences, Debbie, you must see that. So I'm afraid there has to be a punishment. What do you think it should be? I have lots of innovative ideas.'

CHAPTER 17

'We have him!' Charlie Woo stormed into the CID office just as Kate and Hayden arrived in the morning. 'Both of you, upstairs now.'

Deidrie Hennessey was plainly cock-a-hoop when they entered the incident room where the troops were already assembling for what seemed to be an impromptu briefing. They could see that her eyes were practically on fire as she put up a large photograph on the whiteboard to one side of the room.

Dropping into vacant chairs among the rest of their colleagues, they studied the photograph with bated breath.

It was obviously a police custodial mugshot. It showed a lean-faced man in his late teens or early twenties with a pale, almost consumptive looking complexion and prominent cheekbones. He had black curly hair, receding at the front, and dark penetrating eyes that seemed to be alive and staring right back at them all. The thin-lipped mouth was slightly crooked and affected an arrogant, contemptuous sneer that suggested an inherent sense of superiority and his left cheek carried a long, narrow scar from just under his left eye to the corner of his mouth.

And she had seen that face before. Back in Cancun. At the Writer's Retreat. He was a lot younger in the photograph on the whiteboard, of course, but the basic facial characteristics were the same. The effect of the mugshot was to act as a stimulus to the memory she had unwittingly packed away at the back of her mind.

He had called himself Ash and had been quite a vociferous member of her syndicate. She had probably retained her memory of him for the way he had thrown so many personal questions at her at every opportunity in a by now familiar, drawling, sneering tone, regarding her job as a detective rather than about her interest in writing, which was what everyone was there for. Apart from taking her aback a little, she hadn't really read anything into his approach at the time. It had certainly irritated her, but she had simply dismissed him as just one of those people who nursed an obsession about anything to do with the police. Now she thought about it, though, she realised that there had been a point to his questions. He had been building up a profile of her in his mind and he must have been planning his sick game from the very first moment that he had clapped eyes on her. It all fitted perfectly. This was without a doubt the perp they were hunting.

The murmur in the room ceased as Hennessey tapped the photograph with a pointer.

'At last a positive result on the blood trace the forensic team recovered from Detective Sergeant O'Sullivan's car,' she said. 'NDNAD has now confirmed a match to this man whose DNA is on record from an ABH he committed in 1996 as a twenty-one-year-old. His name is Damian Grogan, now aged 47, born 1975. Further inquiries reveal that when convicted, he was a single man, living with his mother at an address on a sink estate in Cardiff and working as an assistant at a local library. His descriptive file then described him as highly intelligent, but a loner suffering from some form of narcissistic personality disorder. The pic you see is obviously very old. It's all we have, though. So you'll need to try and visualise what he will probably look like now. He is known to favour an anorak and a baseball cap. Pretty ordinary, I know, but we also believe he's driving a black Volvo XC40 with a white roof. Unfortunately we don't have an index number. It's possible it is a hired or nicked car. Just keep your eyes open for any vehicle of that description.

'Finally, we have already been in touch with South Wales Police, who will be providing us with more detailed up-to-date background information on Grogan shortly. His recorded home address is being checked out as we speak. All action teams will shortly be provided with copies of this photograph. I am also taking the unprecedented step of circulating this with a public appeal through all media channels and at a specially arranged press conference later today in view of the danger he presents to the public at large.'

She paused to allow her words to sink in, then added with emphasis, 'We have no idea where he has gone to ground, but he must have a bolthole somewhere not too far away from here. So let's get out there and find him before he takes another life. Any questions . . . ?'

Kate felt Hayden's elbow dig her in the ribs and when she glanced at him, he furrowed his brows and flicked his head towards Hennessey. It was plain that he was encouraging her to say her piece about the proposed property checks. But she took no notice and when the briefing was concluded ten to fifteen minutes later, she rose from her chair and followed Hennessey to her office at the end of the room, leaving Hayden to head downstairs, muttering his chagrin at being ignored.

Hennessey shot Kate a curious glance when she knocked on her door. 'What's this, Kate?' she asked. 'Problem?'

Kate smiled. 'No, ma'am, nothing like that. It's just an idea Hayden came up with, and which we have both been working on since to trace our killer.'

'Sounds grand. I'm all ears, so I am.'

Kate quickly explained what she and Hayden had deduced and laid copies of the four properties they had selected on the desk in front of the detective superintendent.

Hennessey scanned each of them in turn, then looked up with a slightly irritated expression. 'So if the pair of you have something to contribute, why didn't youse bring it up at the main briefing just now?'

Kate reddened. 'Hayden wanted to, but personally I wasn't sure how it would be received by everyone after the shitty reputation I seem to have acquired lately. So I thought I'd run it past you first.'

Hennessey smiled. 'Sure, it's not like you to have those sort of qualms, Kate. Where's the dynamic "don't give a damn" Kate I used to know?'

'She's playing things a bit more low-key at the moment.'

'Aha, and I wonder how long that will last,' Hennessey commented with a mischievous glint in her eyes. Then she tapped one of the sheets of paper in front of her. 'But back to this idea youse have been working on. I have to say it seems a wee bit off-the-wall to me, but we can't afford to pass up any chance of feeling this gobshite's collar. So I'm happy for you and Hayden to go ahead with it. I can't spare any more personnel to assist you, though.'

Kate nodded her relief. 'That'll be fine, ma'am.'

'One thing,' Hennessey added sharply. 'Just discreet checks. Nothing more. If you turn up anything, you radio in immediately for backup. This is one occasion when maverick actions are not an option. Is that understood?'

'Completely, ma'am,' Kate replied. She was stung a little by the 'maverick' reference, but nevertheless, she had the fingers of one hand crossed as she left the room.

* * *

It was raining heavily when Kate swung into a gateway near the village of Catcott. The entrance they had just passed was partially hidden by overhanging brambles, but the sign on the tree close to the road had been plain enough.

Walnut Cottage was the third property on their list. The previous two, Faradays and Bentley's Halt, had already been checked out and both found to be empty with no sign of life at either. Just two more properties to go, including this one, and their confidence in striking it lucky was beginning to ebb away.

Kate pulled on her waterproof and glanced critically at Hayden as he sat there staring gloomily out of the car window at the deep puddles already forming in the rutted surface of the road.

'It's only rain,' she joked. 'It'll be over in the morning.'

He scowled at her as he pulled on his own waterproof. 'Very funny,' he retorted. 'I hope you're still smiling when we get to the end of that driveway. It's going to be mud up to the eyeballs after this lot.'

But unbeknown to Hayden, he was about to get a reprieve. Kate had reached for the door handle and was in the process of throwing her door open when the radio suddenly blasted her call sign. Closing the door again, she responded with a quick acknowledgement.

'From Detective Inspector Woo,' the metallic voice said, 'cease present inquiry and attend the *Clarion* building in Bridgwater. Report of suspected kidnapping.'

Kate threw Hayden an astonished glance before confirming their attendance and settling back behind the wheel.

'So near and yet so far,' she muttered as she turned round in the gateway and headed back the way they had come. 'Looks like it's goodbye to further checks today.'

Hayden was suddenly a happy bunny again. 'Could be good news,' he quipped. 'Maybe someone has snatched your bosom pal, Debbie Moreton.'

'If they have, I hope no one pays the ransom!' Kate replied, without the slightest inkling of just how near the mark she was.

* * *

The editor of the *Clarion* was a short, plump individual with a florid face and just a thin frieze of hair around his pink, bald patch. He wore rimless, tinted spectacles and the pale blue eyes behind the lenses seemed to have difficulty meeting her gaze, constantly sliding away from her as he was talking. Not a very nice man, she decided, and not someone she would trust an inch.

He introduced himself as Theodore Rainer when he met them in the foyer, and said abruptly, 'It's Debbie. Debbie Moreton, my crime reporter. She's, er, gone missing. I think she's been abducted by someone.'

Kate stiffened, recalling how she and Hayden had joked about Moreton being the victim of the kidnapping on the way to Bridgwater a short time before.

'What makes you think she's been abducted?' Kate asked.

'I'll show you,' he said and led the way down a flight of concrete stairs on the other side of the reception desk, signed *Basement Car Park*.

Moreton's BMW was parked in a bay at the far end. Kate had seen it before at both the church and cider farm crime scenes and she recognised it immediately. She and Hayden followed Rainer's short quick steps to the driver's side of the car.

'Debbie obviously never went home when she left the office last night,' Rainer said. 'The engine of her car is stone cold and one of my staff found her set of keys lying under it.' He held up a bunch of keys on a ring. 'These keys.'

'How do you know they are hers?'

'Because of this.' He rattled the keys in front of her and shook out a plastic fob that was attached. It bore an unusual floral design, depicting a cluster of green leaves with serrated edges against a black background.

'Debbie once told me that when she was younger, she was well into the alternative or naturalist lifestyle as it is called today, which was originally typified by the sixties hippies culture. I recognised this tab at once,' he said. 'The design is of cannabis leaves.'

Kate nodded, well aware of what the leaves were and unsurprised by the revelation that Moreton had a colourful past.

'We've rung her flat repeatedly to find out why she hasn't come in this morning, but there's no answer.'

'Did anyone see her go?'

'That's the whole point. One of my sub-editors, Phil Maclean, did. He was taking a break at around eight last night after working on today's edition and was having a coffee by the window overlooking the street. He saw Debbie walk out of the car park entrance with a man but didn't think anything of it at the time.'

'Where is this Mr Maclean now?'

'He's upstairs. He had to come in this morning to finish off some work.'

'Then let's go and see him, shall we?'

Phil Maclean was a thin, grey-haired man with a stubbled chin and tobacco-stained teeth. He was smoking a cigarette when they entered the alcove in the corner of the newsroom that obviously served as his office and the front of his blue cardigan was covered in dandruff-like ash.

He smirked when Kate introduced herself and threw a meaningful look in Rainer's direction. Yeah, you bastard, Kate mused, I bet you've both had a pretty good laugh at my expense after all the derogatory comments your newspaper has put out about me. Well, now you need me for a change, so suck on that!

'You saw Debbie leave with a man last night, I understand?' Kate asked without a hint of hostility.

He nodded and stubbed out his cigarette in a tin lid. 'Yeah, around eight o'clock.' He frowned. 'She didn't actually leave *with* him, though. She was in front and he was right up close behind her. It was almost as if he was pushing her on. There's an alleyway down the side of the building and they went into it. Then after a pause I heard a car start up and this big SUV drove out and headed off towards Highbridge.'

Kate started. 'What sort of SUV?'

He shrugged. 'I'm not good on cars, though it looked like a VW or maybe a Volvo. Also, I remember it was black with a white roof.'

Kate glanced quickly at Hayden, then asked, 'You didn't get the number?'

'Why would I bother? As far as I knew, she was going out with some guy, maybe on a date.'

Kate controlled her excitement with an effort. 'Did you see what the man looked like?'

Another shrug. 'Just a tall guy dressed in an anorak and a baseball cap. Didn't notice much else.'

'Any CCTV cameras covering your building?' Hayden put in.

Rainer shook his head. 'We never thought there was any need for them. After all, who would want to break into the offices of a newspaper?'

'Would seem to have been a bit of a short-sighted policy now that this has happened, wouldn't you agree?'

Rainer bristled but didn't respond to Hayden's criticism. Instead he turned to Kate again. 'So what happens now, Sergeant? This is obviously a very worrying situation.'

Kate nodded. 'Well, we'll obviously do all we can to find Miss Moreton, including physically checking her address and circulating her details to all patrols. We'll also be launching a public appeal for information through the media, which you can help us with. But frankly, with the very limited information you've been able to give us, there's not a lot more we can do.'

He shook his head desperately. 'You just don't understand, do you, Sergeant? She is my chief crime reporter and a very good one. As such, she is a vital member of my staff. We need her found quickly, not only for her sake, but for that of this newspaper as well.'

Kate studied him coldly. It was apparent that Rainer's concerns were more to do with the continued operation of the *Clarion* than the welfare of Debbie Moreton.

'We'll do all we can to get her back safely, sir,' she replied, 'and hopefully, your deadlines won't be too badly affected in the meantime.'

His eyes narrowed, plainly not sure how to take her answer. Nevertheless, he let it pass.

'So, what is your opinion on her abduction? Do you think the Levels killer who has been contacting her all the time could be responsible?'

'It's possible, yes, but we have no evidence to support that yet. It's best we keep an open mind.'

'And do you think she could be in any danger?'

Kate nodded grimly, happy to deliver bad news to the nasty, little man who had caused her so much grief.

'I have to be honest, Mr Rainer,' she replied. 'It's very possible that under the circumstances her life could be at real risk. We can only hope we will find her in time.'

'Was it really necessary saying that to Rainer?' Hayden snapped as they left the building.

'No,' Kate said tightly, 'but very satisfying all the same. Anyway, he will be able to draw his own conclusions when he or one of his lackeys attends Deidrie Hennessey's press conference. From what we've learned, however, I think it's fair to assume that Moreton's abduction is down to none other than Grogan. Exactly why he would have chosen to take her is not clear. Especially as she has been functioning as his unofficial biographer up until now. But he obviously had his reasons and knowing his track record, I wouldn't give much for her chances.'

* * *

Debbie Moreton had passed a traumatic night lying curled up on the pile of sacks, listening to the rain on the roof of the barn. Scared of every movement, every rustle or squeak she heard around her. But somehow, despite her nightmare surroundings, she had managed to drift off. She awoke suddenly when she heard the sound of the barn door opening to find that it was daylight and her captor was standing there again, still hooded and studying her fixedly.

She saw that he was carrying a small canvas bag this time.

'Found this in one of the sheds when I first arrived,' he said, delving into the bag. 'Some good tools in here too. It's a crying shame that someone simply chose to dump them.'

Rummaging around inside the bag obviously for effect, he produced a rusted jawed implement of about eight inches in length and held it up in front of her.

'Mini wire cutters, I would think,' he went on. 'But I'm not very good at identifying tools. Not much practice, you see.' He forced them open and ran a finger down the lower jaw. 'Still quite sharp though.'

'Now,' he said, 'are you right or left-handed?' He laid the cutters on the ground and rummaged in his pocket, producing the key to her handcuffs. 'Let's get these cuffs off first and then you can tell me, eh?'

For a moment she just stared at him, her eyes wide with horror as it dawned on her what he was contemplating.

'Please, no,' she choked, levering herself backwards on the heels of her shoes in a desperate attempt to get away from him. Only to find herself up against the wooden pillar behind her.

He made no immediate move towards her. But he shook his head and manufactured a loud sigh. 'Oh dear, so you don't want to tell me, eh? Well, let me put it another way. Do you value your right pinkie finger most or your left?'

CHAPTER 18

George Brompton had been a keen photographer all his life and he had won several prestigious photography awards. Landscapes, wildlife or family portraits were not for him, though. He was into architectural photography. Modern warehouses to ruined country barns, iron bridges to stone viaducts. They were the subjects that captivated him. He would spend hours trying to capture the essence of what they stood for, using a variety of lenses, filters and shutter speeds to create what he saw as the stark beauty of angle and form. He would travel for miles in his home county of Somerset to find the most interesting buildings or other structures and the Somerset Levels always seemed to draw him in. In particular, he found the contrast between the sharp, often ugly angles of the manmade structures that reared up in the mist and the soft, often haunting rural environment of bog and willow totally inspiring. It was small wonder that now retired from his thirty-year 'imprisonment' in a Bristol factory making motor accessories, he spent much of his time wandering the countryside in gumboots and waterproof with his beloved Canon 35 mm camera and a pocket crammed with corned beef sandwiches like the true anorak he was.

But he got more than he bargained for the morning he set out across the Levels from his home in Cheddar to check out the old pumping station near Westonzoyland, and the problem had nothing to do with architectural photography.

To start with, his old Renault hadn't the luxury of sat nav. A committed technophobe, he wouldn't have had a clue as to how to use it anyway. Even the mobile in his pocket was there solely for the purpose of making and receiving calls. So the whole concept of electronic mapping was well beyond him, and as a consequence, he had resorted to the tried and tested method of finding his way with the use of a local map. He managed to get as far as the hamlet of Shapwick. But somehow he must have taken a wrong turn, ending up completely lost on a backroad somewhere within a few miles of his destination. It was then that he spotted the pale figure stumbling unsteadily and seemingly disorientated along the roadside verge in the rain towards him. That it was a young woman on foot was not in itself surprising. That she appeared to be barefoot was a bit more so. But what really held his shocked attention was the fact that she was also completely naked. Then before he could recover from his shock, she stepped out in front of him, and promptly collapsed on to the road. Slamming to a stop, he jumped out of his car and ran over to her, stripping off his coat on the way. As he bent over her, he saw to his horror something else quite gross. She was totally bald, and her scalp was covered in what appeared to be fresh cuts and abrasions suggesting her head had only just been shaved.

Helping her up into a sitting position, he slipped his coat around her shoulders and fumbled for his mobile, holding her there with one arm.

'What on earth's happened to you, love?' he exclaimed, punching the emergency number into the device twice before he could hit the right figures.

'Punished me,' she whispered.

'Who punished you?'

She muttered something he could not catch.

'What's your name?'

'Debbie,' she replied. 'Debbie Moreton.' Then she passed out as the operator on his phone asked sharply, 'Which service do you require?'

'Ambulance,' he replied in a panicky voice, then added, 'and you'd better get the police too.'

* * *

'So how is she?' Woo asked wearily from the corner of his office desk. 'This business gets worse and worse.'

'Under sedation, guv,' Detective Constable Jamie Foster replied. 'Hospital will be keeping her in overnight under observation. They can't find any serious injuries, but they say she's suffering from shock, exposure and some cuts and abrasions to her feet.'

Kate grunted. 'She certainly got plenty of exposure out there starkers in the rain. Her shit of a boss won't be happy about her being kept in, though. As he reminded me, he has a newspaper to run.'

'He was lucky she filed copy for this morning's edition before all this happened,' Hayden put in, nodding towards the paper lying open on Woo's desk. 'Not that the story she has produced does us any favours, and certainly Grogan won't be impressed by it.'

'Did you get anything out of Moreton about what happened?' Woo said to Foster.

'Yeah, a little. After I responded to the three nines, the paramedics crew let me travel in the ambulance with her when I said she needed protection. She told me a man wearing an anorak of some sort and a baseball cap pulled down low over his face, which must have been this arsehole Grogan, forced her into his car at knifepoint. He then blindfolded her and left her handcuffed in some barn out on the Levels. He later returned, hooded this time, and threatened to cut off one of her fingers with a pair of bolt cutters, then changed his mind and shaved off all her hair instead. After that he stripped her, dumped her clothes somewhere and blindfolded her again before abandoning her on the side of the road near where she was spotted by the witness.'

'Did she say why he abducted her in the first place?'

'Some sort of punishment, she said. Something to do with the way she had described him in her newspaper stories. He apparently said he knew where she lived and that next time she offended him he would find her and cut her throat.'

'He obviously stripped her and dumped her there naked as a form of humiliation,' Hayden commented. 'The business with the wire cutters was just to frighten her. The last thing he would have wanted was to cut off her fingers and prevent her continuing to biographise his infamy.'

'A nice beauty. Did she have any idea where he took her?' Woo asked.

Foster shook his head. 'Just a barn somewhere, but it couldn't have been far from where he dropped her as she said it only took a few minutes.'

Woo snorted. 'And what's a few minutes? Ten? Fifteen? Half an hour? If she was blindfolded she couldn't have known for sure, which means he could be hunkered down anywhere.'

'Maybe not, guv,' Kate pointed out. 'Presumably the boss told you Hayd and I had drawn up a list of properties that Grogan could be using as his bolthole?'

Woo nodded. 'Just before she went to her press conference. What about it?'

'Well we were just about to have a look at one called Walnut Cottage near the village of Catcott when we got called to this kidnapping. Then there's another place, Wainwrights at Westonzoyland, closer still to where Moreton's rescuer found her, which could be an even better bet.'

'Okay, then you'd better carry on with what you were doing. We have nothing to lose, have we? In the meantime, I'll have a plod stationed outside Moreton's room at the hospital just in case Grogan decides to show up again and I'll nip upstairs to bring the boss up to date.' He made a face. 'After all, I'm not strictly part of this investigation anymore, am I? And Kate,' he called after her as she and Hayden turned for the door, 'try bringing us all some good news next time, will you?'

* * *

The rain had turned into a penetrating drizzle and Hayden had lapsed into melancholy in the front passenger seat by the time Kate pulled into the gateway opposite the entrance to Walnut Cottage again.

Seeing his depressed mood, she couldn't resist winding him up still more. 'Just think, Hayd,' she said, pulling on her waterproof, 'you won't have to hose the garden tonight.'

He threw her a sour look. 'You never give up, do you?' he growled. 'You really are a laugh a minute.'

Kate was still chuckling when they climbed out of the car and crossed the road, but her laughter soon died when they reached the entrance to the property. She grabbed his arm and squeezed it hard. As Hayden had feared earlier, the ground was sodden from the constant rain, and a line of tell-tale marks was clearly imprinted in the soft, sticky surface.

'Car tyres,' she breathed, peering along the narrow driveway, which tunnelled its way through thick undergrowth. 'Someone's been here recently.'

Hayden bent down to study them. 'Looks like a heavy vehicle,' he said, 'and the lines are irregular and cut across each other, which suggests the same vehicle was driven in and out on more than one occasion.'

They stared at each other and Kate was aware of her quickening heartbeat.

Then Hayden sniffed. 'We shouldn't read too much into a set of tyre marks. Okay, so the other two properties were empty and this one might turn out to be occupied. But so what? It could have been rented quite legitimately.'

She pulled on an overhanging branch. 'Then why haven't they cut back all these brambles? Whoever was here has

206

just forced their car through the narrow gap. You can see that the brambles are broken or torn. It's as if they wanted to keep the driveway obscured.'

He shrugged. 'Maybe they've only just moved in and haven't had time to do the business.'

Kate nodded. 'Or not,' she added. 'So let's take a look, shall we? But in the words of the boss, discreetly.'

The driveway was only a hundred yards or so in length. But going was not easy in the mud and their shoes were plastered by the time they got to the end and emerged from the tunnel.

Walnut Cottage was not a particularly attractive property. It had a red tiled roof and grey stone walls, which were stained with patches of some kind of green mould. It stood in the middle of an overgrown yard with a dismal outlook of marshy fields on three sides and the scrubby woodland, through which they had just made their way, at the front. There was a big, detached barn to one side of the cottage and several small wooden sheds with corrugated iron roofs on the other. The whole place screamed neglect, yet someone was obviously living there, as there was a thin trail of smoke issuing from the single brick chimney.

Kate pointed towards the barn. 'We'll check that first,' she said, 'then make our way around the back.'

To the left of the driveway, the woodland extended along the edge of the yard to a point almost level with the barn. It provided them with some natural cover. But scores of rooks in the branches of the taller trees set up a discordant clamour of alarm the moment they began to push their way through the wet undergrowth. Then they erupted from their nests in panic and began circling noisily above their heads. Forced to freeze for several minutes in the hope that the cawing would die down, they watched the front door of the cottage anxiously to see if the avian outcry had attracted unwelcome attention. No one appeared, however, and they were relieved when the birds suddenly decided to fly off en masse, as if to find someone else to annoy, allowing them to move on. A few more feet and they reached a point almost level with the corner of the building. They stopped again. About a couple of yards of bare ground lay between the woodland and the doors of the barn, which they needed to cross diagonally and in full view of the end window of the cottage. This couldn't have been more risky. But they were left with no other alternative. Kate studied the window for several seconds. Seeing no sign of any movement inside, she turned to Hayden behind her to give the all clear.

Moments later they were at the front of the barn and prising the sliding door open sufficiently to be able to slip through.

'Nothing,' Hayden commented gloomily almost straight-away and Kate grimaced. It was just a typical barn half-filled at one end with bales of rotting straw, an old, overturned cart and bits of rusted machinery. There was no sign of a Volvo car, not even any giveaway tyre marks in the inches-deep filth covering the floor.

'Back to the drawing board then,' Hayden went on, 'unless Wainwrights at Westonzoyland turns up trumps.'

Kate nodded, clearly dispirited, and she was on the point of turning back to the barn door, when something caught her eye. Crossing quickly to a pile of sacks close to the right-hand wall, she jerked her torch from her pocket and bent down to examine it.

'Look at this,' she said triumphantly.

Hayden joined her and stared at the tiny sparkling object in the palm of her hand, which had clearly drawn her to the spot.

'You've got good eyesight,' he commented. 'Looks like an earring.'

'It *is* an earring. A stainless steel stud in the shape of a frog and inlaid with marcasite. I spotted its glitter. Moreton must have lost it when Grogan dumped her in here.'

'How did you make that out? It could be anyone's.'

'I'm a woman, Hayd, and I remember seeing studs like this in Moreton's ears when she accosted me at the cider farm.

They're exactly the sort of weird design I'd have expected someone like her to wear. Also, there's this.' She reached down and held up a handful of something from among the pile of sacks. 'Pink hair, my man. Moreton's pink hair. This is where he cut it off and then shaved her head. We've found him, Hayd. This is the bastard's bolthole.'

Hayden didn't answer. He already had his radio in his hand and was calling up the control room. But it was a call that was suddenly interrupted by the roar of an engine. They both reached the door at the same time. The black XC40 Volvo with the white roof was emerging from somewhere at the back of the cottage and heading out at speed. They were just in time to see it career past them across the rough ground before it disappeared down the driveway towards the main road.

* * *

Patrick O'Leary was tired. He had driven all the way down to Somerset from Liverpool in his big ten-wheeler artic. He'd had very little sleep on the long crossing from Belfast and he could hardly wait to get to his destination at the factory deep in the wilds of the Somerset Levels. He knew the road well. It was a regular route for him and he was fully aware of the fact that the roads across the flat, marshy countryside were poor and liable to subsidence. For that reason he was driving at a sensible speed. But the problem with articulated lorries is the fact that even at reasonable speeds, stopping on a sixpence is impossible. Despite airbrakes, sudden heavy braking could also result in wheel lockup and the dreaded jack knifing of the trailer, especially on a wet road.

He didn't know Walnut Cottage. Why should he? He wasn't even aware of the entrance. For that reason, he was caught completely by surprise when the Volvo emerged from it at speed directly in front of his lorry only yards away. He automatically hit the brakes, but even as he did so, he knew it was too late. The huge rig locked up immediately on the wet, slippery tarmac. Going into a screeching skid, it mounted the verge and ploughed into the woodland bordering the road, taking out fencing, trees and bushes on the way like a runaway tank and sending scores of rooks erupting into the sky with raucous cries. At the same moment the trailer began its inevitable swing across the road, crashing into the car with a force that crumpled the front end like cardboard and slammed it back into the corner of the driveway where it came to rest with its rear end partially buried in the undergrowth.

A brief silence followed, broken only by the hiss of steam rising from the lorry's fractured radiator. Then a series of loud cracks and O'Leary stumbled out of the undergrowth like a drunken man after managing to kick the door of his cab open and clamber out. His face was ashen with shock and he had a large cut to his temple, which was bleeding profusely. But there was a murderous look on his chubby face that boded ill for the person who had just wrecked his lorry and nearly killed him. At the same moment, Kate and Hayden emerged from the driveway at a run, having heard the sound of the collision as they left the barn.

'Bloody eejit,' O'Leary blazed as they all converged on the Volvo. 'Just pulled out in front of me.'

But his words died on his tongue when he joined the two detectives by the car. The engine compartment was unrecognisable as such. It was just a mess of tangled, distorted metal glistening with black diesel. The windscreen was also smashed in and the driver's door badly buckled. Yet the front passenger door was hanging wide open and they could see at a glance that the car was empty. Grogan had disappeared.

* * *

'So how the hell did he get out of that?' DI Don Tappin, exclaimed, arriving at the scene much later. He stared at the wrecked Volvo, which was in the process of being moved by a local garage, then cast a glance at the articulated lorry with its cab still buried in the undergrowth. 'The swine must have a charmed life.'

'I doubt whether he would have survived at all if he'd been in any car other than a Volvo,' Kate commented soberly. 'But SOCO found quite a bit of blood on the driver's seat and dash during their initial examination, so he didn't get off scot-free.'

Tappin threw a quick glance upwards at the police helicopter ascribing a slow circle through the leaden sky. 'He is still away on his toes, though, isn't he? And the chopper will be pulled off when it gets dark.'

Kate bit her lip, acutely conscious once again of how bad things looked. 'Well, we do have roadblocks set up at key points in case he thinks of nicking a car,' she said defensively, 'and dog teams are still out on the marshes doing a sweep. What else can we do?'

Tappin watched the breakdown truck pull away with the Volvo on the back, its amber light contrasting with the flashing strobes of the police traffic cars blocking the road on each side of the accident scene. 'Not a lot, I agree. But I don't think the boss will be too happy to learn what's happened here when she finishes the press conference she's fronting at present. At least those hyenas don't seem to have got wind of it yet, which is one small compensation. When they find out, we'll come in for more stick than ever. We'll be portrayed as a right Fred Karno's outfit.'

'Don't I know it,' Kate muttered. 'Been there already. Got the T-shirt *and* seen the video.'

He grinned. 'So I hear.' He clapped her on the shoulder. 'But don't take it to heart, Kate. You know what they say?'

She threw him a smouldering glance, guessing that he was about to come out with the cynicism she had used so often on others in the past. 'Yeah, I know,' she retorted drily. 'If you can't take a joke, you shouldn't have joined.'

He chuckled. 'Got it in one, girl,' he said, then abruptly changed the subject. 'Do we know how the driver of the artic is?'

Kate shrugged, her disconsolateness plain and Hayden answered for her. 'The ambulance crew reckoned he'd just got a few cuts and bruises, plus some mild concussion, but they're doing the usual tests at the hospital as we speak. As for his wagon, it will be a while before we are able to get it moved and the road reopened, but there's apparently a commercial breakdown truck equipped with heavy lifting equipment on its way.'

'Well, it's good news about the driver anyway. As for the artic, that's plod territory, so I think we can safely leave that with them. Have we had time to check out the property itself yet?'

'We did a cursory sweep with some uniforms. So far we've found evidence to suggest that Debbie Moreton *was* held in the barn. We also stumbled on an incinerator at the back containing the blackened remains of what looked like women's clothes and a wire trap with a couple of dead rooks inside, which explains where the killer sourced his avian calling cards. SOCO are currently carrying out a forensic search of both the cottage and barn, but it's too early for any result yet.'

'And the car?'

'SOCO only did a preliminary scan at the scene. Rain stopped play. They'll do a more thorough job later when the motor is under cover at the car pound.'

He grinned. 'Well, you seem to have covered everything, Kate. We might make a detective of you yet.'

'Two words, guv', she said, raising two fingers. 'First one begins with "P" and the second word is off.'

CHAPTER 19

Grogan was exhausted. He was not built for running. The blisters that had formed on one side of his face from the boiling water that had been thrown over him by Julia Thorogood were burning afresh from the continuous rain, which had already soaked him through to his underclothes. He had also sustained a nasty gash to his temple after impacting something in the car from the collision with the articulated lorry, and the wound continued to smart and bleed.

Just getting clear of the cottage had been the only thought in his head at the time. But the downside was that, although he had managed to get away, he had ended up in just the clothes he stood up in. To make matters worse, half the local police force now seemed to be breathing down his neck. That included a bloody helicopter.

How that bitch of a detective had managed to find him, he just could not understand. He'd got a real shock when he'd glanced out of his living room window to see her and that dipstick of a husband sneaking into his barn. But the upside was that he had at least eluded capture even if he had totalled the Volvo in the process. He snarled defiantly back into the rain. If Kate Lewis thought the game was over because of what had happened, she had another think coming. It went on regardless. He already had his next target in mind. He just needed the time and the place to take stock of the present situation, work out how to overcome this major setback and rebuild his strategy before carrying out that vital next hit.

At which point he was given a stark reminder that this would not be so easy when he was suddenly forced to duck back into the ruins of the abandoned wooden stable in which he had taken temporary refuge as the helicopter swooped in low overhead. Simultaneously he picked up the sound of excited barking a lot too close for comfort. He swore under his breath. First the all-seeing eye in the sky, probably equipped with thermal imaging, and now a load of police dogs closing in on the ground. The odds against him were mounting up. He had to find somewhere safe to lie low. It would be dark soon, which should at least give him a bit of an edge over the police. But it would also present problems of its own. Stumbling around this treacherous countryside with its deep bogs, rhynes and lines of barbed-wire fencing was not to be recommended in the dark. He would have to find shelter and rest up until it was light enough to find his way and he knew just the place for that. Somewhere the police would never expect to find him.

When the 'whoosh, whoosh, whoosh' of the helicopter's rotor faded, he took a chance and stumbled out of cover, heading along a barely discernible track towards a five-barred gate and the warm, dry refuge that awaited him just a few hundred yards away.

* * *

'Gordon Bennett, I think I've cracked it!'

Kate was in a deep sleep when Hayden shot up in bed with an exultant shout and jerked her into instant wakefulness.

'What the hell's the matter with you?' she rapped angrily, her rude awakening almost sending her heart into ectopic overdrive. 'You trying to give me a coronary?'

Glancing at the bedside clock, she saw it was just after midnight. In all the years they had been together she had

214

never known him to wake up in the middle of the night and for a moment she thought he must be having a nightmare. To Hayden, sleep was almost a religion, to be adhered to until well into daylight hours unless he was extracted from what he liked to call his 'pit' by brute force.

He tossed his head impatiently. 'Just listen,' he said. 'Remember you felt there was some sort of connection between Grogan's three main murder victims and asked me to think about it? Well, with all that's been happening in the past twenty-four hours, the whole thing ended up being pushed to the back of my mind. But without my being aware of it, the question must have been whirling round and round in the depths of my subconscious ever since, and it's suddenly come up with the answer.'

She wriggled herself up into a more comfortable position with her back against the headboard, rubbing her eyes. 'What the hell are you gabbling about? I was fast asleep, you pillock.'

He ignored the censure and simply carried on. 'You see, what had been throwing our deliberations out of kilter was the fact that one of the victims was a cleric. It was not difficult to see a connection between a purveyor of alcohol and a prostitute. For a religious purist, prostitution would automatically fall into the Biblical category of lust. The selling and consumption of alcohol would similarly be regarded by many in the church as equally sinful. Perhaps even an extension of the seven deadly sins listed in the Bible. But a priest didn't seem to fit anywhere in this. As far as anyone knew, the Rev Strange was a decent God-fearing man without a stain on his character. So on the face of it, this put paid to your theory of a link between him and the other two victims.'

Kate muttered an expletive at his verbose analysis. 'For flip's sake, get to the point, will you, Hayd.'

'The point, old girl, is that we have been looking at things from entirely the wrong standpoint. The murders have nothing to do with religious fervour. Grogan isn't driven by some personal crusade against sin. His motives are totally personal.

I've just been on the downstairs phone to the incident room night-cover crew. It seems that new information has been received from local police sources re Grogan's background.

'In brief, it reveals that he had a deprived upbringing and suffered neglect and abuse throughout his childhood. This gave rise to mental instability and the narcissistic personality disorder the guv'nor spoke about. His father was a lay preacher at the local church but was a prize hypocrite and was regularly over the side with a number of different women. This "good Christian" also nursed a secret gambling addiction and finally walked out on the family after his debts reduced them to poverty. As for Grogan's mother, she was a violent alcoholic who physically assaulted her son on a regular basis. She also sold herself to successive men to pay for her alcoholism. She apparently broke her neck after mysteriously falling down the stairs some years ago. Her death was recorded as accidental at the inquest, but you have to wonder about that, knowing what we know of Grogan. Do you see where I am heading?'

She was wide awake now. 'We're talking payback time.'

'Exactly. Grogan was not motivated by a personal grudge against the victims themselves. All three were chosen not because of *who* they were, but *what* they were. Everything's been about what they represented in his twisted mind. Occupations he saw as being responsible for the ruination of his childhood and his future ambitions—'

She released her breath in a low whistle. 'The church, hence, the murder of the Rev Strange. Alcohol, which explains why he killed Wilf Carpenter. Prostitution, which indicates why he murdered Marianne Dawson.'

'I rest my case.'

There was an excited glint in her eyes. 'Excellent work, Hayd, I'll give you that. But your analysis only relates to the three targets we know about. He claimed there were going to be six, so what about the other three?'

He grimaced. 'Well, one would possibly be someone involved in the gambling industry, in view of his father's addiction, which impoverished the family.'

'And the other two?'

'Still working on it.'

'Well, following the same train of thought, maybe I can help you there. He was arrested and humiliated in a court of law, wasn't he? How about a judge or an advocate of some sort? Though my money would be on a judge.'

'But which judge?'

'That's the problem. Even if your theory is right, how the hell do we identify his next three hits before he does it for us?'

'He's on the run, Kate. His bolthole is no longer available to him. He has no transport and in this weather, without shelter and a change of clothes, he is likely to die from exposure. He is probably going to save his skin and keep on running.'

She looked doubtful. 'A reassuring thought. Do you really believe that?'

'No, I don't.'

'And neither do I.' She yawned. 'But we can see what the boss thinks in the morning. Now *please*, can we get some sleep.'

He also yawned. 'I won't argue with that.'

* * *

Grogan had seen the convoy of police cars and vans leave Walnut Cottage from his crouched position in the undergrowth opposite the driveway. Then he had waited patiently for an hour before making his move. Darting across the road, he crept through the woodland to within a few yards of the front door where he saw a solitary police patrol car drawn up on the hardstanding with one uniformed copper inside. So the forensic team must have finished its evidence gathering for now and a single officer had been left on site to prevent any unauthorised access. More as a token gesture, he mused. Probably to keep the press out. Well, he wouldn't bother the copper if the copper didn't bother him.

He smiled without humour. He'd taken a gamble on returning to the cottage, but he'd reasoned that it was the last thing the police would expect him to do after he had only just managed to escape from it. Furthermore, he needed some dry clothes, somewhere safe to attend to the gash in his forehead and his facial blisters, and something to eat. What better place for all this than the one he knew so well?

Following the woodland along the edge of the hard-standing to a point level with the barn just as Kate and Hayden had done hours before, he checked to make sure the copper hadn't left his car and loped across the hardstanding to the side of the cottage. Confident that in the darkness and the rain he was all but invisible. He knew the rear bed-room fanlight would be open. He always left it like that for the fresh air. He slipped a hand inside and fiddled with the main window catch until he was able to pull it open. Then he climbed over the sill into the room and shut the window behind him.

Once inside, he quickly stripped off his clothes and gave himself a vigorous rubdown with one of the large towels from the bathroom next door. Next, doctoring the gash on his head with some antiseptic and a plaster, he treated the blisters on his face with some more of the ointment he always carried with him in his haversack.

Then he returned to the bedroom and raided his ward-robe for some fresh warm clothes and a change of shoes. He was already starting to feel a lot better. Moving to the kitchen he helped himself to a couple of pies from the fridge before boiling a kettle for a flask of coffee. All of which he slipped into his haversack with his compass and a detailed map of the local area. He was bolting down a double cheese sandwich when he spotted the glow on the edge of the window. He ducked down just in time. The beam of a powerful torch swept around the kitchen and heavy boots crunched in the gravel outside. The copper didn't stay long but carried on with his circuit of the cottage seconds later, apparently satis-fied all was secure. If only he had known . . .

218

Grogan spent a fitful night in the warmth of the cottage, dossing fully clothed on the settee with one ear cocked for the slightest sound, but he was not disturbed again. Before first light, tired but resolute, he got up and paid a visit to the small freezer in the kitchen. Extracting a small frozen parcel in a plastic bag, he studied it closely for a moment, before slipping it into his haversack. The corpses of the pair of rooks he had trapped and killed a few days before would be nicely thawed by the time he got to where he was going, and the one he was saving for the second hit should keep for another day at least, even if it was a bit ripe by then. Finally, he slipped out the back door and headed across the rear yard of the property to the back gate, clad in a hooded waterproof and baseball cap with the haversack strapped to his back. Once through, he headed off into the weather's cold, wet embrace, a sinister shadow merging into the rain and a newly risen mist like one of the wraiths or will-o'-the-wisps that were said to have haunted this marshy wilderness since time began . . .

* * *

Dominic Martin loved his quarter-acre landscaped garden and the ultra-modern house with its predominance of glass and steel that towered over it. Even in the grey day which had followed the night of heavy rain, it looked special. Reasonably close to the picturesque village of Wedmore, yet still a sensible distance away, it was relatively isolated. This afforded him the privacy that was essential to him. But at the same time it gave him the convenience of the village shops, post office and pubs whenever he needed them. He was very satisfied with the life he shared off and on with a succession of girlfriend visitors and the regular parties he held around the big indoor swimming pool.

As he took his morning shower, he reflected on how good life had been to him since he had thrown up his regular job in accountancy three years before. His manufacturing business, which supplied gaming products, including fruit machines, roulette tables and other related equipment to casinos and amusement arcades throughout the UK from his factories in Bristol and Birmingham, had so far made him one of the richest men in the south west. He couldn't have been more grateful to the naive punters who couldn't resist the lure of his custom-built products with their flashing lights and exciting bell notes. One person's weakness was another's success story, he liked to boast to the young 'fillies' who hung on his every word during their short stays in his luxurious pad. Addictions, he declared, were big money makers and morals were for the birds.

Martin had never met Damian Grogan. Had never even heard of him. He was certainly not the sort of person he would have invited to one of his parties. Damian Grogan didn't know Martin personally either. He had picked out his name and what he did for a living from an old magazine feature on Wedmore during one of his internet searches at the local library, which had also provided him with a nice picture of Martin's house. But as far as Grogan was concerned, it made him a perfect choice for his next hit. Just as the Rev Strange, Wilf Carpenter and Marianne Dawson had been before.

He had not had an opportunity to reconnoitre 'Dollar House', as Martin liked to call his luxurious pad, which obviously made the next job a lot more risky. But he knew that time was running out on him. He could no longer afford to waste it carrying out an initial recce, then a watching brief for an hour or two, as he preferred. He was conscious of the fact that failing to take these preparatory steps had almost ended in disaster for him with his other supplementary hits, like the detective sergeant and the woman with the terrier dog. But he had to take the risk and act quickly and decisively if he was to complete his game successfully and destroy Kate Lewis's reputation for good.

It didn't occur to him that the game itself was no longer just a battle of wits between himself and the female detective he had come to hate so much, but that it involved a whole team of detectives, which meant she would no longer carry the can if the investigation ended in failure. He was no longer thinking rationally, however. His obsession to finish things quickly before the police got lucky had become his main driver and he couldn't see beyond it. Nevertheless, as any wild animal forced into a corner tends to become a lot more dangerous when it has nothing left to lose, so Damian Grogan had become a lot more dangerous than he had ever been, and unfortunately for Dominic Martin, Dollar House was an open invitation to him.

The property was a cinch to get into. No alarms. No guard dogs. Not a single camera. Grogan had arrived on a bicycle stolen from outside a pub, pedalling furiously for twenty-five minutes through the mist along a series of droves and tracks he had already plotted on the Ordnance Survey map in his haversack. He had dumped the bicycle in a nearby rhyne before slipping through a half-open side gate. The sound of loud music had drawn him to the half-open French doors. The conservatory inside turned out to access a huge lounge area, furnished in contemporary style, with brightly painted walls hung with garish, abstract paintings. Half a dozen different slot machines stood somewhat incongruously against one wall, their flashing lights inviting attention. A long green baize table, equipped with a roulette wheel laden with neatly stacked chips and packs of cards stood against another. Obviously Martin liked to gamble with guests in his free time as well as manufacturing gaming products. But where was he? A massive television stood in the centre of the room and was belting out Sky News for all it was worth. Yet there was no one in sight.

Slipping off his haversack and dumping it into a chair by the door, Grogan stared about him with a heavy frown, thrown for a moment. He'd expected to find someone in the room at least. Otherwise, why would the television have been switched on? It didn't make sense. Surely Martin hadn't gone out and left it on by mistake? It was Sunday, so he would hardly be at work. A big maroon Daimler parked in a driveway to the right of the house certainly suggested he was still at home.

The answer came a moment later. 'And who the bloody hell are you?'

The voice was sharp and it came from directly behind him. Wheeling round, he saw a short, chubby man standing in another open doorway on the far side of the room. He was dressed in just a white towelling robe and had been in the process of drying his hair with a towel. Now he froze in the act, his eyes wide with shock.

Who would have reacted next to the situation it is impossible to say, but there was an unexpected intervention. The name 'Damian Grogan' suddenly spat from the television like an expletive. Jerking his head round, Grogan found his own face staring back at him from the screen as the newsreader continued with the story the channel was giving out in the usual dramatic tones: '. . . dangerous man . . . public not to approach . . . ring police immediately . . .' He picked out the words almost in a daze. The police must have matched the blood he'd left in the detective's car. They knew who he was. Worse still, so did his prospective victim.

'You're — you're that man!' Martin gasped.

Grogan tore his gaze from the screen and launched himself across the room even as Martin got the words out. But he was a fraction too late. The door slammed shut in his face. Wrenching it open again, he saw the hem of the white towelling robe disappear through yet another door on the opposite side of a tiled hallway.

Grogan was through the second door before Martin could slam it behind him. He found himself in a small home gym, complete with all the necessary fitness equipment, including a treadmill, barbells in a rack, a rowing machine and a couple of punch bags suspended from the ceiling. He'd expected Martin to be trying to hide somewhere, but he was in for a surprise. The presence of the gym should have told him something, but it just hadn't clicked.

In fact, the little man was standing in the middle of the floor, legs apart, hands on hips, waiting for him with a disturbing air of confidence about him, and a grim smile playing on his lips.

'Come on, big boy,' he invited. 'Why don't you try me out?'

Grogan's rush was met with a pile-driver of a fist, which slammed into his solar plexus. It sent him reeling back against the wall, gasping for breath. Before he could recover, Martin was on to him, fists jabbing repeatedly into his face. One blow caught him in the mouth, another above his right eye and a third on the side of his nose, drawing blood.

As he dropped to one knee in a partial daze, his intended target danced around him in his bare feet, taunting him further.

'Don't work out much, do you,' he sneered. 'I should have warned you I box for my local club. I'm pretty fit too.'

Grogan didn't answer. He didn't waste words. He simply crouched there, hunched over and groaning slightly, as if in pain. Just like the bird that pretends to have broken one wing to entice a predator away from its nest. Martin on the other hand was eagerly waiting for him to get up again. Keen to demonstrate his boxing prowess. Overconfident. Full of himself. Too full in fact. When his downed opponent suddenly threw himself forwards, he was totally unprepared for the move and the knife in Grogan's hand buried itself in the instep of his right foot before he could dance himself away. He was down without realising it, screaming and hugging his foot with both hands in an effort to stem the flow of blood pumping out on to the floor. There was no mercy in Grogan's eyes as he bent over him and jerked the knife free. Hauling him upright by his long fair hair until his neck was nicely stretched, the killer stared meaningfully into his eyes, before abruptly spinning him round to face the right-hand wall. Then in one deft movement he ran the blade across his throat, keeping clear of the jet of blood that he knew would erupt from his severed carotid arteries, before dropping him in a heap to continue to bleed out on the floor.

'And I should have warned you that I don't play by Queensbury Rules,' he said in a soft, sneering reply.

CHAPTER 20

Grogan was in no immediate hurry to leave Martin's house after killing him. In fact, he made a point of sampling a couple of glasses of his twenty-five-year-old Bunnahabhain single malt whisky before having a curious look around the place. It was then that he found the keys to the dead man's maroon Daimler in the pocket of a pair of trousers dumped on the floor of a fancy shower room behind the gym. He extricated them with a triumphant smile.

Finally quitting the house, he took the risk of being spotted by a passing police patrol and headed for the main B3139 in his flashy stolen car, instead of sticking to the backroads. But as it turned out, Somerset's finest were conspicuous by their absence and he got to his next destination without incident.

Mark was said to be the longest village in England and it boasted an ancient church, reputed to date back to the twelfth century, two quaint inns and a post office and shop. But Grogan hardly noticed them as he passed through. His mind was focused on something more important to him.

He finally abandoned the Daimler in a field near the hamlet of Watchfield. The drive in the luxury limo had been exhilarating. But he knew that the car was much too distinctive to hang on to. Its details would almost certainly be circulated by police as soon as they twigged it was gone. So getting rid of it as soon as possible was a priority, even though it meant reverting to shank's pony again.

Doubling back to Mark Causeway on foot afterwards, he turned left into a lane off the main road, which wound its way through open countryside in the general direction of the A38. Within a few minutes he came upon the detached property he was looking for. It stood in its own grounds behind wrought-iron gates and a brass plate attached to one of the gates carried the name *Melton House*. Excellent, he mused. No neighbours, just hedgerows and fields on every side, so no one to worry about.

The gates themselves were shut and plainly meant to be operated electronically. There was a wireless intercom unit attached to one wall pillar with a notice below it stating emphatically: *No Casual Callers. No Jehovah's Witnesses.* He smiled faintly. Obviously this was someone who didn't welcome visitors. That was a pity because he was just about to receive one he definitely would not want to extend a welcome to.

He stood for a few moments under some overhanging trees studying the house cautiously. He was relieved and not a little surprised that he had been able to find it so easily. When he had first arrived in Somerset he'd realised that locating the sort of targets he was looking for was likely to prove difficult. He had never been to the county before, so he had no knowledge of the area. The Ordnance Survey map he had purchased en route to the county was certainly a boon to him. But it didn't help him find people or precise addresses, even if it did enable him to navigate his way around the countryside.

So he had turned for help to a recognised font of local knowledge. The parish library. As an experienced library assistant himself, he'd known exactly where to look for information; such places as internet records, parish notices, newsletters and copies of local newspapers. He had been aided in his searches by directions from the knowledgeable library staff themselves too, and altogether this had provided him with everything he'd needed. The only risk now was that the same staff who had innocently assisted him might recognise his face from the photograph published in the newspapers and on television. But Old Bill already knew who he was so that sort of information wouldn't be of much use to them. Especially since it was now too late for four of the targets he had been searching for to be saved. As for the fifth, they wouldn't know who that was going to be until his corpse was discovered.

He smiled his satisfaction as he thought about what had been achieved so far, though he had to admit the task had not been as difficult as he'd imagined it would be at the start.

His first planned hit on a cleric had simply meant homing in on a conveniently placed village church. In that he had been spoilt for choice. The rest of his victims had only had themselves and the media to blame for being targeted. Wilf Carpenter at Summerdays Cider Farm by drawing attention to his business through the prominent marketing of his cider on billboards and in the press. The high-class whore, Marianne Dawson, by placing her advertisement on the back page of the local newspaper, hinting at the carnal services that were available at her massage parlour. As for the last victim, Dominic Martin, he had made the mistake of listing his 'immoral' gambling business on the business pages of a parish newsletter, which had provoked community outrage in the press. Grogan's next target had similarly guaranteed his selection by announcing in the local rag a talk he was soon to give on crime and punishment in the parish hall. In all, just what the doctor, or in this case the assassin, had ordered, Grogan mused with a grim smile.

* * *

Deidrie Hennessey made no effort to conceal her scepticism. 'I know your suggestion about Grogan's bolthole was dead on, Kate,' she said, sitting back in her office chair, 'but this latest idea of yours seems a bit of a stab in the dark, so it does.'

Kate glanced quickly round the room, first at Hayden sitting beside her and then at Don Tappin making notes as usual in the corner. Still tired after the rude awakening by Hayden the previous night, after which she had found it almost impossible to get back to sleep again, she was determined that her sacrifice would not be wasted and that she would be heard.

'With respect, ma'am, I think it makes perfect sense,' she replied. She suspected that Hennessey was playing devil's advocate to test the strength of the theory she had just put forward on behalf of Hayden and herself. 'As I have indicated, we now know from the new background information we have on Grogan that his childhood years were marred by the appalling behaviour of his parents. Religious hypocrisy, gambling, desertion, alcohol abuse and prostitution they were all there. I believe they rubbed off on him in a big way. Colouring his view of life and people in general. Leading to a deep-seated resentment and hatred of everyone and everything. This inevitably resulted in psychosis and ultimately a dangerous psychopathic disorder.'

'To be sure, Kate,' Hennessey breathed. 'You really have swallowed the psychologist's manual this time, so you have.'

Kate gave her a fleeting smile and glanced sideways at her husband again. 'I'm afraid I can't take the credit for that, ma'am. All of it came from Hayden. But I'm convinced it makes perfect sense. If it is correct, it is logical to assume that Grogan will have chosen his next target from the gambling industry as a kickback against his father. Or alternatively, a member of the judiciary after his own conviction for ABH. In short, he is exacting revenge on the professions he sees as wrecking his life.'

'Hmm. And this "game" youse have talked about before. Where does that fit in?'

Hayden coughed and put in his own two penn'orth. 'I believe he nurses strong feelings of inadequacy after all that has happened to him, ma'am. Consequently, he is desperate to prove he is superior to anyone else. What better way of proving that than outwitting the police, in particular Kate, er Sergeant Lewis, on a major crime investigation?'

'But why Kate more than anyone else?'

'I suspect that some of his inadequacy stems from sexual impotency, which has led to outright misogynistic prejudice. As I understand it, the post-mortem on Marianne Dawson revealed no evidence of recent sexual penetration before she was killed. No allegations of sexual assault have been made by Julia Thorogood or Debbie Moreton either. In fact, I believe Moreton told Jamie Foster when he found her that Grogan had sneered at her and said he had no interest in her body. For a hot-blooded male not to try anything on with a woman he has at his mercy, even after he has stripped her naked, suggests he is not capable of doing anything in the first place.'

'Touch of the old brewer's droop, you mean?' Hennessey responded with a mischievous smile.

Hayden reddened. 'The thing is, when Grogan first observed Sergeant Lewis at the writing school in Cancun, I think he found himself impressed by who she was and what she said at her presentation. Consequently he was drawn towards her. At the same time, though, he despised her as a woman and resented her apparent success in life. These conflicting emotions encouraged him to select her as an unwitting participant in the game that had begun to form in his mind. The object being, as we have discussed before, to rubbish her reputation and demonstrate his own intellectual superiority as well as gaining him the notoriety he craves.'

Hennessey considered his analysis for a moment, then nodded. 'That's all grand, but it doesn't really help us to identify who his next victim might be, does it? You say you think it is either someone in the gaming profession or a member of the judiciary. Well, that gives us pretty wide scope, so it does. Especially in the geographical sense. The Somerset Levels covers a pretty wide area, around a hundred-and-sixty-thousand acres, I'm told. Locating potential targets could be a wee bit difficult.'

Kate shook her head. 'We only need to cover a small area within a short radius of Highbridge, ma'am. All his hits so far have been within just a few miles of here, as I explained once before. The fact that he rented a property just down the road from Catcott supports that fact, and I don't believe he ever intended straying any further out than ten to twelve miles from home.'

Hennessey sighed. 'Okay, you win. Anything is worth trying, so it is. Don here will get one of our staff to do some mapping and sort out possible targets. Doubtless there will be a notables-at-risk list of some sort, covering judges, politicians and such like kept at this nick. Also, there's bound to be a local business directory of some sort, which should shortcut protracted inquiries. Once we have the info, maybe we can get some alerts out just in case, though I still think we're fishing in the dark.'

At which point Hennessey's office telephone rang as if on cue. With an irritable hiss, she reached across her desk to answer it and immediately Kate and Hayden were privy to a startling and dramatic change in her expression. Snapping her fingers in their direction to stop them leaving the room, she set the phone down heavily and stared at them with a new intensity.

'Looks like you'd be justified in saying I told you so,' she said grimly. 'That was Detective Inspector Woo. He's attending another murder scene out on the Levels. SOCO and the forensic pathologist are already en route there.'

'Grogan again?' Hayden hazarded a guess.

Hennessey nodded. 'It appears that the deceased was a fella named Dominic Martin, a well-known manufacturer of, wait for it, *gaming* machines.'

'Victim number four,' Kate breathed.

'Aye,' Hennessey replied as she grabbed her coat from the back of her chair. 'Just two more to go for the half dozen.'

* * *

The corpse of Dominic Martin was not yet completely cold and the young woman who had found him was sitting shaking on a cane settee in the conservatory with a face almost as white as his. A uniformed female officer was sitting beside her, holding her hand.

'Melanie Caulfield, one of Martin's girlfriends,' Woo explained standing with his colleagues in the hallway beyond the living room. 'Came a-calling and found him like this. Quite a shock, I would think. She was almost incoherent on the phone to us.'

Hennessey nodded. 'Sure, that's hardly surprising,' she replied tightly, her gaze fastened on the dead man through the open doorway.

The forensic pathologist and scenes of crime team had not yet arrived and police crime scene tape had been strung out across the door of the room in which Martin's corpse was lying, preventing closer scrutiny.

The former gaming manufacturer was lying on his back in his home gym. His throat had been slit open and his body rested in a pool of blood, which had also heavily spattered a wall on one side and a rack of barbells. A dead rook lay on the floor beside him and his corpse and the floor around him was scattered with scores of coin-like brass discs that glinted under the overhead strip lighting.

'I assume those discs are slot machine tokens,' Hennessey commented. 'I didn't realise tokens like that were still in use nowadays.'

'Amusement arcades tend to use them, though some of the older so-called "penny arcades" continue with coins,' Hayden put in helpfully. 'No doubt Martin catered for both types of machine on his production lines.'

Hennessey threw him a searching glance. 'You're a real font of knowledge, Hayden, so you are,' she said drily. 'Psychology, philosophy, gambling. Is there no limit to what you know?'

'It's all part of my wacky make-up, ma'am,' he sniped back, referring to her previous comment to Kate about him.

'Touché, Detective,' she murmured softly, then went on, 'I don't suppose the young woman who found him saw anything?'

Woo shook his head. 'Unfortunately not, but as you can see, Grogan left his usual crow or rook calling card to tell us the murder is down to him, and it also confirms Kate's original suspicions of a link between his choice of victims. According to the first officer on the scene, Martin was originally positioned ritualistically, with his arms folded across his chest under the rook's corpse with his legs crossed at the ankles. Probably as some kind of a macabre joke. But the disruptive examination of the body by the police surgeon certifying death destroyed the intended effect.'

Hennessey stared first at Kate and then at Hayden. 'Seems youse were right all along,' she said drily. 'Congratulations. So, a cleric, a cider producer, a prostitute and now a gaming manufacturer. All professions Grogan had reason to hate. Rev Strange gets thrown off his church roof, Wilf Carpenter ends up with his skull mashed in one of his cider presses, Marianne Dawson is handcuffed to a frame and suffocated in her own sex parlour. Couldn't be clearer now.'

She turned to Don Tappin, who had just arrived in a separate car. 'What about victim number five? Is someone working on Kate's theory about him being a senior member of the judiciary?'

'Got DS Nicholl in the incident room on the job before I left the nick, ma'am,' he said. 'Nothing back from him yet.'

'Well, tell him he can forget about checking the business directory for this fella.' She waved an arm towards Martin's corpse. 'Wee bit late for that now, so it is. Let's hope we have better luck with the judge.'

'If it *is* a judge and not someone totally unconnected with the judiciary,' Tappin returned.

Hennessey pursed her lips for a moment. 'As of now, I have every faith in Kate's prophetic skills,' she affirmed, tongue-in-cheek.

Kate frowned. 'So, no pressure then, ma'am?' she said.

'Not at all,' Hennessey replied sweetly. 'Only if you turn out to be wrong.'

CHAPTER 21

The message came through on Hennessey's mobile as she was briefing the manager of the newly arrived scenes of crime team in the living room of Dollar House. She summoned Kate from the hallway.

'From Sergeant Nicholl,' she said. 'There is only one former judge living in the area you specified. Sir Richard Stratton Davey, previously of what was originally the Queen's Bench Division, who retired seven years ago. He lives at Melton House on the outskirts of a village called Mark. I have his address and postal code, so you should be able to find him with your sat nav. Be warned, though. It seems he's a bit of an eccentric and very ornery to deal with. Your local intelligence officer, Dave Gort, knew him well when he was the local beat man and gave him crime prevention advice. By rights, he should be safe enough as his place is evidently full of hidden security cameras. He also had a sophisticated alarm system installed recently, which is connected directly to a private security central station after receiving threats from some of the gobshites he put away. But you'd better get out there to check on him anyway.'

'Backup?' Kate asked.

Hennessey thought about that for a second, then shook her head. 'I don't want a blues and twos response at this stage in case we're barking up the wrong tree. We've made enough cock-ups over the last few days and the last thing we need now is an ornery ex-judge breathing fire and brimstone to the local press. But take Hayden with you. Just in case.'

Moments later Kate and Hayden were speeding off across the Levels towards Mark.

* * *

Ignoring the gate and the intercom on the house wall, Grogan walked down a muddy track at the side of the property, looking for another way in. He was in luck. About halfway along there was another gate. This time it was a single and was made of wood. Stepping back slightly, he slammed his foot into it several times until the rusted hasp parted company with the wood and the gate flew open. He was in.

Twenty yards or so in front of him across a manicured lawn graced with a number of stone statues stood a big, grey, stone house with mullion windows. He studied the house carefully. The windows appeared to be closed, which was hardly surprising as it had begun to rain again. But a light glimmered inside through a blind drawn down over one of the ground-floor windows. He took a calculated risk and darted across the lawn to the right-hand corner of the house. There was a single door there and he tried the handle very gently. The door was unlocked.

He took a deep breath and eased it open a crack to peer through. The room beyond was a tiled kitchen equipped with the usual cupboards, a range cooker and an old Belfast sink. The house was plainly very old and no one seemed to have shown any interest in trying to modernise it.

Silence. No one talking. No music playing. Not even the drip of a tap. He stepped through the doorway, crossed the kitchen and exited through a second door immediately opposite into a short hallway. There was a staircase to his right and the front door to his left. An ornate grandfather clock stood against the opposite wall between two more doors, both of which were ajar. There was a further door facing them from his side of the hall. He could hear the clock ticking. Otherwise not a sound.

He crossed the hall to the nearest door and gently pushed it open. A small sitting room lay beyond, furnished with a three-seater settee, two armchairs and a long, old-fashioned sideboard. But the room was empty.

Easing the door open on the other side of the clock, he found himself in a similar size dining room furnished with a long dark wooden table and six high-backed chairs. A large glass-fronted cabinet containing shelves of porcelain figures stood against one wall and a cocktail cabinet occupied a corner. There was no one there either.

Scowling, he returned to the hall and it was then that he noticed the faint chink of light issuing from under the third door on the kitchen side, which was now facing him. He remembered seeing the light glimmering through the blind across one of the lower windows when he'd crossed the lawn a few minutes before. His lips tightened in a smile of anticipation.

The door turned out to access a study with a big walnut desk under the window and shelves on both sides crammed with thick, heavy looking books and bundles of papers. The elderly white-haired man sitting in the bosun's chair, which had been swivelled round to face the door, was thin and gaunt, and predictably he was dressed in faded tweeds and a matching waistcoat. Watery blue eyes, framed by thick horn-rimmed spectacles, peered myopically at his unwelcome visitor from under tufted eyebrows and there was a noticeable tic in the left check of the pale aquiline face, though whether due to fear or down to a permanent affliction was not obvious.

The old man did not make any attempt to speak and Grogan studied him for a moment before his gaze roved around the room and settled on a glass wall cabinet in one corner displaying a gavel and a distinctive white wig on a stand.

Crossing to the cabinet, he pulled it open. Removing the wig, he tossed it on to the old man's lap.

'Put it on,' he instructed and watched while trembling bony fingers complied.

'Very smart,' Grogan mocked. 'I wonder how many people you've put away wearing that thing on your head. Well, now the shoe's on the other foot.'

The old man bent forward and released a racking cough that shook his frame and went on for several seconds until Grogan thought it would never stop.

'What — what are you going to do?' he said in a low, rasping voice.

'Do?' Grogan replied, picking up a heavy cutglass vase from the shelf of one of the bookcases. 'Why, I'm going to kill you, of course.'

* * *

The radio call came through just minutes after Kate and Hayden had pulled away from Dollar House in the CID car.

'Any mobile vicinity of Mark Causeway? Panic alarm call from Melton House, Dutch Road.'

Kate swore and quickly acknowledged attendance as her foot slammed down hard on the accelerator.

'The bastard's in there,' she shouted across at Hayden. 'I knew he wouldn't stop at Martin!'

Hayden fidgeted nervously in the front passenger seat, his right hand gripping the top of his seatbelt. 'At least can we get there in one piece?' he exclaimed. He closed his eyes for a second as the car hurtled past a slow-moving tractor on the approach to a crossroads. 'This is an unmarked car. We don't even have a blue light on the thing.'

Kate threw him a quick sideways glance, her eyes glinting with excitement. 'Do my best, Hayd,' she retorted with a grin. 'But I can't promise anything.'

She didn't make any attempt to slacken their speed and shortly afterwards they were racing through the centre of the village and heading along the Causeway towards the hamlet of Watchfield.

Dutch Road was a narrow lane leading off Mark Causeway to their right, around half a mile from Watchfield itself. Hayden closed his eyes again, convinced that they would never make the turn at their current speed. But even he had to acknowledge his wife's driving skill. She managed the sharp turn under heavy braking and a smooth boost change down the gearbox that sent the car into a momentary quiver before it straightened to the new direction and roared off between tall hedgerows.

Just a couple of hundred yards later they skidded to a halt in front of wrought-iron gates and Kate was out of the car even as the engine died, leaving Hayden to stumble awkwardly after her. Almost immediately she found herself facing a problem. The gates were tightly closed and the intercom unit on one of the pillars indicated that the only way to gain access was by pressing the button or physically climbing over them. Pressing the button was obviously out of the question since it would alert Grogan who was probably already inside, and a climb certainly didn't appeal. The gates matched the seven-foot-high wall and were constructed of tightly patterned wrought iron, which afforded virtually no foothold.

Then she spotted the track down the side of the property, following the line of the enclosing wall, and she was about to turn towards it when to her astonishment the gates started to slowly open. At the same moment she heard the unmistakable sound of a gunshot coming from inside the house.

* * *

'You won't be killing anyone today, my friend,' His Honour Sir Richard Stratton Davey said, a new firmness in his tone and a sudden hardening of his gaze that paused Grogan's move towards him. 'You see, I watched you smash open the side gate on one of my security cameras. With this.' He held up a small mobile device in one hand and turned it towards the killer so he could see the screen. 'I then activated the panic alarm button. The police will be here any second.'

Grogan stiffened, then smirked. 'Not before I cave your head in, old man,' he said.

'Oh, I don't think so,' Davey replied.

He must have had the old Luger pistol concealed under his jacket and letting the device in his hand drop to the floor, he produced the gun with his other hand before Grogan realised what was happening. For a moment the killer froze, taken aback by the sight of the menacing weapon. Then abruptly his thin lips twisted into a sneer.

He could see even from where he was standing that the gun was very old and battered looking and it was wandering and dipping in the bony hand that grasped it, suggesting that Davey was having difficulty holding it securely.

'Careful, Your Honour,' he mocked, 'you could blow your foot off with that thing.'

The old man smiled thinly. 'A Chinese general named Sun Tzu once said, "Know thyself, know thy enemy . . ." That was sound advice, young man. You see, I may be old now, but I was a major in the army well before being called to the bar. This is a Nazi nine millimetre Luger my father took from an officer in the Wehrmacht in the Second World War and he brought it back with him as a souvenir. I have maintained it in good working order ever since and it is now fully loaded. You should bear that in mind.'

'Yeah,' Grogan replied. 'But even if you had the strength to pull the trigger, you couldn't hit a barn door with that relic.'

At which point, he moved slowly forward again, slapping the vase into the palm of his hand at the same time, and stepping from side to side as Davey attempted to keep the pistol lined up on him.

The explosion came suddenly and in the small room the sound was deafening. The flame seemed to leap from the barrel like a live thing and the pungent gunpowder smell that accompanied it filled the room.

The fact that the nine-millimetre shell missed its target was entirely due to a combination of the old man's age, his weak grip, which made him snatch at the trigger instead of pulling it smoothly, and his developing Parkinson's disease. But though the shot did not strike home, Grogan felt it almost part his hair and that was enough for him. As Davey adjusted his grip in preparation for a second attempt, the killer dropped the vase and fled.

Running through the kitchen and out into the garden, he swerved sideways when he saw Kate and Hayden appear around the side of the building and made straight for the gate through which he had forced his entry.

He was conscious of Kate crossing the lawn at an angle in an effort to cut him off, but his long legs easily outstripped hers, even with the haversack on his back. He was through and racing along the track towards the lane even before she reached the gate. Then he heard the scream of sirens and he glimpsed the blue-and-red flashing strobes lighting up the tops of the hedgerows from both ends of the lane as they approached the house at speed. Any moment now he would be trapped between them.

Kate was still doggedly on his tail. But he put on a spurt, emerging from the track well ahead of her. Then almost losing his haversack when one of the straps slipped off his shoulder, he swerved round the bonnet of a police patrol car as it slammed to a stop just before the front entrance to the house. Doors opening, voices shouting intermingled with the metallic clatter of police radios. He dodged the outstretched arms of a uniformed copper. Shouldered another one aside. Then he was across the road, heading back towards Mark Causeway. The entrance to the track or bridleway he had glimpsed on his way in, which had seemed to lead off into a belt of woodland and scrub, was just yards away. He could just make it . . .

He glanced behind and saw that Kate and a raggle-taggle bunch of out-of-condition colleagues had dropped right back. They were no longer a threat. With a sense of relief he swung into the mouth of the track, stumbling into potholes that had plainly been made by horses' hooves. Slithering in the wet earth. Tripping over fallen branches. He heard the sound of racing engines. They were coming after him. He saw a break in the trees to his left and plunged into knee-height undergrowth. A broken-down wire fence was all that separated him from a wide field full of cattle. He scrambled through, spotted a long metal cattle trough a few feet away and headed straight for it.

There was a hollow behind the trough, trampled out by scores of cows over the years. He shook the straps of his haversack off his shoulders, let it fall into the hollow and dropped down beside it, lying full length behind the trough. Cars tearing up the soft earth on the track he had just left. More excited chatter on radios. He remained perfectly still, waiting the situation out. If some enterprising copper decided to check the field, he was done for. He just couldn't run anymore. His chest was on fire and the muscles in his legs and back were so tight that cramp was a real possibility. He gritted his teeth and stayed still.

Now a woman's voice coming from the track on the other side of the belt of trees he had just pushed through to get to the field. Kate Lewis.

'Call up the chopper,' she shouted breathlessly, obviously still on foot. 'And get some dogs out here. He can't have got far.'

There was the staccato sound of a radio blasting again and then a male voice shouting. 'Skipper, they've found Martin's limo in a field at Watchfield.'

'Shit!' Kate said politely. 'Get over there. That must be where he's heading.'

Churning wheels. Doors banging and the whine of car transmissions reversing back towards the road. Silence. They had gone. He had got away.

Nevertheless, he remained lying there a while longer, just in case the police were tucked up somewhere close by waiting for him to show.

As he gradually recovered his stamina, he found himself reflecting on all that had happened. He had fouled up well and truly this time, he knew that. To think that he had been outwitted and sent packing by an old man who had to be well over eighty. It was humiliating and infuriating. But there was nothing he could do about that now. It was done. Okay, so he had failed to take out his fifth target. That was only one, though. He was still ahead of Kate Lewis and the rest of her copper mates. After all, four out of six wasn't a bad score. Especially if he added his other three extra hits to the total. The detective sergeant, the vagrant and the estate agent. That made it a cool seven.

No, he hadn't done too badly at all when he thought about it. But if he wanted to claim a clear victory, he still had one more job to do. Eliminating target number six. He bared his teeth in anticipation, his expression a vengeful mask. It wouldn't be easy. Especially now that he had become the hunted rather than the hunter, which meant that his original carefully thought out plan was in pieces. Yet he had no intention of giving up. He would just have to improvise again. He had no choice. This would require determination, stealth and cunning. But he was confident he had all three in abundance and could carry it off. All he needed was the opportunity and it was up to him to find it. Then he would have truly earned his rightful place in serial killer history and, with the book he was going to write, recognition in the literary world as one of the finest best-selling authors of all time.

CHAPTER 22

'Yet another debacle,' Hennessey said. 'This is getting to be a habit with us.'

Gathered with some of her team in a knot by the front gates of Melton House and trying to ignore the return of a penetrating drizzle, she no longer seemed angry about Grogan's escape. Just resigned to it.

Kate nodded, tight-lipped and pale, but saying nothing.

'At least we managed to prevent another murder,' Don Tappin commented.

'From what I hear, the judge did that for himself,' Hennessey corrected. 'I gather he took a pot-shot at our man. Presumably he missed?'

''Fraid so,' Charlie Woo replied. 'Nice big hole in the doorframe, though. So it was probably close enough to guarantee Grogan now needs a change of underwear.'

'And the firearm?'

Woo shrugged. 'Judge says he hasn't got one and he shouldn't have either, as he hasn't got a licence.'

'How does he account for the sound of a shot being heard?'

Woo grinned. 'Said it must have been a car backfiring.'

'And the hole in the doorframe?'

'Woodworm, he suggested. Or perhaps caused by his late father years ago. Apparently he was a military man who owned a pistol he'd brought back from the war, and it somehow went missing. We found a nine millimetre round buried in the opposite wall, but he claimed it had been there for ages. He inherited the house apparently when his father passed and he used it for years as a sort of country retreat while he was officiating at sessions in the Smoke.'

Hennessey grunted. 'Aye, a man with all the answers, it seems, however ridiculous they might seem. Where is the wee fella now?'

'Having his afternoon nap upstairs. Appeared totally unconcerned about the situation.'

'Have we searched the house?'

'No and he refuses to allow it without a warrant. By which time, of course, he will have got rid of the weapon.'

Hennessey sighed heavily. 'Something for later, I think, much later in view of who he is. For the now, we still have a killer to catch and the press will have another juicy story when they find out about this.'

Hayden, who had been standing to one side saying nothing up until now, chose that moment to contribute to the conversation with one of his flippant remarks. 'Well, at least Grogan succeeded in unwittingly silencing his own biographer by putting her in hospital, so that solves one problem.'

Hennessey raised an eyebrow and turned on him. 'Is that right, Detective? Then I take it you haven't seen this morning's *Bridgwater Clarion*? There's a nice picture and description of Grogan on the front page from our press conference, but also a graphic account inside by a reporter called Debbie Moreton detailing her kidnapping and torture at the hands of someone she now calls the "Beast Man". I've just read the piece. I'm told she dictated the story over the phone to the editor from her hospital bed.'

Woo gave a low whistle. 'Brave girl. Grogan won't like that.'

'I'm sure he won't. That's why I've doubled the police guard on her when she is discharged to her home later today.'

'I don't reckon he'll go after her again,' Kate put in suddenly. 'He's after bigger game now, namely his sixth target.'

Hennessey released her breath in a frustrated hiss. 'Aye,' she said testily, 'and it would be grand if we had the slightest inkling of who that might be, so it would.'

* * *

'Well, what now?' Hayden said when he and Kate got back to the police station in the early evening dusk. 'What's next on our agenda?'

They had returned to Melton House after leading an unsuccessful search of the area with a mix of uniform and CID officers aided by a dog mobile. Hennessey had already left the scene to return to the SIO's office in the incident room and Don Tappin was happy to stand them down, as there was nothing left for them to do at the house.

Kate shrugged. 'That depends on Grogan,' she replied in answer to Hayden's question. 'I can't see him going back to Melton House for a second attempt on the judge. It's too bloody hot now. Unless we can figure out his next move, it looks like we're going to be left with the job of clearing up the mess after his next kill.'

'When he'll be able to say he's outwitted an entire police force and won his twisted game.'

She winced. 'As well as besting his unwilling co-player, yours truly,' she reminded him. 'But what then? He must have something else in mind.'

'Such as?'

'I'll get my crystal ball out of my desk for a quick decko,' she retorted. 'Maybe then I'll be able to tell you.'

Her sarcasm fell on deaf ears and she saw him consult his watch.

'What's up, Hayd?' she asked. 'Belly beginning to remind you that it's after eight?'

'Well, I do need something to eat,' he complained. 'It's well past dinner time.'

She shook her head wearily. 'Okay, you get off home. I don't want to be accused of denying a starving man a crust.'

'What about you?'

'Not hungry. I'll follow on later. I have one or two things to do here first.'

But whatever Kate had intended doing, she never got the opportunity to do it. Charlie Woo walked back into the general office moments after Hayden had left and he flicked his head in the direction of his own office as he strode towards it. A clear instruction that she was to join him.

Once she was there, however, he simply dropped into his swivel chair and withdrew a bottle of Glenfiddich single malt whisky and two glasses from the bottom right-hand drawer of his desk.

'Shut the door and take a seat, Kate,' he said with a grin. 'I think it's time we had one of our special briefings.'

* * *

The night was dry, but cold, with a full moon and a myriad glittering stars. Kate shivered as she finally left the police station and climbed into her car. She should not have accepted Charlie Woo's invitation to a Scotch when she knew she was driving. Especially as she had ended up having two. But she had made sure they were small ones with plenty of water. Anyway, the couple of hours she had spent with him in his office had been more about conversation than drinking. Covering a variety of topics that had had nothing to do with police work. Rather, personal ambitions and life generally. She was confident she was within the alcohol limits for driving. Just. But she still felt guilty as she climbed into her car.

The roads were practically deserted as she drove home. Just an occasional car or truck heading the other way. Hardly surprising really as the clock in the car registered the time as well after midnight. She made a face as she thought of

Hayden probably already tucked up in their nice warm bed, snoring his head off. She was very tired herself and couldn't wait to join him.

It had been helpful talking to Charlie. He had always been a good listener and he'd seemed to understand what she had been going through over the months since her near breakdown. For anyone who had never been through a similar experience, it was difficult to appreciate the debilitating depression that came in waves. The loss of confidence and self-esteem. The nightmare grey world that closed in on the mind, like a tight fist, shutting out all optimism and hope. Charlie had just let her talk. Unload some of her thoughts and feelings without trying to advise, judge or rationalise anything. In the end, encouraging her to answer her own questions herself. She felt somehow unburdened by the experience. That had never happened before. Even by talking to Hayden or her shrink. Maybe Charlie's listening ear on top of the therapeutic effects of getting back into the swing of the job were helping her towards remission from her illness. She certainly felt more like her old self than she had for many months. Maybe Grogan's best efforts to demoralise and destroy her were actually having the opposite effect. She could only hope that was the case, but there was still a way to go yet.

Busy with her thoughts, she almost missed the turning into Burnham Moor Lane and swung off the well-lit main road into its dark mouth at the last minute, vaguely conscious of another vehicle's headlights turning in after her. So there was another dirty stop-out abroad as well as herself, she mused with a smile.

A rabbit bounded across the road in front of her as she straightened up and a couple of bats skimmed past the windscreen, making her jump. The road ahead snaked between tall hedges, which created pools of dark shadow where the moonlight failed to reach. Twice Kate braked sharply as her gaze fastened on a dark lumpy mass resembling a walker hugging the hedgerow on one side. Only to see it disintegrate the next moment before the car's main beam, leaving her shaken and unnerved. Damned whisky, she mused savagely the second time. She was seeing things now.

She made Mark Causeway without problem, passing the entrance to Dutch Road where the last drama with Damian Grogan had played out and shortly afterwards turned right at the crossroads, heading for Burtle village.

The headlights behind her were now much closer, travelling fast. She slowed to allow what seemed to be some sort of van to pull out and overtake. Instead, it just kept going, gaining on her without apparently slackening its speed. Then suddenly the lights were on full main beam and blazing through the back window of her car, blinding her in her rear view mirror.

'What the hell are you playing at?' she shouted, half-turning in her seat to look behind her.

At the last minute the van finally pulled out to overtake. As it passed alongside, she saw that it was an old Transit van. Cursing through her side window at the vehicle, which was too high off the ground for her to see the driver, she hit the brake to let it pass safely. But instead of doing so, it seemed to slow down to match her speed. Then to her horror it suddenly swerved towards her, cannoning into her front off-side wing with a tearing, rending screech of tortured metal, forcing her car off the road completely. She had a vague recollection of the MX-5 pitching nose first into the adjoining rhyne and turning over on to the tip of its front nearside wing. Then nothing as she struck her head on something and blacked out completely.

* * *

Hayden was woken up at around one in the morning by loud hammering on the front door of the cottage. Dragging himself out of bed, still half asleep, he frowned when he saw that Kate was not in bed beside him but assumed she had gone downstairs to answer the door.

He was wrong. She was not down there and the front door was still shut. Opening up, he turned his head away from the glare of a powerful flashlight, glimpsing familiar uniforms behind it.

'Don't you answer your phone?' a voice queried, lowering the flashlight when he waved at it irritably.

The speaker was a uniformed police sergeant.

'What the devil's going on?' he snapped back, turning to glance behind him. Trying to work out through the fog clouding his brain where Kate could have gone.

'Control have been ringing you for the past twenty minutes,' the sergeant continued. 'Is Kate Lewis with you?'

'Kate?' Hayden replied vaguely.

'Your wife, Hayden, remember?'

The fog cleared suddenly from his brain. 'I don't know what you mean.' He turned to peer behind him into the cottage again. 'I thought she was here, but — why, what's happened?'

'We found her car on its side, half in a rhyne off the road between Mark and Burtle. There's blood on the offside door pillar and the windscreen, but no sign of her. When did you last see her?'

Hayden swayed slightly in the doorway, feeling suddenly sick. 'Why, around, er, eight last night at the nick. She told me to go home, but that she had a bit more work to do before leaving.'

The sergeant grunted. 'Well, it looks like another vehicle drove her off the road. We found a bit of bumper bar and a front index plate at the scene and we've got search teams scouring the fields and scrub, looking for her.' His voice softened. 'Sorry, mate, but it doesn't look good.'

Hayden swallowed hard. He was now fully alert and his mind was racing. 'Have you checked out the index plate you found at the scene?'

'Yeah. It belongs to a Ford Transit and the vehicle was reported stolen last night from a smallholding near Mark.'

Hayden grabbed the doorframe for support as the truth hit him. 'Gordon Bennett,' he breathed. '*He's* got her.'

'What do you mean? Who's got her?'

'Damian Grogan,' he replied. 'God help her.'

* * *

Kate slowly surfaced from a bottomless pit towards a pin-point of light that expanded and grew stronger by the second. She slowly opened her eyes, feeling sick and disorientated. There was a dreadful pain in her head and her forehead felt strangely wet.

The face of the moon in all its brilliance stared at her through the glass shards of a broken window high above her head. Its dazzling light spread around the walls of what seemed to be a small bare room. She was lying on her back on what smelled like an old, damp mattress. Her wrists were handcuffed in front of her and her ankles were tied together with some sort of strong thin twine.

She tried to sit up, then fell back again as the pain in her head magnified a hundredfold. For a moment she thought she was going to pass out again but fought against it. Gradually her memory returned with a flashback to the accident with the Transit van. Only it hadn't been an accident, had it? It had been deliberate. Furthermore, she didn't have to be a rocket scientist to work out who had been behind it.

There was a soft chuckle in the shadows to one side of her and a chair scraped on the floor. 'Hello, Kate,' a familiar, hateful voice said. 'Sorry about the sub-standard accommodation. I had originally planned to invite you to the comfort of Walnut Cottage, you see. But I'm afraid your raid on the place put paid to that, so I had to improvise.'

A tall figure, dressed in an anorak and baseball cap, had stepped into view, a torch in one hand. Grogan! He treated her to a gloating smile, his sharp eyes gleaming like polished metal buttons in the bright moonlight. Kate was pleased to see the clearly visible signs of some nasty blistering down his right cheek and part of his neck. Julia Thorogood's pan of boiling soup had obviously done some real damage, she thought with a sense of vindictive satisfaction.

'Where am I, Grogan?' she said.

Another chuckle. 'Well, it's hardly the Ritz, but it will have to do. Still, at least it guarantees absolute privacy. Free from intrusion by your blundering colleagues or anyone else for that matter. In fact, I chose this room on this particular floor specifically for its tucked-away, elevated position. No one will think of looking for us up here.'

'So where is it?'

'Ah, now that would be telling, wouldn't it? How's the head? I can see you have a nasty gash there, I'm afraid. It must hurt a lot.'

'Not as much as your collection of blisters, I bet,' she retorted sarcastically. 'Still, at least the scarring to that side of your face will eventually match the scar you got from the broken bottle on the other side.'

He stared at her silently for a moment. 'Still the same arrogant little bitch, aren't you?' he sneered. 'You were just the same in Cancun. Full of yourself. The ace detective and would-be best-selling novelist who thought she was better than everyone else. That's why I selected you for the game I had devised. The worthy opponent who I knew would turn out to be just another loser.'

'You didn't hit on me because of anything I said or did,' she threw back at him. 'You hit on me because I was a woman, and for no other reason. Don't like women, do you, Grogan? What's the problem? Can't get it up? Or is it because there's nothing there at all, not even the slightest little itch? Maybe you haven't got any balls at all, that would explain it.'

'You'd be well advised to refrain from the childish insults,' he warned. 'You're only going to make things worse for yourself.'

'How much worse can it get? You're going to kill me anyway.'

'How very perceptive of you. But there are many ways in which to die, some a lot more painful than others. You should remember what I have done to those before you to know what I am capable of.'

249

She ignored him. 'And what about those innocent people you slaughtered? Apart from the three who just got in the way, were they picked because you saw them as losers too, even though you'd never met them before? No, they weren't, were they? You chose them solely on the basis of what they did for a living. All held professions which you believed had in one way or another contributed to your ruined childhood. You wanted revenge and as you couldn't mete it out to the actual people you were blaming, like your hypocrite of a father and your drunken prostitute of a mother, you went for them instead.'

'Very good, Sergeant. But they were just pawns. Counters to be played. The fact is, I'd needed a theme for the game. A commonality. Something that linked everything together. To see if you and your dim-witted oppos had the brain power to work it all out. My childhood suffering seemed the ideal thing to go for, so that's what I did. I am just surprised you managed to get there in the end. Pity it's all too late.'

He sighed. 'But at least we are now at the endgame, so I can afford to be a bit more magnanimous in my hour of triumph.'

Kate emitted a humourless laugh. 'Hardly a triumph. Everyone knows who you are, you're on the run with nowhere to go after expertly bungling your last hit, and the net is so tight around you that I'm surprised you can still breathe.'

He hissed his disapproval. 'The judge was just one failure out of six. Not a bad tally, I would suggest, and my successes still put me in the lead.'

'You reckon? So, what about target number six? You still have that one to tick off on your nasty little list, and I don't give much for your chances with the whole area now crawling with police.'

He shook his head. 'You just don't get it, do you? I thought that you of all people would have realised by now. You see, I already have my sixth target.' He flashed his white teeth in a wolfish smile. 'The sixth target is *you*, my dear Kate. You are and always have been the last one on that nasty little list.'

CHAPTER 23

The frost had started to appear at around two in the morning with the sharp drop in temperature. Reducing hedgerows to cringing supplicants and the marshy fields, already tinged with a bluish fire by the moonlight, to a crispness that crackled like breaking twigs underfoot.

The small knot of figures standing by the line of police vehicles shivered and stamped their feet repeatedly on the glistening road. Watching dispiritedly as the handlers returned their panting dogs to their vans and the uniformed Support Group search teams rejoined the big Transits in which they had arrived earlier.

'No trace of her anywhere within the search area, ma'am,' the young inspector said to Deidrie Hennessey. 'At least that's good news anyway.'

Hennessey nodded. 'Aye, in one way, it is, but not in another,' she replied and watched the policeman climb back into the front passenger seat of the leading Transit. Moments later, both Transits pulled away from the verge and followed the dog vans into the night. Heading back towards Highbridge. Their taillights soon disappearing around a bend in the road.

'You okay?' Hennessey asked, turning towards Hayden sitting on the edge of the driver's seat of his red Mk II Jaguar.

He looked up at her, startled for a moment, then ran one hand through his unruly thatch of blond hair. 'Where the hell could he have taken her?' he said.

'It's got to be an empty property, probably another derelict, somewhere not too far away,' Charlie Woo said. 'Guy who owned the stolen Transit said it's an old wagon he just uses around his smallholding and the last time he looked the fuel gauge was on the red. He's apparently been using the vehicle like that for a fortnight but didn't bother to fill up as he's about to sell it for scrap. Grogan wouldn't be able to get far in the thing, that's for sure, and I can't see him trying to fill up at a garage anywhere or resorting to a spot of bilking with Kate on board. He would certainly have been conscious of the risk of running into a police roadblock at any moment if he stayed on the road for longer than was absolutely necessary.'

'Well, it's pretty unlikely he would have decided to return to Walnut Cottage yet again,' Don Tappin commented.

Hayden threw him a quick, curious glance. 'Yet again?' he said. 'What do you mean by "yet again"?'

Tappin shrugged. 'The cheeky bastard actually paid another visit there after scarpering from the place.'

'What? I didn't know that.'

Hennessey interjected quickly. 'Neither did we until late yesterday. SOCO reported that when they went back to the property to finish up, they found evidence of someone having been inside overnight. Window left open. Dirty dishes on the draining board. Blankets and a pillow left in a heap on the settee. Looks like the plod on guard at the front must have been asleep on the job.'

Hayden shook his head in disbelief. 'Unbelievable,' he said bitterly. 'It's as if he's untouchable.'

'Maybe up until now,' Tappin corrected. 'But with all the heat that's on him, it looks as though he's decided against going for the last target in his so-called game. Whoever number six might be.'

'Yeah,' Woo agreed, 'and he's gone for poor old Kate instead—'

'Just a minute,' Hayden cut in, raising a hand, his face creased into a heavy frown. 'Something's just occurred to me. We said that all of Grogan's victims appear to have had the exact same professions as those he considered to have fouled up his life.'

'So?' Hennessey put in carefully. 'What are you thinking?'

Hayden stared at her. 'The last one being a judge . . .' His voice trailed off and he snapped his fingers. 'Do we know who the arresting officer was in his ABH case?'

Tappin nodded, looking puzzled. 'It was a Detective Sergeant Wanda Challenger.'

'And where is she now?'

'Er, she left the force after the case. Apparently, although Grogan was convicted of ABH at his trial, he complained that she'd been prejudiced against him. He alleged that she had refused to arrest the yobos he'd had his confrontation with, even though his face was scarred from a broken bottle wielded by one of them and that they had started the fracas in the first place. There was a subsequent internal investigation and Challenger resigned after it came to light that the kid wielding the bottle was her cousin. Nevertheless, no further action was taken, no new arrests were made and the complaint was filed as unsubstantiated. I suspect she was pressured to resign to save the force from bad publicity.'

'Gordon Bennett, but that's it!' Hayden breathed. 'The complaint was buried instead of being pursued, as it should have been. Don't you see? Grogan was denied proper justice. Unable to find and punish Challenger herself, he's gone for a suitable substitute. Just like he did with all his victims. That substitute is Kate. The sixth target is her!'

* * *

'So, why have you taken all the trouble of bringing me here just to make your confession?' Kate said, playing for time in the hope that her crashed car had been found and that somehow a search team would get to her before it was too

253

late. 'You could have killed me and left me out on the marsh when you totalled my car.'

'Oh, that would have been pointless,' Grogan replied. 'A wasted effort. You are an integral part of the endgame and will be helping me to complete it.'

'Me, help you? You've got to be joking.'

'Oh, I'm not joking, believe me. I'm deadly serious. You see, for me to claim my win in the game, I will have to ensure that there is a very public announcement to that effect so you and your half-witted colleagues won't be able to bury the fact that you lost to a far superior player.'

'And how do you propose doing that from a place like this? Send up smoke signals?'

'Oh, very funny, Sergeant. But no, I have a much more sophisticated means. Let me show you.'

Disappearing back into the shadows, he returned with a haversack, which he placed on the ground in front of her. Then pulling open the straps, he produced a small video camera.

'It's quite simple,' he explained. 'You will sit on the chair over there and admit to the world in front of this camera how you and your colleagues have been outwitted and outclassed by a much cleverer adversary. An adversary who has made fools of an entire police force and taxed your resources to the limit. It is quite shadowy in here in spite of the moonlight, but I have an excellent lighting attachment for the camera, which will solve that problem. It will be a bit like one of those video presentations the terrorists in places like Iraq and Afghanistan have put out to the world. I will ultimately send digital copies to all the main television channels and newspapers.' He emitted a hard laugh. 'You'll be famous, my dear. You should be thrilled.'

'You really are crazy.'

'Not at all. Once I have publicised the truth, I will disappear. To re-emerge once I have completed the book I intend to write on it all and have secured the necessary contract for its publication.'

'When you will be promptly arrested and put away in a loony bin for life.'

'Only if I can be found, which I doubt will happen. But anyway, by then I will have achieved exactly what I set out to achieve when I first embarked on my little game. In short, earning my rightful place in the history of crime as one of the most successful serial killers on record and gaining full literary recognition as one of the greatest true-crime authors of my time.'

Despite the precarious position she was in, Kate made no effort to conceal her incredulity. 'Not only crazy, but totally delusional,' she exclaimed. Her words gave way to cynical laughter. 'And if you think I'm going to do anything to help you with that, you can dream on.'

At once Grogan lost his cool, self-assured demeanour and lurched forward to grasp her chin in one powerful hand. Just as he had with Debbie Moreton.

'Is that right?' he snarled. 'Well, believe me, you will do exactly as I say and you won't be laughing by the time I've finished with you. You will be screaming your head off.'

Returning to his haversack, he rummaged around inside again and when he withdrew his hand he was clutching what Kate instantly recognised as a stubby pair of wire cutters.

He held them up close to her face, then opened and closed the wicked jaws several times. Remembering what Debbie Moreton had said he had threatened to do to her, Kate's blood ran cold.

'Feel like laughing now?' he said. Bending down, he cut through the twine binding her ankles. Then seizing both her legs in a powerful grip, he ripped off her shoes and socks.

'Let's start on your toes, shall we?' he said, grabbing her right foot. 'Your feet will be hidden from the camera, so no one will notice the amputations. We can turn our attention to your fingers later on if that doesn't work. How does that suit you?'

* * *

255

Two tables had been pushed together in the incident room and a large Ordnance Survey map was spread out on top. Hennessey was leaning on the lower edge with both hands, studying it. A number of other figures were gathered around the map, listening to a well-built, fair-haired man dressed in casual clothes, as he briefed them on the designated search area. There was very little that PC Dave Gort, the local intelligence officer, didn't know about the Somerset Levels where he had served for over thirty years and he had willingly turned out from his bed to provide the vital information that was required for the search for Kate. When he had finished, Don Tappin provided a brief summary.

'So we have identified a total of eleven known empty properties where Grogan could be holding DS Lewis,' he said, 'including those Hayden has previously searched, which are deemed worth a second visit. You have all been told the properties that are down to you to check. But I stress the task is not to engage with the target, unless absolutely necessary to save the life of DS Lewis, but to locate, contain if you can, and call up for reinforcements. Any questions?'

'Can we not get the police helicopter airborne?' a uniformed sergeant asked no one in particular. 'It can cover a lot more ground far quicker than foot soldiers.'

Tappin shook his head. 'Already requisitioned for a firearms incident over at Bath, but we're next in line once it is released from that.'

'Unfortunately,' Hennessey added, 'the resources we have at our disposal right now are very limited. But we've pulled in everyone we can and each team will have one local officer attached to it with knowledge of the area. Okay?'

Feet shuffled impatiently on the woodblock floor, like hounds before the hunt, and she nodded. 'Good. Then let's get out there and find DS Lewis.'

'And pray God we're in time,' Charlie Woo muttered under his breath. Deep down, though, he had his doubts.

* * *

'Please, no! I'll do it!' Kate's choking gasp brought a gloating smile to Grogan's face as he put pressure on the jaws of the cutter gripping her little toe.

'You sure?' he asked, tightening the jaws a bit more so that a thin line of blood trickled down her foot on to the floor where the skin had been broken.

'Yes, please, whatever you say.'

He looked disappointed and studied her intently for a moment without making any effort to remove his gruesome 'toy'. Then abruptly he released her toe and sat back on his haunches with a heavy sigh.

'Pity,' he said. 'I would have liked to have tested the amount of pressure needed to sever the bone. Maybe another time . . .'

He stood up suddenly. 'Anyway,' he said. 'Showtime.'

Disappearing once again into the shadows, he returned dragging a rusted metal chair, which he placed facing her about six feet away. He then produced a small, collapsible metal tripod from his haversack, extended it and set it up two to three feet between her and the chair.

As he attached the video camera, he had his back towards Kate and she tensed. She had glimpsed the doorway in the far corner. If she acted quickly, she mused, she might just get past him before he realised what was happening.

'Well organised then?' she said in as even a tone as she could manage to ensure he didn't get suspicious about what she was doing. At the same moment she rolled over on to her left hip and drew her legs up towards her bottom. Then using first her elbow and then her shoulder, she pressed against the wall behind her for leverage and hoisted herself up against the flaking plaster. She was hampered a lot by the handcuffs, which threw her slightly off balance, but she persevered and finally made it to her knees.

'Of course,' he said, replying to her comment. 'Every minor detail carefully planned. Nothing left to chance. You see, when I set everything up at the start, I had no idea where I would eventually end up, so I had to cater for every exigency. Hope you're impressed.'

'I underestimated you,' she said. 'We all did.'

Climbing to her feet, she carefully reached down for her shoes, but almost immediately froze when he spoke, without turning his head.

'You'll never make it, Sergeant, so I wouldn't try if I were you.'

He turned to stare at her. 'Fancy wanting to leave before your TV debut,' he sneered. Then his voice hardened. 'Now, over here and take your seat, and don't get any more silly ideas if you want to avoid that rather drastic pedicure I had in mind for you.'

She reached for her shoes for the second time, but even that was to be denied her.

'Leave those where they are,' he snapped. 'I can't risk you trying to do a runner again, can I? Bit difficult to do that in your bare feet with all this nasty debris lying about.'

Kate soon discovered what he meant, when her bare sole tramped on something hard and sharp as she picked her way towards him through a litter of fallen plaster, broken glass and other rubbish, no doubt accumulated over years of dereliction and decay. But as she bent down to pull the tiny fragment of glass out of her foot, she caught sight of something else and surreptitiously slipped it in-between her cuffed hands as she removed the fragment.

He waited as she hobbled over, then patted the seat and watched critically as she sat down facing the camera.

'Now, all you have to do is read from the prepared script,' he said. He indicated a printed sheet attached to the tripod below the camera, which was clearly illuminated by the spotlight attachment he had fitted.

There was a surge of acid in Kate's stomach. She knew that once she had delivered the prepared statement to the camera she was a dead woman. He would have no further use for her. If she didn't do something now, she would never get another opportunity. But what?

* * *

'Waste of time.' Detective Constable Danny Ferris growled as he was climbing back into the CID car.

Wainwrights was one of the empty properties Kate and Hayden had originally selected as a possible bolthole for Grogan, but the modern three-bedroom house with its double garage and acre of overgrown garden had yielded nothing but mice and brown-and-white spiders with bodies nearly the size of five-penny pieces. It had quickly become apparent that no one had been there for a very long time.

'Just two more derelicts to check then,' Hayden replied, sounding far from optimistic. 'Bentley's Halt at Ashcott first, and what was that place Dave Gort suggested?'

Ferris consulted his list. 'Broad Marsh Court near Street. Some kind of old manor house by the sound of it.'

'And meanwhile, while we waste time stumbling blindly around the Levels looking for a needle in a haystack, that swine could be subjecting Kate to heaven knows what.'

Ferris grimaced. 'Don't torture yourself, mate,' he said, doing his best to console his colleague. 'Don't forget, he's kidnapped her, so it's unlikely he will have, er, you know what I mean . . .' His voice trailed off and he added, 'If he'd wanted to do that, he'd have done it when he forced her off the road.'

'There's other things he could have done apart from killing her.'

Ferris shook his head and with his usual brand of tact and diplomacy, he plunged straight in. 'Screwed her, you mean? Nah, he wouldn't have done that. By all accounts, he's a limp dick merchant.'

Hayden glared at him. 'Thanks, Danny, you really are a tonic. You should have been a trauma counsellor.'

Ferris frowned. 'Do you reckon?'

Hayden shook his head in resignation. 'What do you think?'

* * *

Kate made her move as Grogan stepped forward to switch on the video camera. She had come up with a plan of sorts. It was risky and she knew she would only get one shot at it. Nevertheless, it was all she had and she kept her hands tightly clasped together to avoid dropping the nail she had picked up off the floor on her way to the chair.

'I can't see the words on that sheet properly,' she blurted.

Grogan looked up quickly. 'Don't try that one on me,' he said. 'I'm not an idiot.'

Kate could feel her heart making stressful squishing noises as she carefully manoeuvred the nail between her palms. She took a chance and pushed the sharp sliver of steel outwards between the index finger and the second finger of her left hand rather than her right, so that it protruded about an inch. Then she curled her index finger around the other end to hold it in place, with the head of the nail pressing into her right palm.

'Up to you if I get it all wrong then,' she replied.

She prayed he would not only fall for her ruse, but also approach her chair from the left to check out what she was claiming, rather than from her right, which would have put paid to her risky plan completely.

He studied her for a moment while she waited with bated breath. Then abruptly he scowled. 'This better be legit,' he warned and stepped away from the camera towards her.

To her relief, he did exactly what she had wanted him to do and chose her left side. Exactly where she needed him to be. Then he bent down to put himself at roughly the same height as her to study the script. He couldn't have been more obliging.

'You should be able to read that,' he said, turning his head towards her with obvious suspicion. At which point she acted. Swinging her cuffed wrists to the left in a hard jabbing motion towards his face, she felt the nail head dig painfully into her right palm as it struck home.

She knew that the move was clumsy, desperate and offered only a minimal chance of success. But for a change, luck was with her. With an agonised scream, he staggered back clutching his right eye, which was already spurting blood. At the same time, the nail slipped through his bloodied fingers and dropped to the floor with a metallic 'ding'. Tripping over the splayed legs of the camera tripod, he sent it crashing to the concrete floor. Then losing his balance, he collided with the wall and fell heavily on top of it, still clutching his eye, moaning and cursing.

Springing past him, she headed for the doorway at an awkward stumbling run. Thrown off balance by the handcuffs binding her wrists, she was unable to match the panic that drove her with any real speed for fear of pitching over. At the same time, she couldn't help her involuntary cries of pain as the debris littering the floor in places jabbed painfully at the soles of her bare feet. But she clenched her teeth and ran on, intent only on putting as much distance between Grogan and herself as possible. And in the shortest possible time.

Ahead of her stretched a long corridor with doors opening off on both sides and ugly lagged pipes running its length close to the ceiling. Moisture ran down the peeling plaster walls and dripped on her from above. It formed pools on the stone floor, which gleamed yellow in the bright moonlight streaming through broken high-level windows. An abandoned steel trolley and then a wheelchair missing a wheel reared up in front of her, forcing her to take avoiding action. Through a couple of the doorways she ran past she glimpsed rooms containing naked iron bed frames and rows of baths and in one room what looked like a long examination table and a broken porcelain sink unit. She had to be in some sort of derelict hospital, but where, that was the point, and how the hell was anyone going to find her here?

Even as that last thought occurred to her, she heard heavy feet pounding along the corridor behind her. Glancing quickly over her shoulder, she saw a sinister black figure loping along in pursuit with the determination of a predatory beast.

CHAPTER 24

Debbie Moreton left her flat as soon as she got the 'whisper' from her regular source inside Highbridge police station about the new developments regarding the hunt for the serial killer the police had named as Damian Grogan. So Kate Lewis had been taken by him, had she? Just as Debbie had previously. Well, that was a turnup for the books. No wonder the whatnot had hit the fan.

Moreton had been given explicit instructions by the hospital doctor to rest. But as a journalist who ate, slept and breathed her job, the principle of rest was not in her psyche. Furthermore, after what Grogan had done to her, there was no way she was going to just sit back and do nothing. Especially as it would have meant missing out on a follow-up to her feature in the *Clarion* about her kidnap ordeal. She would never forget the trauma and humiliation Grogan had subjected her to. Far from being intimidated by the threats he had made after torturing her, she was motivated by a burning desire for revenge. Her shaven head still carried the painful scars from his scissors and razor and her feet the cuts and abrasions from the road surface. But she had no intention of letting such minor discomforts deter her from getting her own back.

She headed for Highbridge police station first. She was lucky enough to be parked up outside when a convoy of police cars and Ford Transits pulled out from the back yard, splitting into two groups when they got to the junction with the main road and heading in two different directions. That presented her with a dilemma. Which group to follow? Then she spotted Hayden Lewis at the wheel of one of the plain CID cars and it was no contest. She stayed with him.

She followed the CID car at a discreet distance all the way to Wainwrights at Westonzoyland. Then hiding among some bushes at the main entrance, she overheard the conversation between Hayden and Danny Ferris when they returned to their car after a fruitless search.

So, only two more derelicts on their list, she mused, as they pulled away again. The second of the two she was already familiar with after ironically covering it in a historical feature a couple of years before as a junior reporter. She just hoped she hadn't backed the wrong horse and that one of the other search teams didn't end up hitting the jackpot.

Her disappointment was magnified when the next property, Bentley's Halt, produced a similar negative result. The place was deserted. Things were beginning to look bleak. However, she was committed and she had no option but to pin her hopes on the very last check. A case of 'in for a penny' . . .

* * *

Kate could hardly feel her feet now. They were like blocks of ice. So much so, that they had become more or less numbed to the pain that should have been so noticeable after their contact with the sharp objects on the floor. Her breathing had become ragged and her chest so constricted that she feared her lungs were about ready to burst. She couldn't keep up the pace much longer. But she could still hear Grogan's pounding feet behind her and they seemed to be gaining on her.

She reached a cross section and turned into an even narrower corridor striking off on her right. She passed two more doors. Then with her legs threatening to buckle under her, she swerved left through a third open doorway into a room piled high with old mattresses. There was a vertical gap between them. She forced herself into it until she could go no further and the mattresses folded around her. They were damp and torn in places, giving off a foul smell. But at least they provided temporary concealment. She could only hope that Grogan wouldn't suspect where she had gone.

Then she froze as heavy footsteps skidded to a halt further back along the corridor. Silence. She guessed Grogan had stopped at the cross section, unsure which way she had gone. He was obviously listening for the faintest sound that would give her away. She held her breath, conscious of her heart pounding as her lungs desperately cried out for oxygen, but fearing the sound the gasp building in her throat would make if she gave in.

Her head was swimming. The stench from the mattresses was enveloping her, forcing itself up her nostrils. Threatening to choke her. She couldn't hold her breath any longer. She was done . . .

At which point there was the sudden scrape of shoes on the gritty floor, followed by the sound of heavy feet moving off slowly in the opposite direction.

The explosive release of air from her oxygen-starved lungs came at the same moment. But to her relief the departing footsteps didn't falter, and gradually faded into nothing. He had gone, leaving her noisily hyperventilating as she clawed herself free of the mattresses' suffocating embrace. Then she stood in the doorway, bent over at the waist as she desperately tried to control the muscular spasms in her legs.

It was several minutes before she felt confident enough to move on. But that's where her confidence ended. Although instinctively turning left to continue following the corridor, she hadn't the slightest inkling of where it led. She assumed somehow that she was on the top floor of the building. But the top floor of how many floors? Two? Three? Four? All the windows she had seen so far had been up high and too close to the ceiling for her to see enough of the outside to be able to judge. Yet there had to be a staircase down to the lower level or levels somewhere.

She needed to find that staircase and find it quickly. But that looked like being even more challenging in this moonlit labyrinth than she had imagined. Then the corridor she was following came to an abrupt end before yet another door. Frowning, she pushed through and found herself in a virtually bare room with the same ubiquitous high-level windows.

Suddenly she froze. The footfall had not been loud, but in this empty building any sound was magnified. Heaven help her! Grogan was somewhere nearby. Creeping up on her. She swallowed hard. How on earth had he found her so easily after she had managed to elude him so effectively earlier? It was as if she had some sort of tracker device fitted to her, which was emitting a tell-tale signal.

Then she happened to glance down and her stomach chilled. Her feet had evidently been bleeding profusely from all the cuts and abrasions she had suffered and there was a line of bloody imprints across the floor from the doorway behind her to where she was standing. He must have missed them at the start, then spotted the imprints shortly after realising somehow that he had been hoodwinked into heading in the wrong direction. After that, all he'd had to do was follow the trail she had left behind. Even as the fact dawned on her, a dark figure pushed through the doorway through which she had just come.

* * *

'This must be it,' Danny Ferris commented as Hayden pulled into a turning circle at the end of the narrow lane they had been following.

Before them a pair of seven-foot-high wrought-iron gates set between massive stone pillars barred their way. The headlights of the car blazing through the gates revealed a long driveway stretching away between tall poplar trees to a circular forecourt with a big stone statue mounted on a plinth in the centre. Beyond the forecourt a massive three-storey building reared up in the moonlight, as if challenging them to enter. To the right of the gates a big blue sign with faded white lettering declared:

Broad Marsh Court Psychiatric Hospital. Restricted Area.

'Shit sticks!' Danny Ferris exclaimed. 'It's a bleedin' nut house.'

'If Grogan's in there, then he should feel right at home,' Hayden commented grimly, switching off the engine and lights before they both climbed out of the car.

The gates had been secured with a business-like padlock and chain below a notice warning: *Keep Out. Dangerous Building.* But someone, possibly vandals or thieves, had already disregarded the instruction and the padlock now hung down limply still attached to one of the links in the chain, which had been severed, no doubt by powerful wire or bolt cutters.

Ferris examined the chain with his torch and held it up for Hayden to inspect. 'Looks recent to me,' he said. 'Whoever did this must have come prepared with the right kit.'

Hayden grunted and stared at the building again. 'Hardly just vandals then,' he said, grabbing one of the half-open gates and pulling it wider on protesting hinges.

Squeezing through the gap, they immediately found further encouraging evidence. Deep tyre tracks seemingly caused by the wheels of a heavy vehicle biting into the soft shingle driveway under hard acceleration.

'Grogan?' Ferris suggested.

Hayden met his excited gaze. 'So, let's find out, shall we?' he said softly. As they both set off up the driveway towards the brooding building, they were completely unaware of the fact that another figure, dressed in a dark hoodie and jeans, hugged the shadows cast by the poplar trees in their wake.

* * *

Damian Grogan had been hurt badly. His face still streamed with blood, which ran down his neck into the collar of his coat. His right eye was trying to focus on Kate through a glistening mess from which part of his torn eyelid protruded grotesquely.

'Well, bitch,' he snarled. 'Satisfied now, are you? You've probably blinded me, but that's nothing compared to what I'm going to do to you.'

The moonlight glinted on the large knife he was holding out in front of him. He ran the back of the same hand across the gory wound he had sustained to clear his vision. Kate glanced desperately around the room in which she had ended up. Looking for another way out. She noticed the second door almost immediately. It was partially blocked by a rusted metal chair in the corner behind her. Jerking round, she went for it at a run, bypassed the chair and with a strength born of panic, kicked it back behind her. She had the satisfaction of hearing Grogan swear as it must have cannoned into his legs. But then she had the door open and was through, hauling it shut behind her.

She found herself in yet another long corridor striking off to her right. Bare, save for bits of debris on the floor. But she was only interested in the door a couple of yards to her left. It admitted a flood of moonlight, and there was a familiar metal bar across the middle and a sign at the top, carrying the most welcome of words, *Fire Escape*. At last.

She almost threw herself at it and pushed the panic bar hard, using all her strength to force the rusted hinges open. The next second she gulped down great lungfuls of clean night air as she stumbled through. She found herself on a wrought-iron walkway, which ran the whole length of the wall outside, linking several other doors. There was an angled staircase at the far end, dropping to the ground with a small platform at each of three levels. She felt a sense of relief at her miraculous escape and breathed a prayer of thanks to the panoply of stars. But that relief abruptly turned to alarm as the walkway began to stir uneasily beneath her feet. Then emitting a loud groan, part of it moved sideways as the rusted bolts holding it in place started to come adrift from the wall. To her horror, she realised it was on the verge of breaking away completely.

* * *

It was Ferris who first saw the Ford Transit. It had been driven into an open-fronted shed to one side of the forecourt, partially hidden from view by tall shrubs.

'Well spotted, Danny,' Hayden exclaimed as they ran over to it.

Ferris checked the rear number plate. 'It's the right motor,' he said.

Hayden nodded grimly. 'He obviously stuck it in here so it wouldn't be spotted by police patrols or the chopper.'

Ferris bent down with his pocket knife and deflated each of the tyres in turn. 'Well, it ain't done him no good. He ain't going nowhere now.'

Hayden pressed the transmit button of his radio. 'So let's flush the swine out,' he grated, and sending a terse message to the control room, he was gratified moments later to hear the broadcast made to all units. But even as the terse metallic voices, giving ETAs of five, ten and twelve minutes, came back over the radio, the business of flushing Grogan out of his last bolthole proved to be unnecessary.

The crash of a heavy door slamming was not that loud, but sound carried a long way on the still night air and the desperate involuntary cry that followed drew both detectives out of the shed at a run.

They spotted Kate immediately and it was a sight calculated to forever haunt Hayden's dreams. She was clearly visible in the moonlight on a fire escape three storeys up at the very top of the building. Hanging on to the outer rail of a wrought-iron walkway from which an angled staircase dropped away to a concrete base far below. She was not alone either. A tall figure was advancing slowly along the walkway towards her. Grogan!

For a moment neither Hayden nor Ferris could understand why she hadn't turned and fled and then the reason was made plain. The walkway on which she stood was visibly shaking and they could hear the agonised groan of fracturing metal and the sound of steel bolts snapping under the strain. The whole structure was close to collapse and three storeys up, Kate had no chance of survival when it did.

Some twenty yards back from Hayden and Ferris, a figure in a hoodie stared up at the drama being played out at the side of the building. Then making a sudden decision, the onlooker took off at full speed in the opposite direction, keeping to the grassy edge of the forecourt to deaden the sound of their shoes. They finally disappeared through a wide, covered opening at the front of the building where faded white lettering on the concrete said: *Ambulances Only*. The figure was then swallowed up in the creepy darkness.

* * *

Grogan was motivated by an all-consuming hatred ten times more potent than anything that had driven him before. He had lost the game, he knew that now. There was no way he was going to be able to force Kate Lewis to do what he had so meticulously planned for her to do. His camera had been smashed anyway when he'd fallen on it. He was out of options. Facing failure and ignominy on a grand scale. Something he had had to put up with all his life. He could still get away and write his book, of course. *If* his injured eye would let him. But who would be interested in him now anyway? He had become just another ruthless killer. Without meaning or purpose. A killer who had been vanquished by of all people a female protagonist and was on the run from the police like so many others. And what about his eye? If he needed surgery, that would raise impossible questions and probably mean a major operation to save his sight. It would almost certainly result in a call to the police and in his subsequent arrest, followed by a life sentence in some hideous prison full of nonces and drug addicts. And it was all Kate Lewis's fault. She had done this to him. Killing her was going to be a real pleasure. He stared at her now, edging away from him along the wrought-iron walkway, and the hand that gripped the large knife trembled with anticipation.

'What's the matter, Kate?' he shouted. 'Don't want to play anymore?'

'Game's over, arsehole, and you lost,' she shouted back. 'How's the eye?'

Despite the outward defiance of her response, there was an almost tangible fear evident in the tone. A fear that communicated itself to him across the yards of rusted Victorian ironwork. He soon realised why. The walkway beneath his feet was shaking, as if under an earthquake tremor. A loud cracking noise followed, as a bolt must have sheared, and part of the walkway close to him parted company with the wall. In that brief terrifying moment he felt the icy hand of death on his shoulder and at once he lost interest in Kate in favour of his own salvation.

Kate also heard the walkway start to tear itself free with a feeling of dread. But for a second her legs refused to function. Then there was a violent lurching motion and she was pitched sideways against the outer rail as the walkway dipped on the same side. Desperately clinging to the rail with both her cuffed hands, she heard more cracking sounds and saw the platform below her pull away. The whole structure was about to collapse like a pack of cards. Snapping out of her temporary paralysis, she went for the stairs in a panic-stricken run as the whole thing began to break up around her.

At the top of the fire escape Grogan made a grab at the rail as the walkway slanted at a sharp angle away from the wall. He saw Kate start to run. But he knew he would never make the stairs. Forcing himself back the way he had come by hauling on the rail hand over hand like a climber negotiating a steep mountainside on a rope, he reached the fire exit door just as the walkway gave a tremendous heave in its death throes. He took a wild dive at the door. But it was tightly closed. As he began to slide back across the walkway, he managed to grab the external handle. At the same moment, a figure in a dark hoodie materialised behind the door inside the room and stared at him through the glass panel.

'Open the door!' he practically screamed. 'Please! I can't hold on much longer.'

For reply, the figure slipped the hood back to reveal the familiar face of a young woman he had never thought to see again. Dark eyes bored into him from a pale, mask-like face and in the blaze of moonlight the livid scars on the grotesquely shaved head stood out like disfiguring birthmarks. Then as the walkway slewed from under his feet with a nightmare rending of tortured metal and his grip slipped off the door handle, she treated him to a cold humourless smile and raised an erect middle finger in a cynical farewell salute.

Perhaps a hundred yards away from the corner of the building, Hayden and Danny Ferris witnessed with a sense of horror the beginning of the end for what had once been seen as a tribute to the success of Victorian engineering. As the walkway finally tore itself away from the wall completely, leaving the upper part of the fire escape tottering on the slender struts of the slowly buckling ironwork beneath it, both detectives launched themselves across the forecourt in a desperate attempt to get to Kate in time.

Despite his bulk, Ferris was a much fitter, more powerful man than his overweight, out-of-condition colleague. In a few strides he was way ahead of Hayden, leaving him stumbling along, panting and coughing in his wake. But even Ferris was not quite fast enough. He got to the foot of the fire escape and was on his way up when he ran out of time. For a few brief seconds both he and Kate were plainly visible to Hayden on the shuddering staircase just below the first-floor platform. Then the whole structure finally folded in on itself and she and her would-be rescuer disappeared under an avalanche of dismembered ironwork and clouds of choking dust kicked up by the lethal debris as it slammed into the concrete below.

* * *

Pulsing blue and red lights. Warbling sirens. A convoy of police vehicles racing up the driveway of Broad Marsh Court. Swerving and slithering in the gravel as they came to a stop. Then the banging of doors and the metallic chatter of police radios. A mix of uniformed and plainclothes officers racing across the forecourt in front of the building. All heading towards the wreckage of the fire escape. There a solitary, dishevelled figure could be seen bending over the heap of twisted wrought iron by the wall of the building, tugging at it with his bare hands. Hayden was bleeding profusely from a number of wounds to his head, and his jacket and shirt were filthy and badly torn. But he seemed unaware of his condition. His face was set in a savage mask as he futilely tried to haul the heavy struts and plates aside.

'Kate and Danny,' he shouted like a man demented. 'They must be underneath. For God's sake help me!'

Looking at the mass of tangled metal, his colleagues exchanged grim, pessimistic glances, knowing full well that if they were under there, the chances of finding either of them alive were likely to be nil. Nevertheless, they set to with a will and it wasn't long before they found one broken dismembered body. It was that of Damian Grogan. A splintered length of metal had driven into his abdomen and his head had been partially severed from his body, his injured eyeball bulging from its socket through a bloody, leaking crust like something out of a horror film.

But of Kate and Danny there was no sign.

'So where the hell is she?' Hayden choked. 'I saw her running down the stairs just as the whole lot fell apart. Danny got there just as it happened.'

For a moment there was absolute silence among the searchers and they cast hopeless glances around them, throwing occasional meaningful looks at each other.

'Hayden,' Charlie Woo said quietly, placing a hand on his shoulder. 'Come on, old son. Let's get you back to my car. There's nothing we can do here until the fire service arrives.'

'NO!' Hayden almost screamed, shaking his arm away. 'I won't leave her. She's here, I know she is.'

'Hayden,' Hennessey said gently. 'Listen to me.'

That was as far as she got. 'Over here!' someone shouted. 'They're over here!'

Wheeling round, they spotted a uniformed woman officer a few yards away from where they stood. She was standing close to the wall waving both arms excitedly above her head. They scrambled back over the wreckage towards her, with Hayden this time way ahead of anyone.

There had obviously once been a door in the wall at this point, possibly accessing a basement or coal hole. But it had been bricked up, creating an alcove maybe just over two feet deep. Through the tangle of ironwork piled up in front of it, they could see in the powerful beams of several Bardic lamps the head and shoulders of an auburn-haired woman, scrunched up in the corner, facing them, with the heavy-set body of a man lying face-down on top of her. Neither showed any signs of life.

'Holy Mary,' Hennessey breathed. 'He was shielding her with his own body, so he was.'

Further down the lane outside the derelict building, Debbie Moreton pulled off her hoodie and slipped behind the wheel of her car. No one saw her leave, and she was on her way home well before the ambulances arrived. Busy with her own selfish thoughts.

It was too late to supply any copy for the *Clarion*'s morning edition. But she was thinking that maybe, just maybe, she wouldn't give it to them anyway. It was time for her to free herself from the clutches of the odious Theodore Rainer and strike out on her own as a freelancer. And before that, it would be an excellent idea to write a book on the Grogan case. After all, she had enough material and she wouldn't have to put *everything* in it, would she? No one ever need to know about her last goodbye to him. That was her secret. Okay, so the book would not be written as Grogan would have written it. But what the hell. There was such a thing as freedom of expression, wasn't there?

AFTER THE FACT

Kate Lewis felt as if she had been hit by a train. Her left arm was broken and in plaster. Nasty cuts, abrasions and a plentiful array of purplish bruises covered various parts of her face and body and her feet were heavily bandaged from the abuse they had suffered at Broad Marsh Court.

Sitting in the wheelchair beside her hospital bed, she looked in a real sorry state. Nevertheless, she still managed to smile at Hayden as he sat on the edge of the bed beside her, holding the hand of her sound arm in both of his own.

'How do you feel?' he asked, concern etched into his expression.

'Like shit,' she replied pleasantly.

He frowned at her use of the word. 'Still have the same unique mastery of the English language then?' he said sarcastically.

Her smile broadened, then was abruptly replaced by a wince of pain, and she carefully adjusted her position in the chair.

'Well, I could think of a worse description to come out with,' she replied. 'But at least I'm still alive. More than that bastard Grogan is.'

He grunted. 'Grogan got what he deserved all right and at least you'll no longer have his shadow over you.'

She gave a little shiver and changed the subject. 'How's Danny? I understand he saved my life.'

He nodded. 'Got to you just as the fire escape collapsed completely. Picked you up and jumped with you in his arms from the last level into an alcove at the foot of the staircase. Then he crushed you against the wall at the back of it and shielded you with his own body against all the bits that were coming down. Broke both his legs, fractured part of his spine and suffered multiple other more minor injuries to his neck and back. Brave man, that. I'll never call him a waste of a skin again.'

Kate shook her head in disbelief. 'You can say that again. I'd like to see him.'

He shook his head. 'He's sedated and in a lot of pain. No visitors at the moment apparently. Though he did ask me to give you a message when they were wheeling him in.'

She looked puzzled. 'Message?'

He grinned. 'Yes, he said, "I told you I owed you one, didn't I? Now we're quits".'

Kate didn't know whether to laugh or cry as she remembered his embarrassment over the postcard incident. 'Big dumb gorilla,' she whispered affectionately, wiping her eyes on the sleeve of her hospital gown. 'Will he be okay?'

'Doc says so. It will apparently take a few months all told, but his injuries are not thought to be life-threatening. They have had to break the tragic news to him, though, that whisky is definitely off limits for the foreseeable future.'

He raised a hand before she could ask any more questions. 'Oh, by the way, all the lads and lassies have clubbed together to buy you a present.'

'A present? I don't understand. What sort of a present?'

He bent down at the foot of the bed and picked up a parcel wrapped in brown paper, which he carefully placed in her lap.

'They thought it might help you to concentrate on something to keep you out of trouble while you are off sick, er, yet again.'

Intrigued, Kate tore off the wrapping paper of what was obviously some kind of book. She stared at it in astonishment before releasing an incredulous laugh. It was indeed a book. A very thick book. The latest edition of the annual *Writers' & Artists' Yearbook*.

There was a card with it too, which read:

We thought this little gift might help you in the new career you might be contemplating as a crime novelist. We're quite sure your friend, the DCI, would consider that to be a much better career for you than real-life criminal investigations.

Still chuckling, Kate tossed the book on to the bed beside her. 'You can tell them all, Hayd,' she replied, 'that I will definitely be staying on as a police detective. I think my days of crime writing are well and truly over. Especially as it was the writing that got me into trouble in the first place.'

'Thank the Lord for that,' he replied. 'Alleluia!'

THE END

ABOUT THE AUTHOR

David Hodges is a former police superintendent with thirty years' service. Since 'turning to crime', he has received critical media acclaim, including a welcome accolade from Inspector Morse's creator, the late great Colin Dexter, and he is now a prolific novelist with sixteen published crime novels and an autobiography on his police career to his credit. He has written a number of stand-alone thrillers and his Somerset Levels Murder Series, published by Joffe Books, which features feisty young detective sergeant, Kate Lewis and her laidback partner, Hayden, has attracted a particularly strong following, not only throughout the UK, but also in Europe, the United States, Canada and Australia.

David has two married daughters and four grandchildren and lives in the UK with his wife, Elizabeth, where he continues to indulge his passion for thriller writing and pursue his keen interest in the countryside.

He is a member of the Crime Writers Association, The Crime Readers Association, The Society of Authors and International Thriller Writers Inc.

THE JOFFE BOOKS STORY

We began in 2014 when Jasper agreed to publish his mum's much-rejected romance novel and it became a bestseller.

Since then we've grown into the largest independent publisher in the UK. We're extremely proud to publish some of the very best writers in the world, including Joy Ellis, Faith Martin, Caro Ramsay, Helen Forrester, Simon Brett and Robert Goddard. Everyone at Joffe Books loves reading and we never forget that it all begins with the magic of an author telling a story.

We are proud to publish talented first-time authors, as well as established writers whose books we love introducing to a new generation of readers.

We have been shortlisted for Independent Publisher of the Year at the British Book Awards three times, in 2020, 2021 and 2022, and for the Diversity and Inclusivity Award at the Independent Publishing Awards in 2022.

We built this company with your help, and we love to hear from you, so please email us about absolutely anything bookish at feedback@joffebooks.com

If you want to receive free books every Friday and hear about all our new releases, join our mailing list: www.joffebooks.com/contact

And when you tell your friends about us, just remember: it's pronounced Joffe as in coffee or toffee!

Ingram Content Group UK Ltd.
Milton Keynes UK
UKHW011125180423
420361UK00004B/482